Make It Last

Also by Megan Erickson

Make It Right
Make It Count

Make It Last

A BOWLER UNIVERSITY NOVEL

MEGAN ERICKSON

WILLIAM MORROW IMPULSE
An Imprint of HarperCollinsPublishers

Excerpt from *Make It Count* copyright © 2014 by Megan Erickson.
Excerpt from *Make It Right* copyright © 2014 by Megan Erickson.
Excerpt from *Holding Holly* copyright © 2014 by Julie Revell Benjamin.
Excerpt from *It's a Wonderful Fireman* copyright © 2014 by Jennifer Bernard.
Excerpt from *Once Upon a Highland Christmas* copyright © 2014 by Lecia Cotton Cornwall.
Excerpt from *Running Hot* copyright © 2014 by HelenKay Dimon.
Excerpt from *Sinful Rewards 1* copyright © 2014 by Cynthia Sax.
Excerpt from *Return to Clan Sinclair* copyright © 2014 by Karen Ranney LLC.
Excerpt from *Return of the Bad Girl* copyright © 2014 by Codi Gary.

EPub Edition JANUARY 2015 ISBN: 9780062353535
Print Edition ISBN: 9780062353542

10 9 8 7 6 5 4 3 2 1

This book is for all my readers, who've stuck with me and grown with me throughout this series.

Acknowledgments

THIS IS ONE of the fastest books I've ever written, and that's because Cam started speaking in my head pretty loudly. Then Tate piped up, not wanting to be overshadowed. And their story poured out of me. I love these characters and the whole crew of the Bowler U series. I've had a blast writing these books.

I want to thank my readers. Because without the excitement and cheering, the grind of writing my first series might have gotten to me. But instead, I was excited to write these books because *you* were excited. For an author, there's nothing better.

Amanda Bergeron, you continue to be one of the best people I've met, not only in this industry, but in life. You're sweet and encouraging and smart. I love working with you, and I can hear your little editor voice in my head while I'm writing. I love knowing that you're in my corner.

Marisa Corvisiero, my agent, this book might not exist at all if it weren't for you. It was your idea to give Cam a book. You mentioned it, and the ideas started flowing, and here it is. I hope you love him.

Jessie Edwards—your encouragement and publicity help made all the difference with this series. I can't thank you enough for your kind e-mails and your push to get the word out about these books.

My critique partners—Natalie Blitt and AJ Pine —I love you ladies! You are everything to me and I would not be here without you. One of the best things about this writing gig is gaining you both as friends. Natalie, you are my plot whisperer. Never leave me!

Lia Riley – you are the Kristan Higgins to my Jill Shalvis. Next year, 2015, is *so* our year.

I've received so much support from bloggers, for which I'm immensely grateful. You know who you are— you've made me teasers and you tweeted and you've squeed. I love you all!

As always, Lucas Hargis, you are my spirit animal and I can always count on you for a smile when I'm feeling low. Thank you to my friends in NAAU, my Debut '14 girls, and all the BuBs who've known me since I was a stressed out pregnant lady.

Neal—you are the reason I can do this, write about love. Because I wake up to you every day. Thanks for putting up with me when my head is distracted with character voices. I love you.

My kiddos—I love you. It's pretty cool to pick my son

up at the end of the day and have him ask, "Did you write a book today, Mommy?"

To my friends and family—your support means everything. Thank you! With this book especially, I pulled a lot of experiences of my own from college. Maybe I'll tell you all one day, and maybe I won't, haha.

And Andi, don't forget, you'll never be one of the "little people."

Chapter 1

HE'D BEEN HOME three weeks before he could no longer avoid this place.

And the worst part was, it hadn't changed. Not one bit. Not the red pleather booths lining the wall—even the corner one still had its trademark X in silver duct tape covering a wicked tear. Not the robin's egg blue Formica countertops. Not the silver rotating stools at the counter. Not even the temperamental soft-serve ice cream machine, which a waitress currently wrestled with while a salivating kid watched.

Not the flickering PARADISE DINER sign out front, the second A blown out so it looked like PARDISE. Which wasn't far off in this western Maryland town where everyone blurred their syllables. *You're not from Pardise, are you?*

It was like he'd pressed PAUSE while playing Utope, freezing every character in the game into status quo indefinitely.

Cam Ruiz didn't know whether the static nature of this damn place was comforting or infuriating. Because all of it reminded him of her. Her little black apron covering little black shorts. Those damn wedge sandals that she said made her calves and ass look good so she got better tips. Her laugh when he'd sit at the counter right before she got off her shift, sucking down a milk shake while she mopped up the spills, shooting him flirty smiles.

Fuck, it'd been four, going on five years now. Why couldn't he just forget?

Now, he had chosen a booth he didn't think he'd ever occupied back in high school, right near the front door. He sipped from his plastic cup of water and looked down at his watch, then at the door. There weren't tons of places open at noon to eat, so when his friend and old college roommate, Max Payton, called and asked where to meet, Cam had frozen. Then his mom yelled, "Pardise Diner!" in the background. Max had heard, and the meeting location was decided.

Through the dirty windows of the diner, Cam saw the rusted piece-of-crap truck Max drove rumble in. His friend hopped out of the truck, sunglasses in place as he squinted at the sign and then helped his girlfriend, Lea, hop down out of the passenger side. She looked good, her limp slight, her dark hair shining in the early June sun.

Max held open the door and a bell tinkled overhead. Lea spotted Cam right away, and he stood so she could hug him. He greeted Max with a handshake and back slap. As they slid into the booth, Cam on one side and Max and Lea on the other, a commotion at the counter caught his attention. A squeak followed by harsh whispers. He turned his head and all he saw were the doors to the kitchen, swinging back and forth. He shrugged and turned back to his friends.

"Thanks for visiting me," he said.

Max laid his arm behind Lea along the back of the booth. "Wanted to see the town that raised the great Cam Ruiz."

Cam rolled his eyes.

"It's definitely small," Lea said. "But I like it. Very welcoming and homey."

He guessed so, if moving back didn't make him feel like he was taking a step backward. Like a reset button wiping away the basic training for the Air National Guard, the weekends at drill, the three and a half years he busted his ass to graduate college early.

A waitress he'd never met came to take their orders, her eyes lingering a little long on Cam. Not in a flirty way, like he was used to. Plus she was probably his mom's age and wore a wedding band. But she studied his face and his clothes and it made him uncomfortable. He wanted to ask if he had something on his face or in his teeth.

After they ordered, Max turned to Cam. "So how's your mom?"

She was the reason Cam had come back. The only reason he'd return to Paradise. He shrugged. "She's all right. She's got this thing . . . called fibromyalgia. Basically, she's in a lot of pain. It's hard for her to keep a job. So she's out of one right now and she's collecting disability." He waved a hand toward the door of the diner. "Not like there are tons of jobs around here for her to pick from anyway."

The waitress delivered their drinks and when she walked away, Lea placed her hand on top of Cam's where he twisted his straw wrapper in his fingers. "Anything we can do to help while we're here?"

Cam shook his head. "Nah, it's cool. I got a job and our rent is cheap."

Max took a gulp of water and crushed ice between his molars. "What job did ya get?"

Cam couldn't stop the growl in the back of his throat. He had a bachelor's degree and he was a . . . "Bouncer. At a bar in town."

Max's eyes widened, but then his face quickly shuttered. "Bet you squeeze into a black T-shirt and let the tats peek out and all these rednecks scatter, huh?"

Cam laughed. "I just started last week. It's mostly girls from the community college looking to dance and stuff. I even have this fancy machine I run their IDs through to make sure they aren't fake."

"Why the hell didn't the bars at Bowler have that? Kat used her fake all the time." Max frowned.

"Until Alec shredded it." Lea snickered.

Max threw back his head and laughed. "Oh man. Apparently Kat and Alec are at her beach house with her family, and Alec is worried her brother is going to drown him in the ocean."

Lea wrinkled her nose. "Which is stupid because Marc likes Alec. He's just being paranoid."

The waitress delivered their food, and even the sound

of the melamine plates sliding across the table as she announced the orders brought back memories.

He picked at his bun while Max demolished a burger. In between bites, Max stole a handful of fries from Lea's chicken salad sandwich.

"Seriously?" Lea glared at him. "You have your own."

"But yours taste better," Max said around a mouthful of fries.

"That doesn't make any sense," she grumbled. "Don't make me kick your ass."

He grinned. "Maybe I want you to kick my ass. My favorite foreplay."

Cam groaned. "That's enough, guys, I'm going to lose my appetite."

Neither looked apologetic.

Cam ate his burger while he chatted with Max and Lea about their trip. They planned to head up into Pennsylvania and then Massachusetts. A road trip for just the two of them, since next year was going to be rough. Lea started a teaching job in the fall, and Max would be completing his last semester at Bowler University student teaching.

Max picked up the tab, which made Cam bristle a little, but Max assured him it was just to thank him for taking them out in his hometown.

Cam followed them out of the diner and Lea hugged him before climbing into Max's truck. Max watched her through the windshield as she buckled her seat belt, then leaned a hand on his hood and turned to Cam. His eyes traveled over Cam's shoulder to the diner and then squinted at the sparse traffic on the street.

Finally his eyes met Cam's. "You sure this is what you need to be doing?"

No, he wasn't sure, but he'd committed now, hadn't he? "I need to help my mom with the bills. She worked two jobs when I was a kid, just to keep food on our table and a roof over our heads. What am I gonna do, leave her?"

Max ran his tongue over his teeth. "You could have maybe gotten a job and sent money . . ."

Cam shook his head. "I thought about that, but . . . I wanted to make sure she was okay. And I think she's glad that we're getting some time together, you know?"

Max watched him for a minute, then gave a curt nod. He slapped Cam on the shoulder. "All right, man. You need anything, you call me or Alec, all right?"

He wouldn't. "Sure."

Max got into his truck and pulled out onto Main Street.

Cam sighed, feeling the weight of responsibility pressing down on his shoulders. But if he didn't help his mom, who would?

He jingled his keys in his pocket and turned to walk toward his truck. It was nice of Max and Lea to visit him on their road trip. College had been some of the best years of his life. Great friends, fun parties, hot girls.

But now it felt like a small blip, like a week vacation instead of three and a half years. And now he was right back where he started.

As he walked by the alley beside the restaurant, something flickered out of the corner of his eye.

He turned and spotted her legs first. One foot bent at the knee and braced on the brick wall, the other flat on the ground. Her head was bent, a curtain of hair blocking her face. But he knew those legs. He knew those hands. And he knew that hair, a light brown that held just a glint of strawberry in the sun. He knew by the end of August it'd be lighter and redder and she'd laugh about that time she put lemon juice in it. It'd backfired and turned her hair orange.

The light flickered again but it was something weird and artificial, not like the menthols she had smoked. Back when he knew her.

As she lowered her hand down to her side, he caught sight of the small white cylinder. It was an electronic cigarette. She'd quit.

She raised her head then, like she knew someone watched her, and he wanted to keep walking, avoid this awkward moment. Avoid those eyes he didn't think he'd ever see again and never thought he'd wanted to see again. But now that his eyes locked on her hazel eyes— the ones he knew began as green on the outside of her iris and darkened to brown by the time they met her pupil—he couldn't look away. His boots wouldn't move.

The small cigarette fell to the ground with a soft click and she straightened, both her feet on the ground.

And that was when he noticed the wedge shoes. And the black apron. What was she doing here?

"Camilo."

Other than his mom, she was the only one who used his full name. He'd heard her say it while laughing. He'd her moan it while he was inside her. He'd heard her sigh it with an eye roll when he made a bad joke. But he'd never heard it the way she said it now, with a little bit of fear and anxiety and . . . longing? He took a deep breath to steady his voice. "Tatum."

He hadn't spoken her name since that night Trevor called him and told him what she did. The night the future that he'd set out for himself and for her completely changed course.

She'd lost some weight in the four years since he'd last seen her. He'd always loved her curves. She had it all— thighs, ass and tits in abundance. Naked, she was a fucking vision.

Damn it, he wasn't going there.

But now her face looked thinner, her clothes hung a little loose and he didn't like this look as much. Not that she probably gave a fuck about his opinion anymore.

She still had her gorgeous hair, pinned up halfway with a bump in front, and a smattering of freckles across the bridge of her nose and on her cheekbones. And she still wore her makeup exactly the same—thickly mascaraed eyelashes, heavy eyeliner that stretched to a point on the outside of her eyes, like a modern-day Audrey Hepburn.

She was still beautiful. And she still took his breath away.

And his heart felt like it was breaking all over again.

And he hated her even more for that.

Her eyes were wide. "What are you doing here?"

Something in him bristled at that. Maybe it was because he didn't feel like he belonged here. But then, she didn't either. She never did. *They* never did.

But there was no longer a *they*.

"I was hungry," he grunted.

She pursed her lips and narrowed those hazel eyes. "I mean, what are you doing here, in Paradise?"

He raised his eyebrows. "I'm not allowed back here or something?"

She took a deep breath. "Can you stop getting defensive? I just wanted—"

"What are *you* doing here?" he countered. After she backed out of following him to Bowler University, he'd heard she'd gone to her second choice college in Pennsylvania. Shouldn't she be out of this town working a fancy job with her fancy new degree? But here she was, in that same damn apron. Why was she wearing that apron?

Her posture deflated, and she fiddled with the hem of her shirt. "Did you graduate?" she asked, ignoring his question.

He wanted to tell her it was none of her business, but instead, he nodded. "Busted my ass to get out in three and a half years." He was in basic training the first semester. When she . . .

Nope, not going there either.

She flinched ever so slightly, then rolled her lips between her teeth and nodded back, gaze drifting to the ground at her feet. "Good," she whispered so softly, he barely heard her. "That's good."

He stared at the top of her head. When he heard a soft sound and saw a jerk of her head, his heart lurched. All these years, and he still knew the quiet sounds of Tate crying.

Maybe because he grew up with a single mom, women's emotions never scared him away. He didn't always care, but he wasn't one of those guys who panicked at the sight of tears.

But he always cared about Tate crying. Always. He would place her head on his shoulder, where it fit just right, and he'd run his fingers through her hair, massaging her scalp. Then he'd retrieve the water and pain reliever because crying always gave her a headache.

It was like his body had muscle memory, because every one screamed at him to move and cradle her. She was trying to keep it in, he could see it.

"Tate," he said, and her head shot up, eyes wide and wet.

But he managed to hold firm. Because she'd chosen this consequence the day she decided to sleep with another man.

He gave her a quick two-fingered salute. "See you around."

And then he walked away.

Chapter 2

TATE SCRUBBED THE counter with the damp rag. She was pretty sure there was a spot on the counter, but it was hard to tell with her eyes being all leaky and blurry and emotional and stuff.

She huffed and leaned her head back. Deep breaths. In and out. In and out.

Sometimes it felt like she hadn't taken a decent breath in four years.

She blinked her eyes at the ceiling, steeling herself. It'd been a long time since she cried. Despite wanting to every night when she collapsed exhausted and heartbroken in her bed.

But of course he had to come back. Waltzing down the street like he fucking owned it. Looking better than he ever did.

Back when he was hers.

Before she blew it.

She willed the tears back and renewed her efforts scrubbing the countertop.

Cam had always been attractive, but he always had this look about him, and she knew he'd be downright gorgeous once he grew into his body.

She'd been right.

His hair was shorter now—military shorter—but he'd put his earrings back in his ears. He had those same dark eyes and beautiful skin. And now he had bigger muscles, and she swore she saw a tattoo peeking out of the sleeve of his T-shirt. Probably his new girlfriend's name or something. She was probably *perfect*.

"Did you just growl?"

Tate snapped her head up to see her coworker Anne. "I didn't growl."

Anne crossed her arms over her well-endowed bosom. "You growled at the countertop."

Tate narrowed her eyes. "You its defender or something?"

Anne reached over and gently plucked the rag from Tate's hand. Tate blew a strand of hair out of her face and turned to fiddle with the soft-serve machine.

"I saw him," Anne's voice said softly behind her.

And those three words, said with a mix of pity and something else, slammed into Tate like a sucker punch. Her hand slipped off the knob and cracked down on the old metal tray below the nozzles, taking a chunk out of her palm in the process.

"Shit!" Pain radiated into her fingers and down her arm.

She cradled her palm in her other hand and clutched it to her stomach, clenching her teeth, wishing this whole day would just fucking go away.

"Tate, for God's sake!" Anne tutted, tugging on her elbow until Tate relinquished her arm to the mother hen she'd known and worked with at the diner since she was sixteen.

Anne didn't say anything else to Tate, just picked up a clean rag and wrapped it around Tate's hand while asking Margo to make sure the machine was clean of blood, before leading Tate to the break room.

Tate pulled on her arm, but Anne held fast, shooting a stern look at Tate.

Tate sighed. *Whatever.*

She let Anne sit her down on the couch and clean the cut with hydrogen peroxide.

After Anne bandaged it, she patted Tate on the shoulder. "All right, well, we'll take it from here. Why don't you head home?"

Tate jerked her head. "What? Why?"

Anne stood before her, hands on her ample hips, and purposefully looked at Tate's bandaged hand, currently lax in her lap.

"Oh this?" Tate said, holding up her hand. "Just a flesh wound."

"Tate."

"Anne."

"Go home."

And sit around the house with her sick father and her old memories? No thank you.

"I need the money." That, too.

Anne pursed her lips. "You'll get paid for the full shift—"

"But I didn't—"

"Tate, if you don't go home right now, I swear to God, I'll put you over my knee!"

Tate widened her eyes, because Anne looked so serious. And frankly, even though Anne had seventy-five pounds on her, Tate made up for her small size with scrappiness. She'd really love to see Anne try to spank her. She began to giggle. Which made Anne glare harder.

Then Tate was laughing, big heaving chuckles, while Anne shook her head, smiling slightly.

Tate finally calmed and wiped her hands over her eyes. "Thanks for that visual, Mama Bear."

Anne sighed. "I love you, Tate."

Tate ducked her head and dug her fingernail along the edge of the bandage on her hand. "I know."

"Quit picking at it."

Tate rolled her eyes. "I'm twenty-three, you know."

"You'll always be sixteen to me." Anne's smile faded, her eyes softening.

Tate looked away, staring at the calendar on the wall. It was June now. The calendar needed to be changed from May. The calendar was full of drawings of cats in yoga positions. The cat had its paws above its head, one leg bent at knee, foot flat on the other inner thigh.

Who thought of calendars like this?

"Do you want to talk about it?" Anne asked softly.

Tate wished Anne was asking about her hand, or even the stupid cat calendar, but Tate knew she wasn't. "No."

"How long is he in town?"

"I don't know." He'd always wanted to live in a big city, be some big hotshot detective or private investigator or something. They'd had so many dreams . . .

"I saw him in the diner, eating with friends. It's why . . . I told you to take a break. But then I heard voices and saw you outside talking to him, so I guess my plan didn't work."

She'd quit smoking years ago, but all today she'd felt off. And that was when she turned to the electronic cigarettes. Just holding them helped ease her anxiety. Still a poor substitute for the real thing, but she'd never pick one up again. Tate shrugged and gave Anne a weak smile. "It's okay. I appreciate you trying to protect me from an awkward situation."

Anne bit her lip. "Go home, sweetie."

This time Tate didn't argue. She hugged Anne and waved good-bye to Margo. She went to the bathroom, managing to wash her hands without getting her bandage wet. When she looked in the mirror, she saw dark circles under her eyes, freckles so stark against her pale skin. She needed to get some sun. Lie out in her backyard or something. She snorted. When did she have time for that?

As she walked to her Jeep, she untied her apron strings, cursing when her fingernails kept slipping on the tight knot, her movements awkward with the bandage. When she reached her old red Jeep, the rust spots near the tires growing each day, she wrenched open the door, hopped inside and slammed the door shut. She threw the apron into the backseat and leaned her head back, rubbing her hands over her face.

It was only two hours away from the end of her shift, but routine was everything in Tate's life right now. Her dad didn't expect her home until after work. She could ... go to the lake. Or go shopping. Or ... something for herself. Her fingers gripped the steering wheel as the birds in her rib cage beat against the bones. Maybe that's what she needed to feel like herself again.

Her phone rang. She dug into her purse and answered it without looking at the caller ID. "Hello?"

"You need to come home."

Her brother's voice, irritated and maybe a little panicked, shot those birds down. They flopped to the bottom of her stomach. Dead weight in her gut.

"Is he okay?" she asked, jamming the key in the ignition and praying this wasn't the day old Jeep gave up the good life. The engine turned over and Cecil purred her broken rattle.

"I don't know. He fell in the bathtub. I mean, he wasn't taking a shower or whatever. He was in there and somehow tripped on the mat and into the tub. And he's heavy and it's awkward and I can't lift him." The frustration was clear in Jamie's voice, and Tate floored Cecil, rocks pinging the brick wall of the diner as she roared out of the lot.

"I'll be home in five, Jamie. Just stay with him."

She pushed the thought of a lazy day at the lake out of her mind, way out. Those dreams were for another time. Another life.

This was her life now.

She pulled into her driveway and hopped out of her Jeep, hitting the ground running. She took the porch stairs into her house two at a time and threw open the front door.

Deep voices sounded from the direction of the bathroom and her heart pounded. Two voices, two conscious voices, so that was a good sign.

She pounded down the hall and skidded to a stop in the doorway of the bathroom, breathing hard with anxiety and exertion. Scared to death she was going to see her father bleeding or broken.

Instead, she saw Jamie sitting cross-legged in one end of the bathtub and her father sitting in the other end, legs stretched out in front of him.

And they were both licking spoons. A carton of nearly empty ice cream between them.

She blinked.

"Hey baby," her dad wheezed.

"Yo," Jamie said, lapping happily at his spoon like a damn dog.

Once Tate unhinged her jaw from the shock of what she was seeing, she narrowed her eyes at the two men in the tub. "Are you fucking kidding me right now?"

"Language," her dad warned.

Tate threw up her hands. "I was scared out of my mind! I raced home, pushing Cecil way past her limits because I was worried about you, and you two are here enjoying a treat!"

Jamie held his spoon out to her. "Want some?"

Tate tried to kill him with a death glare.

Jamie scrunched his lips to the side and then lowered his hand back into his lap. "That's okay, it's a little freezer-burnt anyway."

Their dad nodded at Jamie. "And I like moose tracks better than Neapolitan. Baby," he said, turning to Tate, "put some moose tracks ice cream on the grocery list, will you?"

Tate ignored him and pointed at Jamie. "You. Out of the tub."

"But I'm not done my ice—"

"Get. Out."

Jamie wrinkled his nose and stepped out onto the bathmat, grumbling.

"Now help me get Dad out of the tub," Tate ordered.

"I'm comfy where I am," her dad said.

Tate ignored him and ordered Jamie to stand beside her. Bracing their feet against the base of the tub, they hauled their father to a standing position by pulling on his arms.

He tried to shrug them off weakly. "I can step out myself."

"Oh really?" Tate said. "Just like you got into it so gracefully?"

He huffed, and she rolled her eyes.

With Jamie's help, they were able to help him out of the tub. They led him down the hallway and deposited him in his recliner.

Jamie left to throw away the ice cream container while Tate stood in front of her father, hands on her hips.

"What happened?" she asked.

He eyed the bandage on her hand. "What happened to you?"

"I asked first."

"I'm older than you."

Tate sighed. "I cut my hand on that dumb ice cream machine. So I'm not too happy with the ice cream gods today."

He squinted up at her. "So does that mean no moose tracks?"

"Dad—"

He held up his hand with a chuckle, then winced and tucked his elbow into his side.

Tate took a step and knelt down beside the chair. "Dad, come on, tell me. What happened?"

He didn't look at her when he talked, but stared at the blank TV screen. "I was in the bathroom, using the facilities, and I guess I slipped on the tub. I caught myself with one arm on the bar but I banged the hell out of my elbow."

Tate angled his arm to get a look at the joint. The area was already swelling, a bruise starting to form. As if he didn't have enough to deal with already, who knew how long this would set his recovery back. But she didn't say that. "Okay, Dad, give me a minute and I'll get you some frozen peas."

"I think we only have corn."

"Fine, then, corn."

In the kitchen, Jamie was rummaging in the fridge.

"Hand me some peas or corn or whatever we have, will you?" Tate asked.

Jamie opened the freezer and tossed a bag of frozen peas at her. She caught it as it hit her chest. "Ow."

"Sorry."

She smacked the bag on the counter to break up the frozen pea clumps. "His elbow is pretty wrecked."

Jamie didn't say anything, his movements jerky at as he pulled out a packet of sliced turkey to make a sandwich.

Tate took a step closer. "Hey, he's okay—"

The slam of a fist on the counter cut her off. "He's not okay, Tate. He'll never be the same."

Jamie's hazel eyes were pained and pissed and Tate hated seeing him like this. He'd been such a sweet kid, but the last four years had been hard on them, and he'd grown into a brooding and out-of-control seventeen-year-old. She didn't know what to do with him.

"Look, Jamie—"

He whirled on her, the knife in his hand flinging mayo on the counter. "I'm done talking about it."

She kept on, despite the angry flush rising up his neck like fire. "I'm glad you called me. I get that you were freaked out—"

Jamie slapped his sandwich together and turned to walk out of the kitchen.

"Jamie—"

He glared at her over his shoulder. "Quit acting like the glass is half full, Tate. It's empty, and no matter how much sunny optimism you pour in it, it's just going to keep leaking."

And then he was gone. She flinched when his bedroom door slammed.

She wanted the time to fall apart, to curl up in a ball and cry and feel sorry for herself, but she didn't have that luxury.

She had to work. And take care of her father, whose body had been ravaged by lung cancer and was now currently in a remission that felt as fragile as an egg. And parent a seventeen-year-old boy-man who looked at her like an annoying sister rather than the closest thing to a proper guardian he had.

She grabbed her father's oxygen tank from the corner of the living room. They still had it from when his condition was worse and she liked to think it gave him a boost when he was feeling weak.

He rolled his eyes when he saw it, but kept quiet as she wrapped the bag of peas in a towel, then placed it on the arm of his chair. She nestled his elbow onto the makeshift cold pack. "At least twenty minutes, okay?" she said, handing him the remote.

He nodded and then took the nasal cannula from her, placing it in his nose while she started his oxygen.

"You should be careful when you're in the bathroom," she said quietly.

She made sure he was settled and as she turned to leave, he muttered, "I'm sorry."

Tate closed her eyes as the word pierced her chest. She didn't know what he was apologizing for. Smoking a pack a day for years. Not taking care of himself. Falling. It didn't matter. She loved him with everything she had. She didn't blame him for her life. It was what it was.

"I love you," she said, brushing her lips across his forehead.

"Love you, too, baby," he answered, his breathing evening out with the extra help.

She walked down the hallway of their small rancher as the sounds of deep bass pounded through the thin walls of her brother's room. She checked her bandage in the bathroom, glad to see the bleeding had stopped. Then she sequestered herself in her room and shut the door.

She unstrapped her shoes and collapsed onto her bed on her back, staring at the ceiling. Her whole body felt like it weighed three hundred pounds and she wanted to melt into her mattress, let her skin fuse to the fabric so she never had to get up again.

Her fingers itched for a cigarette, even though she hadn't smoked since the day after they'd gotten the diagnosis. She'd burned through the rest of her pack, literally, alone in a secluded area of a local park. Crying as she stomped on the last butt, she'd vowed never to smoke again. And she didn't, except for the electronic cigarettes every once in a while. Like today.

She rolled her head and stared at her small television set in her room, her eyes scanning her video game system, Catharsis, and stack of games. She sat up with a groan and reached out to look through the discs, trying to decide which game she could get lost in for a little while. To forget about real life.

Her gaze was drawn to the one game she'd hidden behind all her others. Utope sat dusty and lonely in its spot out of view. She'd thought about throwing it away so many times. But a part of her took comfort in knowing that imaginary life was still there if she ever wanted to return to it.

Of course, it was just all pixels and coding, but in that world, she and Cam had a house and a dog and money. And a leopard-print rug in the bedroom that Cam had hated but she'd insisted looked perfect.

Her hand stretched toward Utope. Maybe she could pop in the game just for a little. She hadn't played it in four years, thinking it was really creepy to return to the game where she and Cam had created a whole fictional life they'd eventually hoped to make nonfictional.

But then her father's voice called to her through her bedroom door. And she snapped her hand back. And returned her thoughts to the real world where they belonged.

Chapter 3

CAM TOSSED HIS keys into the metal dish on the table beside the front door and toed off his boots. "Ma!" he called, and listened for her answer.

"In here!" came her voice from the direction of her bedroom. Cam walked up the stairs of their small, two-bedroom town house they'd rented since he was in high school. He heard rummaging and cursing and rolled his eyes.

He stopped in her doorway and leaned a shoulder against it, crossing his arms over his chest. His mother was bent over, digging in her closet like some sort of gopher. "Ma, what're you doing?"

She straightened, her gray-streaked black hair escaping the headband decorated with a large fake flower bloom. She wore a flowing flower-print dress that would have been ugly on anyone else. But not his ma.

"I'm looking for my sandals," she answered, jutting a

hip out and putting a fist on it in classic Teresa Ruiz–annoyed mode.

"Your sandals," he parroted.

"The ones with the big flowers on the top," she added.

He gestured toward her dress and headband. "I'm thinking you can chill out on the flower theme."

She narrowed her eyes and stomped her right bare foot, because the left one was still swollen from her sprain when she tripped down the stairs. "Camilo!"

"Ma!"

"I want those sandals," she muttered, turning back to her closet and biting her lip.

It'd always been just them. His dad had been some drifter who'd never stuck around after his mom found out she was pregnant. So, whatever, he'd had a sperm donor. But his mom did her best to make up for his lack of a father. She worked hard—two, three jobs sometimes when he was a kid, and she loved the hell out of him.

She'd begun to complain of pain when he was in middle school, and by high school, it'd become unbearable. Test after test revealed nothing until one doctor suspected fibromyalgia, a syndrome associated with chronic muscle pain, depression and fatigue. After numerous visits with a specialist, his mom was diagnosed with it.

She'd been put on several medications to help battle the pain and depression. It'd been a long road to find the right balance of doses. And sometimes those still needed to be altered. Since he'd been home, her drug cocktail had changed again and they were both hoping this one would stick for a while.

And at times like these, when his whip-smart and quick-witted mom looked lost, he wanted to punch a wall, or claw through the "fibro fog" that gripped her brain sometimes and made her brain work a little slower than normal.

He sighed. "I think they're in the blue container on the shelf in your closet."

She squinted at him, then turned to look up at the shelf. "They are?"

"I put all your summer shoes up there last fall."

She frowned, then her face lightened and she turned to him with a smile. "Well, then get them down for me, will you?"

He smiled back. "Sure, Ma."

Cam hauled the box down and helped her dig through it until she found the god-awful sandals with the huge pink flower on the top. She sat down on the edge of her bed, slipped them on her feet and wiggled her toes. "I forgot how much these made me happy," she said softly.

Cam sat down beside her and brushed his lips on his mother's temple. "How are you feeling?"

She had good days and bad days—when the pain was less but she was anxious and depressed. Or the pain and fatigue crippled her but yet her spirits were up. Today seemed like a better day than most. She confirmed that by saying, "I'm feeling pretty well today."

"Your ankle?" he asked, twisting his neck to eye her foot. The bruise seemed to be healing although he was irritated she wouldn't wear the brace.

She rotated her ankle a little. "It's healing." She reached

up and placed a palm on his cheek. "Did you have a nice lunch with your friends?"

"Yeah."

"How's Max?" A smile touched her lips.

Cam rolled his eyes and nudged her. "He's got a girlfriend now. Get over your crush."

She laughed, her eyes sparkling. She'd always had a soft spot for the big guy.

Her face softened and her eyes searched his, like she was expecting something. And that's when he knew.

"Why didn't you tell me?" he asked.

"Tell you what?" she said innocently.

"She's still here. In town."

Her eyes shuttered, and she turned away. One of the biggest battles in his life had been balancing his mom and Tate. Two strong women who butted heads and never saw eye to eye. Who both thought they knew what was best for him and went to war against each other without consulting him. He sure as hell didn't miss that clusterfuck.

His mom fidgeted with the fabric of her dress. "It's been four years, I didn't even think about it."

Cam raised an eyebrow. "Really."

Her head turned and she skewered him with those dark eyes. "Did you talk to her?"

"Briefly."

She hummed under her breath and slipped her sandals off her feet.

"Mom, what—"

She laid a hand on his forearm. "How long do you plan to stay?"

The change in her line of questioning caught him off guard. "What?"

"How long before you take that job in New York?"

The job offer in New York. His dream come true, working for a private security firm.

But then Cam's mom had fallen down the stairs, and he couldn't leave her alone. Despite her insistence she was fine, he just couldn't. He returned home after graduation and found she hadn't been able to hold down a job and the bills were piling up. After all she'd done for him growing up, he couldn't abandon her now.

They'd given him the summer to decide before they found someone else to fill the job. Every time he thought about his fall deadline, a rock settled into his gut. He didn't want to talk about it. "I don't know. They said I could take the summer to decide and—"

"So come fall, you'll take the job," she stated.

Cam furrowed his brow. "Yeah, probably. It depends how you're doing here—"

"I never asked you to come home and take care of me."

What was going on here? And why did she keep interrupting him? "I know that, Ma, but you're in pain and you're not working. I couldn't just take a job states away and leave you here all alone."

She was silent for a minute. "So as long as I'm okay, then you'll take the job? The job you wouldn't stop talking about when you got the offer? Your dream job?"

He didn't mean to, but a growl rumbled in his throat. "Ma—"

She held a hand up. "Sorry. I shouldn't have grilled you like that."

But she looked sad. Not sorry.

"I want to make sure you're still looking out for your future."

"I am."

That seemed to pacify her. "I'm going to lie down for a little, okay?" She patted his knee.

"Yeah, you need anything?"

She shook her head.

He stood to leave as she scooted under her covers. "I have to leave at six to head to work," he said.

"Okay, have a good night," she said, laying her head on her pillow and closing her eyes.

He leaned down to give her another kiss. "Love you."

"Love you too," she mumbled back. He walked out and closed the door behind him and then went to his own room.

He sat down on his bed and picked at the calluses on his hands. In high school, he'd taken a career placement test to determine what he wanted to do. And he found that he loved to research and observe. Solve puzzles. He shadowed a local security firm in town that also completed investigative work for a law firm. And he was hooked. He wanted to be one of the guys behind the computer, finding inconsistencies in pay stubs or accounting records or databases. Digging up criminal histories and background checks. He knew he'd never afford school and didn't want the loans, so he'd joined the Air National

Guard. They paid his tuition, plus gave him a monthly stipend if he attended a monthly drill weekend. It'd been hard and grueling, but he'd learned discipline and a lot of other technology skills.

His last semester of college, as part of a class, he'd spent two weeks in New York at a detective agency. He had a chance to actually do some of the things he'd always dreamed of doing, and he was hooked. The owner, Vince Marino, had taken a liking to him, and offered to interview him after graduation. They'd done a phone interview the week of finals, and Mr. Marino had offered him a job.

He stood up and walked over to the shelves around his TV, picking through video games and books. There were novels he hadn't read yet, but nothing sounded appealing. Nothing promised to make him forget everything in his life for a couple of hours until he had to go to a job he had no desire to be doing. But that paid the bills.

He brushed a stack of CDs and they clattered to the ground. He picked them up and stacked them in his arms, but when he went to place them on the shelf, a familiar case caught his eye.

The green and blue logo of Utope.

Damn, he hadn't touched the game since he left for basic. He'd thought about it though, plenty of times. He'd thought about their little pale blue house. And their dog. And the rain forest in the backyard with poison dart frogs. He snorted a laugh when he remembered how many dogs they'd gone through before they learned to erect a fence around their deadly rain forest.

In high school, his best friend, Trevor Ames, had looked at him like he was crazy when he talked about playing Utope with Tate. It was a simulation game, where the player could create individualized avatars, build houses and communities. Trevor preferred Grand Theft Auto and Call of Duty. Cam liked those, too, but there was nothing like the escape of playing Utope with Tate.

When they imagined what life they'd have, far from the soul-sucking Paradise.

He slammed the CDs back in front, hiding Utope from his view.

That was all gone, every dream they'd had. Vanished. But why couldn't he get over it? He'd spent four years trying to get the taste of Tate out of his mouth but she was always there under his tongue, seeping out when he least expected it.

He could get through this summer. He could get through dealing with seeing Tate. He was twenty-three. He had exes in college. He could deal with it.

But as the blue and green colors of the video game burned into his retinas, he couldn't deny that there was always something different and special about Tate Ellison.

DEKE'S BAR WAS kind of a dive.

Well, most places in Paradise were dives, so Deke's was no exception. There was also no Deke. The owner of the bar was Cynthia Parker and before that it'd been her father, Richard Parker. Cam figured Richard was trying to attract the biker crowd by naming it something like

Deke's Bar, but instead it'd turned into the bar where all the kids from the local community college gravitated. Trevor, a bartender at Deke's, said the patrons mostly played pool and sang "Sweet Caroline" and danced. Then there were Taco Tuesdays, when Cynthia had a waitress scoop ground meat out of a flowered slow cooker into soft shells, and sold them two for a dollar.

The public area of Deke's was one big room, with the bar along one end, then a small dance floor surrounded by tables. On a platform on the other end were a couple of pool tables and a digital jukebox.

This was only Cam's second day on the job as a bouncer/ID checker/heavy-lifter guy. It wasn't what he wanted to do, but the job wasn't hard and it paid pretty well for such a hole in the wall. Plus he got to work with Trevor.

He'd been friends with Trevor since middle school, when they were paired up on the soccer team, Trevor with the gloves guarding the goal, Cam in front of him as the last defender.

They'd both been sullen, pissed-off, fatherless teenagers, but as they'd learned how to communicate with each other on the field, it'd translated to off the field as well. On the field, they could read body language so well, they'd been called The Wall. No ball got past Ames and Ruiz. Hell, they'd taken Paradise to the Maryland state championship senior year.

As much as Cam loved Max and Alec and the friends he'd made in the military, Trevor was the one person he felt he could count on the most.

His best friend was currently wiping down the shelves behind the bar and getting it ready for when the doors opened at seven.

Cam picked at the sleeve of his T-shirt. Max was right—it was tight and black and didn't hide his tattoo. He'd gotten three phone numbers on napkins shoved into the front pocket—labeled Deke's Bar—on his first day.

In college, he would have been happy about it. But he didn't have time to play around here at home. And now it felt especially weird, knowing that Tate was still in town.

Why was that?

Trevor dropped the rag into the sink behind the bar. "Wanna help me lower the chairs?"

"Sure," Cam said, and followed Trevor as he began picking up the chairs off the tables and placing them on the floor.

"How's your mom?" Trevor asked.

Cam shrugged. "She's all right."

"Yeah?" Trevor said, raising an eyebrow.

"Yeah, I think so. Just tired a lot, but her pain seems better. The pill combination she's on now seems to be working."

Trevor nodded. "That's good."

While Cam had been off at college, his mom had become progressively worse. She'd hid it from him, not wanting him to drop out or transfer closer to home. Trevor went to the community college and lived in his own apartment, so he'd help out Teresa when he could. He'd been the one to finally come to Cam and let him know just how bad it'd been. Cam had dropped every-thing to come home, but his mom refused to let him stay. So he'd busted his ass to get out in three and a half se-mesters.

"Thanks for putting in the word for me to get the job."

Trevor shrugged. "No big deal. It just lucked out that Roy got that factory job and had to move. He was a shitty bouncer anyway. If you slipped him in a twenty, he'd let you get in without ID."

Cam wrinkled his nose.

"That was my reaction." Trevor laughed.

Cam owed Trevor. A lot. But he was still rankled about what happened earlier. "You know, I ate at the diner today."

Trev's hands paused, then he resumed lowering the chairs from the tables onto the floor. "Oh yeah?"

Cam leaned a hip on the table and watched as Trevor moved on to another table. "Yeah. So why didn't you tell me she was still here?"

Trevor took a deep breath before answering. "Because you said you didn't want to hear about her. You said you didn't want to hear her name again."

Cam ran his tongue over his teeth. "What's she doing here?"

Trevor spat out a dry laugh. "You don't own this town, Cam. She's allowed to live here. She never left."

An odd chill ran down Cam's spine. "What the fuck? She went to school in—"

"No." Trev's voice cut through the chill like a hot knife." She never went to school."

What? Cam thought she'd gone to Tucker U. None of this made sense. "But—"

Trev whirled on him then, his dark eyes flashing in the dim light. "Man, you don't know what happened. All you can focus on is the fact she cheated on you. And fine, okay? Be pissed about that. But what's going on right now with her isn't about you. She's got much bigger problems than something she did four years ago." Trev's voice was shaking by the end. And that knife burned hot in Cam's gut, slicing muscle as it cut deeper.

"Did you sleep with her?" He didn't want to ask, but he had to know. That didn't stop the words from slicing tiny cuts in his mouth on the way out.

Trev froze with his back to Cam, then slowly turned his head, so Cam could see only his profile. "What did you just say to me?"

Cam licked his lips. This was a bad idea to go toe to toe with Trevor. The guy had probably fifty pounds on him. But that knife was burning, burning and Cam needed the truth. "Did you get with Tate? Is that why you're so worked up about defending her?"

In one step, Trevor was in Cam's face, their chests brushing, Trev's jaw clenching. "You're one dumb fuck."

"Answer the question," Cam gritted out.

And then Trevor laughed, that sad, ironic laugh. "This is so messed up. I thought you went to college and fucked her out of your system, but I guess not. You're still torn up about her, aren't you?"

The words twisted that knife until Cam swore a limb had been cut off. "Trev—"

Trev pushed his chest into Cam's, sending him stumbling back a few feet. Trev turned and kept arranging the chairs. "No, I didn't sleep with her. Ever. We're friends. I've been helping her out, is all, when she needs it."

Trevor the white knight. Helping all the women in Cam's life. The knife had eased up somewhat. "Helping her with what?"

Trev shot him a look. "You wanna know about her life, you talk to her."

"I don't—"

"Don't act like you don't want to." Trev pointed a finger in Cam's face. "This isn't resolved. I know it and you know it. Talk to her."

Cam chewed on the inside of his cheek. "So if she didn't go to school, she's been working . . ."

" . . . at the diner," Trev finished, walking toward the bar.

Cam followed him. "Why didn't she get a better job?"

Trev scoffed. "What do you expect her to do? Be an accountant? An astronaut? Fuck, she has a high school degree, she has no trade education, and we live in shithole Paradise."

"Why didn't she leave—"

Trev slammed a glass on the bar, and Cam flinched. "I'm done with this conversation, Ruiz. I swear to God. You're my best friend, but I'm not doing this with you. You wanna know anything else about Tate Ellison, you get it straight from the source. Get me?"

Cam swallowed and whispered, "I get you."

Trev stared at him for a beat, then nodded. "Go in the

back and get a couple bottles of Jack Daniel's for the bar, will ya?"

"Sure," Cam said, heading toward the back room.

"Hey," Trev called.

Cam stopped and turned around.

"You get in my face again," Trev smiled. "And I'll knock you out. *Capisce?*"

Cam chuckled. "*Comprende.*"

Trev gave him a smirk and a chin lift, and Cam went to retrieve the whiskey.

Chapter 4

IT WAS AFTER ten when she walked in. Tight jeans, heels,
and a low-cut racer-back tank top. She was with a couple
of girls he didn't recognize, and linked arms with her
best friend, Vanessa. She'd been friends with Van as long
as he'd known her. Van was also Trevor's sister.

Cam was on his break when she walked in, so Trevor
took their drink orders at the bar, not bothering to check
their IDs since he knew them. Cam hung out in a dark
corner, drinking a glass of lukewarm water.

He and Tate drank at high school parties, sneaking crappy
blackberry schnapps and chasing it down with fruit punch.
But she never drank when he wasn't around, saying she was
only comfortable letting go of her inhibitions around him.
She knew he'd watch out for her. He always did.

She didn't trust the guys in their school and frankly,
Cam didn't either. There were tons of assholes in their
class that wanted the "spic's chick."

He was hidden in his little alcove, so he could watch undetected as Tate ordered a round of shots, two for herself. Cam gripped his empty glass tighter as she threw them back like they were water. He remembered how she used to sputter and sneeze when they drank in high school, and he'd always laugh because she sneezed three times in a row.

He blew out a breath. These memories had to stop.

After ordering more drinks—not shots—the group retreated to a table at the back of the bar near the pool tables. Its vacancy in the rapidly filling bar gave Cam the impression that was "their" table.

Did Tate drink a lot?

Cam stood up and walked to the bar, leaning against the flip top. "Tate come in here a lot?" he asked Trevor.

His friend didn't answer him, even though he wasn't serving anyone at the moment and was only washing glasses.

"Hey, Trev—"

"I heard you." Trevor emphasized each word, his voice full of irritation.

Cam bit the inside of his cheek. "Are you going to answer?"

Trevor licked his lips, leaned his head back and stared at the ceiling, like he was praying for patience, then he took a step toward Cam and leaned on the bar. "I'm not answering anything else about Tate until you talk to her."

Cam glared. "You're a jerk."

Trevor laughed and went back to washing glasses. "No, I'm not. And you know that. I'm the best friend you've got."

Cam pushed off the bar and retreated to his post at the door, propping himself on the stool and crossing his arms over his chest. He was hidden a little in the doorway, so he could spy on Tate without her watching.

Damn, he was a creeper.

An hour later, he was still at the door, checking IDs. Tate and her friends had gone through two more drinks and all of them were getting louder and louder. None of them had noticed Cam, in his little hidey-hole, dressed in his black shirt and dark jeans. He was practically part of the decor, the way all bouncers seemed to blend in to the place they guarded.

Deke's Bar had a digital jukebox and someone put on a club hit. Cam recognized it and enjoyed a little eye candy as some cute girls began to dance.

And then Tate stood up, starting that hip sway, and he braced.

And panicked.

Tate outside the diner? Drinking in a bar?

He could handle that.

But watching her dance? Those hips and that hair and that ass? And possibly . . . for fuck's sake . . . another guy touching her?

Cam might burn this motherfucking bar down.

He didn't even want to analyze the way his fingers curled into fists and his knuckles kneaded his thighs. The uneasiness that swept over him, beading his brow with sweat.

Tate looked over her shoulder, shooting Van a brilliant, loose smile, reaching her arm back as her friend slipped her hand into Tate's. Tate led the way onto the dance floor, as Van held her other arm over her head with a piercing "whoop!"

Cam inhaled sharply. Tate and Van were a force together. Van was tall and curvy as hell. Skin dark like her brother's, with natural hair she teased out around her head.

In high school, Cam and Tate used to get drunk and perform dance routines that they had learned when they took jazz dance classes together. It was ridiculous, and silly, and half the time one of them would trip and fall into the other until they both ended up in a pile on the floor, giggling and snorting.

And no one gave them crap because no one really wanted to mess with Trevor or Cam.

They'd all had each other's backs. Until they graduated high school and went their separate ways and the ties that held them stretched so far that they snapped.

Cam held his breath as the girls started dancing, the beat pounding into his head as the vision of Tate's hips swirled in front of his eyes. She still moved the same, and it was crazy how he could practically feel that ass snugging up against him as she moved, like it was just yesterday.

He glanced at the bar, but Trevor was busy pouring a beer and chatting with customers.

Cam crossed his arms over his chest and thunked his head back into the wall behind him.

This night—fuck, maybe this whole goddamn summer—was going to be torture.

THINGS WERE A little blurry.

Van's laugh sounded extra loud in Tate's ears as they both moved to the beat. Tate wobbled a little on her heels. It'd been so long since she had a night out like this, and the alcohol made the three-inch spikes tricky little buggers.

And the whole night, she'd felt this weird presence sliding over her skin. She chalked it up to the residual agitation of running into Cam, but the feeling only got worse as the night went on.

She turned and looped her arms around Van's neck, slowing her dancing to small shifts of her hips. Van loved to dance, and loved girls, a fact that hindered her love life in this small town. Van was currently working at a department store, saving money to head to California to try to model.

"Wanna go sit and get another drink?" Tate asked over the pounding music.

Van frowned down at her, placing her hands on her hips. "Is that you, Tate Ellison?"

Tate scowled. "Yes, why?"

"You're throwing in the dancing towel after two songs?"

Tate rolled her eyes and pinched the back of her friend's neck.

"Hey!" Van said with a mixture of annoyance and laughter. "Don't pinch me!"

"I'm tired." Tate pouted. "Don't give me crap."

Van's face softened. "Oh right, you had a blast from the past today."

Tate tried not to wince at Cam simply being referred to as her *past*. Even if it was true. "*And* cutting my hand *and* the panicked phone call from my brother which ended up being a bathtub ice cream social."

"Poor baby," Van said in baby talk.

Tate held her fingers up in a pincer grip. "You're asking for it."

Van laughed and pushed at Tate's shoulders, so she turned around and walked off the dance floor.

"I'm going to get our drinks. Go on and sit down and put your legs up, old lady," Van said.

Tate gave her the finger, and Van stuck out her tongue.

Tate walked along the wall on the way back to the table with the rest of their friends, fingertips brushing the old wood paneling to keep herself steady. Damn, why did she drink so much?

Her dad had said he was fine, that he was just going to sleep, so Tate could go out and enjoy some time with her friends. It still hadn't stopped her from checking her phone constantly like a doctor on call.

She totally *was* an old lady.

Her eyes were on the floor in front of her, so she saw the shadow first as it crossed her path. "Tate," said a familiar voice, and she stopped dead. Her skin prickled. And she wondered if this was the source of that weird feeling she'd had all night.

Marcus Olsen. Another mistake she regretted. Who the hell did she piss off that all of her worst decisions were biting her in the ass today? Really. A girl could take only so much.

And where was Van with those drinks?

"Tate," Marcus said again, and Tate sighed, looking up into his blue eyes.

"Hi," she said lamely, tucking a stray piece of hair behind her ear and bracing herself on the wall with her other arm.

Marcus leaned one shoulder against the wall in front of her, letting her know he was settling in for some Tate-Marcus chat time. Oh goody.

His eyes flicked down her body. "Lookin' good."

She wanted to wrinkle her nose, but she resisted. "Thanks."

"Wanna dance?"

"I hurt my ankle."

"Wanna smoke?"

"I quit."

"Wanna drink?"

"Not thirsty."

Marcus inhaled and exhaled slowly. "Why we gotta play this game?"

Tate narrowed her eyes. "There's no game."

Marcus barked that condescending laugh he had. "You played hard to get for a while and then finally backed down. I don't really want to play this game again, but I'll do it if it gets you in my bed again."

Tate wanted to vomit. Like in one of those romantic comedies where the heroine spews all over the lobby of her new school within the first ten minutes of the movie, and then spends the next hour and ninety minutes reviving her reputation from the ashes with pluck and a great wardrobe.

Wouldn't that be awesome? If she could throw up all over Marcus's shoes, and then she could begin her life over? And end up with a healthy dad and mature brother and guy of her dreams?

Movies were awesome. But they weren't real life.

And sleeping with Marcus last year had been a big, fat mistake.

"Look, Marcus, there is no *game*. That was a one-time thing. It was great, we both got what we wanted, but it's not something I'm going to revisit, okay?"

Marcus bent his head, watching his boot as he ground it into the floor, like he was putting out a cigarette butt. Tate's fingers twitched.

He raised his head slightly, eyeing her. "I'm not big on giving up when I really want something."

Why the hell did he want her? Honest to God, she had nothing to offer. Nothing. Okay, except sex. But he could get that from some other girl. She was closed for business.

She shook her head and leaned off the wall. "Well, nice talking to you, but I'd like to get back to my table."

Marcus straightened. "Tate, come on—"

"Marcus, please. No. Just no. Not now, not ever. And I'm sorry if I led you to believe there would ever be something between us, but I'm making it clear now. No."

Marcus's blue eyes swirled and his mouth tightened. "Tate." He took a step forward and grabbed her hand, not noticing the bandage on it from where she cut it earlier. His thumb pressed into the injury, and she cried out in pain.

Marcus jerked back, his mouth open in shock as he

stared at her hand. He looked like he was going to apologize but he never got the chance. Because another body was now between them.

A big one. In a black shirt. And this body was now pressing Marcus into the wall.

Tate clutched her hand to her stomach and groaned. Apparently this night could get worse.

Camilo was here.

The two men faced each other, Cam looking like he wanted to bite Marcus's head off. Marcus held his hands up at his head and looked so visibly freaked that Tate wanted to laugh. The guys had known each other in high school, but Tate didn't think they'd ever been friends.

They were talking heatedly and Tate clued in to the conversation.

"—she said no," Cam growled.

"I'm not a moron, Ruiz. I heard her."

"Then why did you grab her hand so hard that you hurt her?"

"I didn't—"

"I heard her cry out in pain, Olsen."

Tate froze at that. He heard her? Where the hell had he been standing? It wasn't like she'd screamed. As much as she enjoyed Marcus getting pinned to the wall, she thought it was time she stepped in.

"It's okay, Cam." She stepped forward, placing a hand on his arm. She opened her mouth to keep talking but lost her train of thought when Cam's head whipped to the side and he stared at her, eyes wide, wild and pissed off.

Oh shit.

"You said no and he laid a hand on you," Cam said through clenched teeth.

Damage control, Tate thought. As much as Marcus didn't know when to back off, he hadn't tried to hurt her. "I know. He grabbed my hand, which he shouldn't have done and I'm sure he'll apologize for, but the only reason it hurt was because I cut it earlier today. He didn't grab me hard."

Cam's eyes flicked down to her bandaged hand. Tate held it up and wriggled her fingers. "See? The soft-serve ice cream machine attacked me." She smiled weakly.

Cam didn't smile back. But at least his posture lost some of its aggressiveness. Didn't the military teach them to be cool under pressure? Jeesh. Cam was never a hot-head.

"I'm sorry, Tate, honest." Marcus spoke up. "I didn't know about your hand. But I shouldn't have grabbed you."

Tate nodded. "It's okay."

No one moved.

"Ruiz, pretty sure you can stand down now." Marcus glared at him.

Cam stepped back a foot, and Marcus eased off the wall. He turned to Tate and licked his lips, looking like he wanted to say something else. But Cam's presence, his thick arms crossed over his chest as he stared at Marcus, seemed to unnerve the guy. Marcus rolled his eyes and began to back away. "Whatever. See ya around, Tate. Have fun with your bodyguard."

And then he left Tate alone in a dark corner of the bar with Cam.

Tate rubbed her temples where a headache was forming. Today was the fucking worst. She exhaled slowly and focused on Cam, who stood before her with his arms crossed over his chest and still a little pissed off.

Which pissed *her* off. Because really, who did he think he was? Rolling back into Paradise with his fancy college degree, thinking she needed some sort of help or protection or what the hell ever.

Well she didn't. She'd been taking care of her family all this time on her own, working her ass off at the diner. The last thing she needed was Cam Ruiz thinking she owed him anything. "Well, thanks a lot for your tactic at disarming the enemy, but I think I have it from here." Tate made to walk past him, but he took a step, blocking her path.

She pulled up abruptly and glared at him, placing a hand on her hip. "Excuse me?"

Cam's jaw flexed. "How's your hand?"

"It's fine."

"Do you need stitches?"

Tate inhaled through her nose and out through her mouth and prayed for patience. "Nope, it's fine. It'll scab over and heal and be good as new. We done with the questions now?"

Cam gestured behind him in the direction Marcus left. "What was that about?"

Tate hadn't wanted to get into this, because that would just prolong this conversation, but it'd been a long day, and she was a little drunk. "Seriously? Look, Cam, I appreciate the concern, but I don't need this. I don't need a bodyguard or whatever. So just finish your visit in town and mosey on out to your big, hotshot job and forget about me like you did for the last four years, okay?"

Cam flinched slightly, dropping his hands at his sides, and that's when she saw the logo on the breast pocket of his shirt.

It burned into her eyes, and she felt a headache spreading from her temples toward the base of her skull.

She pointed at his shirt. "Why are you wearing that?" *Please, please, please—*

"I work here."

Three words. Three words that tilted her world on its side. And physically her world was tilting because she felt an arm around her waist, catching her before she hit the floor in an unceremonious puddle of Shocked Tatum.

And then her back was against the wall, and Cam was inches away, his face no longer pissed off, but concerned.

She blinked slowly. "Cam?" He was still so gorgeous. With those full lips and perfect skin and large dark eyes. His eyelashes were so full and thick, she used to joke about him wearing mascara. Her breath hitched. She could press forward, just a little bit, touch her lips to his. Just once. It'd been so long, and maybe she could claim she was drunk . . .

"You okay?" he asked, taking her attention off his mouth.

She focused on his eyes with his dark brows furrowed, and she recalled the reason she'd temporarily lost her standing ability. "Why are you working here?"

His lips shifted, like he was biting the inside of his

cheek. Then he licked his lips. "Because I needed a job. I'm the new bouncer."

That headache was a wrecking ball between her ears. None of this made sense. Cam was always going to go on to big things. He was always going to get out of this town. Why was he here? Working as a bouncer in a dive bar? "But you joined the military so they'd pay for your school. And you went to school. And you graduated magna cum laude. And you . . ." How could she make him see he was better than this? "You shouldn't be here," she whispered.

Cam frowned, but didn't step back. "I'm here to help my mom." He still had a strong arm around her waist, and her hand rested on his biceps, which had gotten much bigger since she'd last seen him.

She wanted to cry. Just burst into salty vodka tears right here in this bar because this couldn't be happening. She'd done all this for him, so he would be free.

And now he was back.

Shackled to this town.

How could this have all gotten so fucked up? She needed to get away from him. She needed to be alone where she could break down into a sobbing mess in private like a responsible adult. She pushed on his arms. "Please let go of me."

His arm loosened, but he didn't step back. "Okay, I hear you, but can you stand? You almost fell and—"

She pushed harder. "I'm fine!" Her voice was louder than she meant it to be, a shout, right in his face.

She froze. And he froze.

And then her phone rang, vibrating in her back pocket, its trill ring cutting the silence between them.

Chapter 5

HER EYES WERE huge, barely any hazel showing in the dark light. Her cheeks were flushed from the alcohol, her lips parted in rapid breaths.

Her phone continued to ring in her back pocket, but it was like they'd slowed down the action in Utope. Everything around them was slow motion as they stared at each other, as Cam's mind replayed their conversation, trying to figure out why Tate was worked up.

Other than the awkwardness, why did she care so much that he was back? And why the hell did she care where he was working? He felt like he was missing something, as Tate shook in his arms and visibly blinked hard to beat back tears.

"Tate—"

She ripped herself from his grasp and grabbed her phone out of her pocket, not looking at the caller ID as she answered it.

Her voice was shaky when she answered. "Hello?"

Both of them were silent as the voice on the other end spoke. Tate's face slackened as the color drained, and then it roared back to life as she clenched her jaw. "Are you fucking kidding me, Jamie? Hold on, I can't hear you. I'm going outside." Without looking at Cam, she took off, albeit a little wobbly, for the door.

Cam told himself to stay put. Not to get involved in Tate's personal life. But she'd said *Jamie*. That name tugged on his heart. Jamie had been like his little brother for years, and breaking up with Tate had felt like a divorce because of the kid. Cam wanted to know how he was, what he looked like.

And that was why Cam's feet began to move after her. Why he stuffed down the resentment he still felt over what she did. He did it because of Jamie. And because Tate looked half dead on her feet and her eyes were in shadows.

Cam followed her outside, where she was shouting into the phone. "You're lucky! You're so goddamn lucky they let you off with a warning. What the hell, Jamie? And I have to pick you up *now*? Right this minute?"

A pause and then Tate let out a frustrated growl, bracing herself with a hand on the side of the brick building. "Fine, I'll be there as soon as I can. I should let you stew in a holding cell. You owe me!"

She dropped the hand holding the phone at her side, her back to Cam, and he watched her slender shoulders rise and fall with deep breaths. Her shoulder blades poked through her thin shirt. Was she eating? Damn, she was thin.

And then she reared her hand back, like she was going to throw the phone, and Cam stepped in. He grabbed her elbow and cupped the phone in her hand so she didn't hurl it.

A gasp escaped her and she whirled around, Cam's hand on her elbow.

"Oh my God, what are you doing following me around? Looking for all the ways to save me?" The tears were there in her eyes now. "Big, smart, important Cam relishing how far Tate has fallen, huh? Is that it?"

Her words were furious, each one a fastball to his sensitive flesh, like he was naked at home plate and she was pitching them as hard as she could.

"Stop it," he said, slightly shaking her arm. She snapped her jaw shut and glared at him as he kept talking. "You think I . . . what? You think I came back here to gloat or something? I'm not gonna lie, I'm not over what you did. And I'm not gonna lie and say I'm ever gonna be. But that doesn't mean I don't care. And that doesn't mean that when you need me, I'm not gonna step up and be there for you. Like right now." He pulled his keys out of his pocket. "Where we going?"

Tate started to shake her head.

He cut her off. "I gather we gotta go pick up Jamie?"

She stared at him mutinously before giving him a small nod.

"Okay, and you've been drinking, so you can't drive. I can. Just let me tell Trev I got to go."

She crossed her arms over her chest and glared at the street.

"Wait right here, okay?"

Another nod.

Cam ran inside the bar, let Trev know he had to leave early to drive Tate and then tore back out of the bar, convinced Tate wouldn't be there.

But she was right where he had left her, looking deflated and not at all willing to battle him. When he reached her, he slung an arm around her shoulders and directed her to the car. "So, where to?"

CAM DROVE, SNEAKING glances at Tate. She was silent on the drive, but not still. She fingered a lock of hair at her shoulder, twirling it in her fingers. She rubbed her knuckles on the leg of her jeans, and slipped her feet in and out of her heels.

She sighed a lot, and sometimes she opened her mouth like she was going to speak, but then shut it again and stared out the window.

But her head kept drifting toward him and he could feel her eyes on him. His face, his hands, his arms.

Then, a featherlight brush on the arm of his shirt and she pulled up the fabric to look at the tattoo on his biceps. It was a simple set of wings he'd gotten with a couple of friends after they'd graduated basic. He and Tate used to talk about how they would get tattoos together when they were older and had money. It had been one of his fuck-yous to her he wasn't necessarily proud of. But girls dug it in college so it ended up being all right.

Finally, she turned to him. "So how long do you plan to be in town? What's going on with your mom?"

Cam tapped his fingers on the steering wheel as he halted at a stop sign and looked both ways. He began talking once the truck was rolling again. "She's got fibromyalgia. Some days are good and others are bad. She's on a new mixture of medication, so we are hoping that helps her out with the pain, mood and sleep issues."

"I'm sorry to hear about that. I didn't realize."

That was nice of her to say in light of her rocky past with his mom. "It is what it is."

She was silent for a minute and when he glanced at her, she was biting her lip. "So how long will you be in Paradise?"

"Not sure. I have a job offer in New York at a security firm. So as long as Mom is okay by then, I hope to take it."

"New York." Tate's voice was soft, almost reverent. "Good, that's good. You should take that job."

This conversation about his future, with the girl he always thought would be in it, was uncomfortable. They fell into an awkward silence, and Cam fidgeted with the radio, turning it up to drown out his thoughts. When that didn't work, he turned it back down. Finally, he spoke. "What's going on with Jamie?"

When Cam left for basic training, Jamie had been thirteen. He'd grown out of that weird preteen stage, and although he had his rebellious moments, he loved his dad and worshipped Tate. She was the mother he never had, since their mom had passed away from a heart attack soon after Jamie was born.

"He was drinking at a friend's house and a neighbor called the cops. The friend is a judge's son so that's the only reason we aren't picking him up at the police station right now."

Cam wasn't dumb, and he knew a lot could change in four years, but he never thought Jamie would be that seventeen-year-old kid caught drinking at a high school party by the cops. "Seriously?"

Tate stared out the window and when Cam glanced at her, she was rolling her lips between her teeth. "Tate?"

She started and glanced at him, then looked at her hands in her lap. "He's . . . having a rough time."

"Drinking? What the hell, Tate?"

Her head whipped to face him and those almond-shaped eyes were fierce. "I'm doing the best I can."

Cam held up a hand. "I never said you weren't. And what do you mean *I*? What about your dad? Shit, I'm just trying to get caught up on everything that happened since I've been gone—"

"There's really no reason you need to be caught up—"

"Damn it, Tate!" He banged a hand on the steering wheel and she jumped in her seat, but shut her mouth. "Why won't you let me help you?"

Her lips were pressed in a thin line until she spoke. Her voice was barely above a whisper. "You have to know it's killing me to be near you again."

He didn't know how to interpret that. All he knew was that he was conflicted. Because while he still wasn't over her betrayal, he also wasn't over how he felt about her. What a shitty situation—that he could never again be with the only girl he ever truly wanted. So he stayed silent. And Tate stared out of the windshield as they drove through the night to pick up her brother.

The house where they needed to pick up Jamie was on a good side of town, where a lot of people lived who commuted from higher-paying jobs in the city. They pulled up outside a large, two-story brownstone. Two cop cars were parked in the driveway, and a couple of kids were sitting on the curb, two cops standing behind them.

"I'm going to kill Jamie," Tate mumbled, staring at the cluster of teenagers with bowed heads.

It took Cam a minute to spot him. The porch lights from the house glinted off his dark blond hair. It was long, bangs hanging in his eyes, so when he looked up, he had to toss his head to the side to see.

They made eye contact, and if it wasn't for his unmistakable Tate-like face, Cam wasn't sure he'd know it was Jamie. Because those eyes, which were usually full of contentment, with a touch of snark, were full of anger and hurt, and Cam had to tense so he didn't flinch. What the hell had happened to this family?

And finally a thought occurred to him. "Wait," Cam said, turning to Tate as she placed a hand on her door to get out of the truck. "Why isn't your dad here?"

Tate froze, then opened up the door. "Can we just get him and go home, please?" she shot over her shoulder, and slammed the truck door behind her.

Cam winced and patted the dashboard. He'd have to talk to Tate about being nicer to his baby.

He hopped down out of the truck and strode toward

Jamie as Tate spoke to the police officers. She seemed to sober up since the situation called for it.

Cam stopped in front of Jamie and crossed his arms over his chest. The kid stared at up at him, eyes narrowed, lip curled into a sneer. "What the fuck are you doing here?"

It took every ounce of Cam's strength not to falter back a step at the force of Jamie's words. He was no longer a sweet young teenager who thought Cam and Tate walked on water. He looked like he wanted to drown them instead.

Cam leaned down slightly so he didn't have to yell. "You watch your mouth."

Jamie snorted. "I don't have to listen to you. You'll be gone again soon anyway, I'm sure."

Cam frowned. These poison barbs Jamie threw made no sense. "What the hell—?"

"Come on," Tate said, appearing beside Jamie and hauling him up with a hand wrapped around his biceps. "You're damn lucky this party was at a judge's house so these cops let you all off with a warning. I don't even want to know what would have happened if you lost your license."

Jamie didn't say anything but shot another glare at Cam as he walked by, allowing himself to be dragged by his sister. She directed him into a seat in the cab of Cam's truck. Cam slid into the driver's seat and looked in the rearview mirror. "Seat belt, Jamie."

Jamie didn't move.

"Put on your fucking seat belt, Jamie, or I'll have those

officers handcuff you and put you in the back of their car," Cam said.

When Cam heard the click, he put the truck in drive and headed for Tate's house.

It was muscle memory, all the turns he had to make, which potholes to avoid. He managed to make it there in fifteen minutes, despite the tension so thick in the car he could barely breathe.

When Cam pulled into the driveway, Jamie was out of the truck before Cam had it in park. "Hey!" he called after Jamie sharply, but the kid was already sprinting into the house. Tate followed more slowly, her heels in one hand, her purse dangling from the other.

Cam got down out of the truck and walked in front of her, checking the ground to make sure she didn't step on anything, like broken glass or a nail or a rock.

She followed along behind him hesitantly and when they reached the front door, she didn't open it right away.

"You need help with anything? Want me to do damage control with your dad?" Why was Cam volunteering to get so involved again in her life? He wanted to smack himself; at the same time he wanted to offer more, get on his knees and do anything so that she would let him chase away the shadows in her eyes and the anger in Jamie's.

She shook her head vigorously.

Cam looked around their yard and frowned. "Is the Civic your dad's car?" The Ellisons didn't have a garage, so Tate's old Jeep and the Civic sat in the driveway. Tate's dad drove an old Crown Victoria.

Tate shook her head. "No, that's Jamie's. We got rid of the Crown Vic."

Cam cocked his head. "What does your dad drive now?"

Tate bit her lip and looked down at her bare toes. "Look, it's been a long day, okay? I need to get inside and check on Jamie and . . ." She let her voice trail off. And Cam knew she was hiding something.

He took a step closer and gripped her chin lightly, tilting her head back so he could look in her eyes. She continued to worry her lip, her gaze darting back and forth between his eyes.

"I'm going to be here the whole summer. And as much as I wanna say, 'Screw you,' I can't. Because you're Tate and I'm Cam and this is what we do. Help each other."

It'd been that way since they were kids, when Cam didn't have a dad and Tate didn't have a mom. So together they made their own little family of sorts.

Her eyes closed slowly and then snapped back open. He wondered what it would be like to kiss Tate again. She'd been his first kiss. She'd been his first everything.

Why was he torturing himself like this?

Because his heart gave him no other choice. He saw something wrong with a family who'd been everything to him once. And he had to do everything he could to fix it.

He closed the gap between them and rested his forehead on hers. Maybe they could do this. And just be friends. They'd been best friends once.

"You'll let me help?" he whispered.

She licked her lips, and he felt a slight swipe of her tongue on his bottom lip. "Why do you want to?"

He shook his head, still connected to her with his hand at her chin, his forehead touching hers. "I don't know. But it feels like that's what I should be doing."

She inhaled sharply and then exhaled slowly. "Okay."

And before he did something crazy like kiss her or let his hand wander, he pulled back. "You know where to find me. And tell Jamie he and I are going to have a chat."

She nodded and he turned to walk down the porch steps.

"Camilo," she said softly, and he looked over his shoulder. "Drive safe."

He smiled. "Sure."

Chapter 6

TATE BLINKED AT the TV in her dark room, running her
fingers over the button of her Catharsis controller.

The opening screen of Utope flashed in front of her
eyes, little characters on the screen making dinner and
shopping and diving into their backyard pools. In Utope,
players created characters from scratch—choosing their
hair, eye and skin color; their wardrobe; their jobs.

She hadn't played this game since Cam left for basic.
She hadn't been able to look at the house they created
together, a two-story with a two-car garage and roaring
fireplace.

A dog and a cat.

A swimming pool with a grotto.

And that rain forest with colorful poison dart frogs.

She dug her nail into the plastic seam of the controller and bit her lip. This had been their escape, when the
pressures of school and no money and racist assholes got

to them. It was where they dreamed of what they wanted, once they graduated college.

But then Tate's dad got sick, and she made a bad decision and those dreams were gone.

Except they weren't erased. Because they were here, in this stupid video game.

Tate straightened her spine and hit the START button, pulling up her saved games. She clicked on the saved Ruiz game, typed in the password—*pinkiepie*, after her favorite My Little Pony character—and then there it was. Their blue house with the yellow gerbera daisies in the front garden.

All the characters could be controlled by the same user. Or, since the game was connected online, they'd often played together when Cam was at his house and she was at hers. It was fun to "talk" to each other through the characters.

As Tate stared at the TV with her stomach churning, the game resumed where they'd left it the day before Cam left. Their two characters sat on the front porch swing, drinking beer together, Tate's head on Cam's shoulder.

She laughed, because Cam wore only a pair of camo shorts and work boots, which was the closest they could come to a military uniform in the game. She wore black pants and a black shirt and a black veil, "in mourning" because he was leaving. Cam had laughed when he'd seen her outfit, and then his character kissed hers, and then they kissed in real life and it'd been a while before they'd picked up their controllers again.

She pressed the A button on her controller, which brought

up suggested dialogue, as well as a blank box for her to type in her own. She hesitated. If Cam signed in to the game, he could see anything she did, replaying previous scenes with a click of a button. But he probably didn't even have the game anymore. And if he did, there was no way he'd sign in.

There were many things she wanted to say to Cam, but after last night, she knew what she wanted to say most at this moment. She clicked on it.

Her character in the game raised her head, looked at Cam, and said, "Thank you."

Afterward, Tate saved the game and shut it off, then crawled into bed and hugged her pillow. She closed her eyes and pictured Cam's face when he had looked at her on the front porch, so close to hers, his lips parted. She swore he was going to kiss her, and there was no way she'd recover from that.

Seeing Cam again made her want all the things she couldn't have. And that was a distraction. She needed to stay home and take care of her dad and Jamie. She couldn't live that life with Cam they'd dreamed of.

But Cam deserved those dreams. He was a good man. A brilliant, determined man. And he should have that cute house and dog and swimming pool. A girl he loved who loved him back.

He shouldn't be here in this town. The thought of him living here again, working as a bouncer after everything they'd been through, made her blood pump hot with anger. She hadn't realized his mom was struggling. Not that his mother would let Tate know anyway since she never liked Tate in the first place.

Accepting Cam's help wasn't an easy choice. She wanted to resist because, come fall, he'd probably be gone, starting his future in the Big Apple with his fancy job. And she was happy for him. But she'd still be here in this town, with only a high school diploma, working at a diner while trying to keep her dad alive and her brother out of jail.

Tate considered herself a strong person, but she'd been strong once—or so she thought—and look where it had gotten her.

Cam was her weakness. And she resigned herself to the fact he always would be.

She didn't know how long she lay there in the early morning, drifting in and out of sleep, between the real world in her bedroom and the dream world where she was on a porch swing with Cam.

Eventually the noises of her household set her permanently in the real world. She stretched and rose, padding out of her room and down the hall to the bathroom. While doing her business, she wondered how the hell she was going to deal with Jamie today. Last night, he'd shut himself in his room by the time she made it back in the house, and she was too tired and drained at the time to deal with him. Today, though? That was another story.

When she walked out of the bathroom, her father was on his way toward her. "You need help?" she asked.

"I'm good, baby."

Tate walked past Jamie's door, which was still shut. She was tempted to bang on the door and drag him out by his hair or his ear or his ankle, whichever was more painful, but she needed coffee first.

She'd at least been conscious enough to make the coffee last night so all she had to do was press the START button. She stood in front of it, staring at it as it brewed, like that would make it work faster.

She heard her father shuffle into the kitchen and lower himself on a chair at the table. "Toast okay?" she asked him.

"Do we still have some of that quince jelly?" His voice was hopeful and although she hated to give him the sugar, it made him happy.

"Just had Anne pick up some more."

Her father made a face she couldn't decipher, and Tate turned away from him so he didn't see her smile. She always thought Anne and her father had feelings for each other, but neither was willing to make the first move.

Except for this weird quince jelly arrangement. Which Tate didn't think was very romantic, but whatever.

Her father was a month out from his second round of chemotherapy. It had taken a while to get his strength up to begin this second round and he was slowly starting to come back into himself. She hoped this was it, that he'd beaten the lung cancer once and for all. But she knew he'd never fully recover. He'd lost too much weight and muscle mass.

They had some pension money from his factory job, but they had to budget everything down to pennies. Which was one reason they sold her father's car. He never drove much anyway. Jamie had bought his old sedan for less than a thousand dollars, and he needed it for his pizza delivery job.

Tate had thought about finding another job, but the

diner paid her well and gave her the flexibility to take her father to his appointments. And when her whole life was spinning out of control, it was nice to have a place that grounded her. Where she knew exactly where she was supposed to be and what she was supposed to be doing.

She poured herself a cup of coffee and turned around, eyeing her dad over the rim of her mug as she took a sip. "How are ya feeling today?"

He shrugged as the toaster popped. Tate slathered it with margarine and quince jelly and slid the plate in front of him along with a large glass of apple juice.

He picked up a slice, which Tate cut into triangles just to annoy him, and took a bite. "Fine," he mumbled around a mouthful of bread and jelly. "Did you have a good time last night?"

Her father didn't always sleep well, a mixture of feeling ill and the medication he was on, which gave him the jitters, but apparently last night, some god had smiled on her, because he seemed not to have a clue what had gone on.

She took another sip of her coffee. "Yep." She glared down the hallway, silently daring Jamie to show his face right now so she could tear him a new asshole.

But he didn't show. And so she silently seethed.

There was a knock at the front door and a feminine "Hello?" Then Van came into the kitchen holding a wax paper bag, large sunglasses covering her eyes. She plopped the bag on the counter and then took her glasses off, sliding one end into her shirt. "I brought doughnuts and—" She held up her hand as Tate opened her mouth. "Your father can have one measly doughnut hole."

"I want more than a doughnut hole," he grumbled.

"You just eat your toast," Tate shot at him.

Van pulled out the doughnuts and plopped one on Tate's father's plate. Then she licked her fingers and dug out a chocolate glazed. Tate bit into a Boston creme.

Van chewed and swallowed. "So, wanna talk about how Cam's back?"

Tate began to choke on her bite of doughnut, and Van slapped her back until Tate held up a hand.

"Cam's back?" her father said, his mouth hanging open in wonder. Because back in the day, he and Cam each had this mutual hero worship thing going on. At the time it warmed her heart. And now it soured her stomach.

"You couldn't lead in with a 'How are ya?' or a 'Good morning'?" Tate asked. "You had to ruin our lovely and pleasant doughnut breakfast by hopping right into the big questions?"

Van popped the last bite of her doughnut in her mouth. "I'm still having a lovely and pleasant time." She turned to Tate's dad. "Aren't you, Ted?"

He nodded vigorously. "Quite pleasant. Never been pleasanter."

Tate glared at both of them. "I don't like when you two team up."

Van wobbled her head and made a face. "Whatever. So, Cam?"

"I have a bone to pick with you about that anyway." Tate pointed at her friend. "How could you not tell me he's back and working with Trevor?"

Van wrinkled her nose. "Trev never told me. He's not going to be happy with the words I plan to say to his fact-omitting ass."

Tate snorted, and then picked at the icing on her doughnut. There were things she wanted to say, but not in front of her dad. Actually, she wasn't sure she wanted to say them out loud . . .

Her father cleared his throat and rose from the table. "Well, I'll leave you two to do your girl talk—"

"Dad, you don't have to do that." Tate grabbed his plates and placed them in the sink. "You can stay to chat—"

He held up his hand with a chuckle. "I can see this is a time where your old man isn't wanted. All I want to say is that I'd love to say hi to Cam sometime. Maybe bring him around?"

Oh jeez. Oh shit. That's exactly what she wanted to avoid. But instead, she bit her lip and nodded.

Her father gave her a smile and then walked out of the kitchen.

Tate collapsed into a kitchen chair and propped her chin in her hand. Van settled down beside her with another doughnut.

"So Cam helped you with Jamie or something?"

Tate gave her a brief rundown of last night's events, including Cam's insistence on helping her.

"Well that's good, right?" Van's face brightened. "That he wants to help? You could sure use it."

Tate sighed and raised her hand, fingered a dent in the wooden tabletop. "But that's the problem, Van. I could use it. And then what happens when he leaves again?" She lowered her voice. "And he doesn't know about Dad."

Van cocked her head. "Then tell him. He'd want to know. Especially now that your dad took chemo so well."

Tate pursed her lips. Cam back in town and inserting himself in her life was complicated. It dredged up all the old memories and mistakes and decisions. She'd finally come to terms with her life and her responsibilities. And the fact that none of her new life involved Cam.

But now he was back, making her want things. Making her wish she'd done things differently.

And it hurt. It hurt places she swore she'd caulked until they were sealed airtight.

But Cam always had a way of worming himself inside.

A door slammed open and Jamie stomped down the hall. Tate rose. "Jamie, we need—"

"Gotta go." He didn't even look at her as he made his way to her front door, keys jingling in his hand.

"Excuse me?" Tate didn't have to force the attitude in her tone. It was there as she cocked out a hip and placed a hand on it.

"Sorry. Got an appointment." And then he was out the door.

Tate contemplated running after him and slashing his tires or something drastic. Instead, she stamped her foot and growled in frustration. Then she sat down on her chair and stuffed a doughnut hole in her mouth.

"What the hell is his problem?"

"I don't know," Tate said through a mouthful of sweet carbs. She brushed glaze crumbs off the table. "But we still need to talk about what happened last night. He's obviously avoiding that conversation. Hell, I don't want to have it, but it needs to be done."

"You going to tell your dad?"

Tate shrugged. "Yeah, but after I talk to Jamie and get things settled. I don't want my dad to have to deal with this stress."

"I'm sorry." Van placed a hand on Tate's forearm.

She sighed. "Yeah, me too. Story of my life."

Operation Catch Jamie, Avoid Cam, Help Dad was in effect. Easy-peasy.

Chapter 7

CAM STARED AT the TV in his room. He hadn't touched it since he'd been home. They'd canceled cable long ago to save money, since his mother's only source of income right now was disability. And his TV only made him think of video games. And Utope.

And Tate.

He closed his eyes and sighed. The pain of what she'd done had been so fresh yesterday when he first saw her. But now that he'd seen she had a lot going on in her life, his feelings had shifted.

He'd always want to be there for her. He'd always want to help.

Before he could think too much about what he was doing, he sat up and grabbed the case for Utope and slipped the disc into the game system. He gripped the Catharsis controller and lay on his bed on his stomach, propped on his elbows and started the game.

His fingers hovered over the START button and he pressed it, then pulled up the Ruiz saved game, typing in the password.

And there they were. Avatar Cam and Avatar Tate, together on the porch swing. They were just pixels of CMYK, but Cam could still close his eyes and feel the weight of Tate's head on his shoulder, the smell of her hair, the feel of her skin.

A notification popped up in the lower right-hand corner, letting him know there'd been activity on this game since he last checked in.

Had Tate . . . ? No, she probably took this game and smashed it or something.

But no one else knew the password . . .

He clicked on it and the past scene replayed. Tate raised her head and looked at his avatar in the game, and a little speech bubble appeared over her head. *Thank you.*

Cam's whole body jolted and he nearly fell off the bed. He scrambled to his feet and then slid to his knees in front of the TV. He replayed the scene again.

Thank you.

And again.

Thank you.

And that was it. That's all she'd done. But she'd done it. He frantically pulled up the menu to see when she'd played it last. The time stamp showed that it'd been done about three hours earlier. Only three hours ago. She'd been awake, and she'd played the game just to tell Cam thank you. And before that, she hadn't played this game since the day before he left for basic.

He'd run miles with a fifty-pound ruck on his back, and he'd entered battle simulations and he'd shot a gun at targets but he wasn't sure his heart had ever beat this fast. If his hands had ever been this clammy.

He dropped the controller and placed his palms on his thighs, breathing deeply, feeling the ache in his chest, the pull toward Tate. Sometime in the last twelve hours, she'd hooked her chain to his heart again. And she was reeling it in.

He couldn't deny it. And he didn't know what to do about it.

When he got his heartbeat and breathing under control, he picked up the controller, clicked Z for action and B for speech.

His character kissed Tate softly on the forehead and said, "Always."

CAM GLANCED AT the clock as he drank his coffee and figured it was about time to check on his mom. She was usually awake by now. Part of him wanted to put it off and just wait for her to come out on her own, all chipper and moving freely with no pain.

But that was wishful thinking.

He sighed and walked down the hall, touching her door with the tips of his fingertips so it slowly swung open.

His mom lay on her side, staring at the door. When she smiled at him, it was strained.

"Mom?" Cam said, walking in and taking care to sit on the bed gently so he didn't rock her.

She blinked a couple of times and licked her lips. "No laundry today, Camilo."

Cam exhaled roughly and fisted the sheet so he didn't punch a wall. That was their code phrase for a bad pain day. Fibromyalgia was a tricky bitch. And anything that involved his mom moving her arms a lot, especially over her head, caused extreme neck and shoulder pain. He glanced at a basket of folded laundry in the corner and pursed his lips. "I told you I'd do that."

"You were working."

"Damn it, Ma!" Cam's voice rose and when she flinched at his tone, he took a deep breath to calm himself before he spoke again. "That's why I'm here. To do things for you, like fold laundry so we don't have days like this."

She walked her fingers forward until she covered his hand with her own. She squeezed gently until he relaxed his fist. Then he turned his palm upward and twined his fingers with hers.

"I've been dealing with this for years. I can handle it. It's just going to be a bad day."

"But I want to help—"

"You're not going to be here forever. And I don't want you to be. You need to live your own life."

He clenched his jaw. "Right now, my life is here with you."

When she smiled, it was sad. Wasn't she happy that he was home to take care of her? He was sacrificing a lot to be here, so he at least wanted her to appreciate the help.

He pushed that thought aside. "Do you need anything? I don't have to work until later."

"I think we need some groceries. You mind running to the store?"

Good, a job. A task that she needed completed. He could do this. He nodded eagerly. "Of course. Do you have a list?"

"On the notepad on the fridge."

He leaned down and kissed her forehead. "Want me to get you something to eat?"

She shook her head. "I'll get it myself. Just going to lie here for a bit."

He frowned. "You sure?"

"I'm sure."

He stood up and fixed the covers over her shoulders. She huffed at him and rolled her eyes but he ignored her. "Call me if you need anything, okay?" He made sure her phone was within easy reach.

"Just go already."

"Okay, I am!"

He was wearing only a pair of camo shorts, so he went into his room and slipped on a shirt and an old pair of sneakers.

As he walked out the front door, he called out, "Be back soon!" And waited for an answer. When he heard, "Drive safe!" he smiled and walked outside.

At ten in the morning, the June sun was out in full force. The air in his truck was thick and hot and he turned up the air-conditioning full force, letting the vents blast the air in his face as it cooled. He reached for his sunglasses in the center console and accidentally knocked them on the floor of the passenger side. When he reached for them, he spotted the keychain first, a plastic My Little Pony charm he'd given Tate for her seventeenth birthday. He picked up the set of keys, running his finger over the face of the pony. Pinkie Pie. Tate's favorite. Their Utope password. She loved the toys when she was a kid and still watched the cartoon.

Her keys must have fallen out of her purse last night. Jamie and gone into the house first, so Tate might not have realized she didn't have them. "Shit," he muttered. He'd have to take them to her.

He glanced at the time, figuring she worked a later shift today if she went out last night. But even if she wasn't home, hopefully he could catch her dad or brother.

So when he backed out of the driveway, he headed away from the grocery store, and toward Tate's house.

He pulled into the driveway behind Tate's Jeep, but he didn't see Jamie's car anywhere, which kind of pissed Cam off. He wanted to have words with the kid where he wasn't drunk and angry. He'd have to talk to Tate about maybe taking the kid out for lunch or dinner. A neutral place where Cam could figure out where the hell all his anger was coming from.

He knocked on the door and waited, shifting his weight from foot to foot and jingling Tate's keys. When no one came to the door, he tried again.

Finally he heard footsteps and then the door swung open. "Van, why bother knocking now—"

Tate's voice cut off and her eyes went wide when she spotted Cam on the doorstep.

And he stared. Because she was wearing teeny-tiny

shorts that showed off her long, tan legs and a tight tank top that clearly let him know she wasn't wearing a bra.

He didn't mean to stare at her chest, but holy hell. She might have lost weight other places but not there. Damn.

"Cam?"

His gaze shot up to her face. And he cleared his throat in an effort to hide his blush. He held up her keys. "Uh, you left Pinkie Pie and her friends in my car, so . . ."

He waggled them and shot her a grin. She blinked at the keys, then at his face, then smiled slightly and reached for her keys. "Oh wow, I can't believe I didn't notice."

"It was pretty hot in my truck, so might want to give Pinkie Pie some water, make sure she isn't dehydrated."

Tate chuckled softly; her head dipped as she fingered the keychain. "Okay, I'll do that."

A shuffling sound came from inside the house, and Cam craned his neck to see inside. "Hey, is your dad here?"

Tate straightened and closed the door so he could barely see inside at all. "Um, he's busy doing . . . stuff . . . so, I appreciate you bring my keys over—"

"Cam?" came a deep voice from inside.

Tate whirled her head around, so her loose ponytail on top of her head flopped. "Dad, I think he needs to go—"

"I can stay for a little and say hi to your dad—"

"But—"

"Baby, open up the door!" There were some whispered words, and then the door opened wider. Tate stood off to the side, fidgeting uncomfortably as Ted's figure filled the door frame.

And it took all of Cam's self-control not to gasp.

Because this was not the large, muscled man he remembered. The man who worked at a factory building high-end motorcycles.

His hair was mostly gone. He had no mustache or five o'clock shadow. He probably weighed half what he did the last time Cam had seen him.

But he still had that smile and those bright hazel eyes Tate had inherited. "Cam." He extended a thin, wrinkled hand. "Good to see you, son."

Cam shook his hand, feeling a slight tremor in the body of the other man. "Come on in," Ted said, waving him in. Cam followed him inside, shooting Tate a what-the-fuck look behind his back. She at least had the decency to look ashamed.

Ted took a seat on a recliner and Cam's eyes fell on an oxygen tank beside him.

"Van brought some doughnuts this morning. Baby, why don't you get me another doughnut hole? And offer one of those apple fritters to Cam. He always liked those."

"Okay, Dad." Tate arranged a blanket around his frail legs and then without a look at Cam, turned and walked into the kitchen.

Cam took a deep breath and followed her.

In the kitchen, she set out plates and began placing doughnuts on them. Her hands were shaking and she was biting her lip.

"Tate—"

"Do you still like apple fritters?"

"Tate—!"

"I don't know why Van even gets them. You're the only person I know who ever ate them."

"Tate, for fuck's sake, what's going on?"

Tate stared at the doughnut on the plate in front of her, breathing deeply. And Cam waited. Ted had always treated him like another son. He'd been so accepting of his daughter dating one of the few minorities in this town. And to see him looking . . . so weak . . . made Cam sick to his stomach. He certainly didn't want a fucking doughnut. Apple fritter or not.

"He has lung cancer." Tate's voice was soft. She picked off a flake of glaze from one of the doughnuts and stuck it in her mouth. "Diagnosed a couple of years ago. He just had his second round of chemo. They'll test soon to see if it worked."

He glanced at her trembling fingers, remembering how she used to smoke. "Is that why you quit?"

She nodded, picking more glaze off the doughnut.

"I'm so sorry."

Tate looked up at him. "Thank you."

Cam rested a hand on the counter and leaned closer. "I feel like when I was gone, no one told me anything about what was going on back here. How come no one told me about his cancer?"

Cam shrugged jerkily. "I think you made it clear that anything about me was no longer your concern."

He threw up a hand. "Seriously? Your dad has cancer and because we broke up, you think I didn't care about him anymore? What kind of robot do you think I am?"

Tate placed one foot on top of the other and scratched

her cheek. "I don't think you're a robot. I just . . . Everything happened so fast. He got diagnosed and then it was this whirlwind. We were caught up in the tornado of cancer treatments, and I don't think we've touched the ground yet. Sometimes I wonder if we're just in the eye of the storm right now. Where it's calm before all hell breaks loose."

"Did you think about what I said? I'll help, Tate." They could be friends, couldn't they? And her family meant something to him.

Tate pursed her lips. Then picked up a doughnut and took a big bite. Once she chewed and swallowed, she gave him a small smile. "I'll think about it." She was being evasive. She was brushing him off. But he wasn't giving up, especially not now that he knew what she'd been dealing with since he'd been gone.

Cam broke off a piece of fritter. Because even though his stomach hurt, it smelled good and Tate's smile was easing that sick feeling in his gut. "I can drive him to appointments or anything. Whatever."

"I said I'd think about it." Tate's voice was edged with irritation.

"Hey, where's my treat!" Ted called in from the living room.

Tate laughed, the first real laugh he'd heard from her since he'd been home. "We're coming, keep your pants on!"

Cam spent the next hour eating doughnuts and drinking coffee with Tate and her dad. They caught him up on the new businesses in town, and he told them stories about Alec and Max. Tate took an interest in Kat, Alec's girlfriend, and said she'd love to meet her.

When he left the house, he called his mom.

She answered the phone. "Did you get lost at the grocery store?"

Cam laughed. "No, I had to stop at Tate's house." He turned on his truck and sat back in his seat. "So, how come you never told me about Tate's dad?"

His mom was quiet for a moment. "It's complicated."

"How is it complicated? You call me and say, 'Hey, Camilo, Tate's dad has cancer.' You had to have known. This whole town is one dysfunctional family."

She sighed. "I know, and I'm sorry."

"I know you don't necessarily like Tate—"

"I don't dislike her," his mom grumbled.

Cam signed and ran a hand over the steering wheel. "Makes me feel weird, being gone and missing everything."

"You were off living your life. Getting a degree. That's better than most people in this town."

He bit his lip, because it wasn't like he deserved it more than anyone else here. "Okay, well, I'm heading to the grocery store now. You okay?"

"I'm fine. Go and make sure the ice cream doesn't melt."

Cam laughed. "Okay, Ma."

Chapter 8

TATE GLANCED UP at the sound of the bell over the door of the diner and watched as Cam sauntered inside. He glanced around at the half-full tables and then swung his gaze to where she stood behind the counter.

A small smile touched his lips, and then he made his way toward her. He slid into a chair opposite her at the counter and jerked his chin to the ice cream machine. "Behaving itself today?"

Tate rubbed the small scar on her hand. "I guess so. Temperamental bitch."

Cam laughed. "Well, I won't make you do battle with it today. Burger and a Coke?"

Tate nodded and wrote it down on a slip of paper, then slapped it on the counter behind her for the kitchen. "Order!"

It'd been this way for about a week. This tentative truce. Cam showed up at her work, dropped off take-out dinners at her house, anything he could do to help. Even though she hadn't asked for a thing. But he was pushing his way into her life again without her knowing when it had started. She knew she should put a stop to it. Tell him to back off and deal with his mother and his own life.

But she hadn't. And she didn't intend to. Maybe she was a masochist because she knew how this would end when he left. But the instant gratification of having him now won out.

Anne walked out from the back room, smoothing down her apron. "Hey there, Cam."

"Looking good, Anne. You just had a birthday, right? Twenty-five?"

Anne psshed. "That charm and those dimples, boy. Gonna get you in trouble one day."

"Already has." Cam winked and took a sip of the soda Tate slid in front of him.

"Trouble," Anne muttered, but her smile let Tate know she enjoyed the teasing.

Tate grabbed the bin of silverware and began rolling them in napkins before the lunch rush.

"You talk to Jamie yet?"

Tate dropped a knife and it clattered on the counter. She picked it up and placed it in the napkin with its friends, the spoon and the fork. "He's avoiding me."

"Well, make him *not* avoid you."

"It's not that easy. I don't want to get Dad involved right now, so unless I go make a scene at his job, it's hard." She dropped a silverware package in another bin and eyed Cam. "Oh, and he's got a girlfriend."

Cam raised his eyebrows and took another sip of his soda, crunching an ice cube. "Yeah? That good or bad?"

"I don't know. I haven't met her yet but he's spending the night there. So that's a whole other issue I have to deal with." She leaned closer and spoke lower. "I need to make sure he's being smart and using protection."

Cam pointed at her. "Okay, I'll make you a deal. I'll talk to Jamie about the drinking and the screwing. But you have to tell your dad, too. If I know Ted, he'd be hurt about being kept in the dark."

Tate's hackles rose. "You think I don't know my dad? I'm trying to make the right decision—"

"Tate." Cam's voice was firm. "I'm not judging you. I'm trying to help, okay?"

She deflated a little. "Okay."

"And hopefully Jamie will listen to me. He did when he was thirteen."

Tate looked up at him through her lashes as she continued to roll silverware. "Yeah, well, thirteen seems like a lifetime ago."

"We'll figure it out, okay?"

Tate nodded, a pricking starting behind her eyes. All this *we* talk was hard to hear from Cam's mouth. As much as she appreciated having him back in her life as a friend, it was hard to deny she was still in love with him. She'd repressed her libido for so long and one look at Cam in his tight T-shirts, those full lips grinning, those earrings she wanted to nibble, was almost too much.

The day he started dating someone else, she might have to drive to the ocean and fling herself into it.

Of course she knew he dated girls in college. She'd seen the pictures on Facebook when she snooped. Which was rare because it put her in a depression for about a week.

But he'd never been around the same girl for long, thank God. She could deal with him doing his thing, playing the field. But him getting serious with someone? The jealousy screaming through her body was no joke.

But he'd be gone by fall. To a big city. He'd meet some amazing girl, probably a Latina hottie with a great ass, and they'd make cute little Latino babies. But at least she wouldn't have to see them walking down the streets of Paradise together. Hopefully.

For now, though, she'd take him how she could. And if that was friends, at least she had him in her life somehow. They'd been friends first. In fifth grade, Cam had been small and scrawny. He'd been bullied for being different, for having a last name that stood out. He'd had his lunch stolen almost every day, until Tate sat beside him one afternoon and shared her peanut butter and marshmallow sandwich. He'd taken it with a quiet thank-you, and they ate in silence.

Every day after that, she shared her lunch with him, growing wiser and packing two sandwiches for him. Until the bullies stopped bothering him because Cam wasn't suffering from their theft.

And then they'd played pick-up games of soccer together. And then they'd studied together. Until they had their first kiss over top of a biology textbook in high school, and they'd been together ever since.

So she could do this again—be friends with Cam.

As long as there were no biology textbooks.

She rolled the last of the silverware and plopped it in the bin. Margo called Cam's order and Tate reached for the plate, then set it in front of Cam.

It was crazy how she could predict his actions for the next thirty seconds, and she watched his hands. Take the bun off. Remove onions. Rearrange lettuce and tomato. Take top bun. Shake a dollop of ketchup on top in an expanding swirl. Plop bun back on burger. Smoosh. Pick up. Take a bite.

She smiled to herself as he hummed and chewed at the same time. "Is that all you plan to eat all summer? Burgers? You're going to lose that physique the armed forces worked so hard on."

Cam pointed a finger at her. "Mind your own business. In fact, you could stand to eat a burger or two."

She propped a hand on her hip. "Excuse me?"

Cam looked a little chagrined as he pushed his fries around on his plate. "Just saying you lost weight is all."

He was right. Tate only knew because her clothes had been fitting a little bit different. "Guess I need to eat more doughnuts."

Cam smiled.

She stacked the glasses under the counter, then unstacked them and then did it again. Needing something to do with her hands to avoid looking at him when she spoke next. To pretend it wasn't such a big deal. "I . . . uh . . . actually I do have a favor to ask."

He looked up expectantly. "Yeah?" His voice was tempered, she could tell, like he was worried if he showed too much excitement, she'd retreat.

She shoved the cups away and began folding clean rags. "Next Wednesday, can you drive my dad to an appointment? He might only have to stay for a couple of hours, or they might keep him overnight for some tests. Jamie and I have to work. Normally, I'd ask Anne or something but she has to work too . . ."

Cam held up his hand. "No problem. I don't work Wednesdays."

She dipped her head. "Yeah, I know. I had Van check Trevor's schedule."

"You could have called me or texted me. My number hasn't changed. Unless you deleted it from your phone."

Of course she hadn't. She lived in fear of drunk texting him, but couldn't bring herself to delete it. "No, I didn't."

He shook his head, his smile a little sad. "Yeah, me either."

LATER THAT NIGHT, Cam signed into Utope, thinking maybe he should feed their dog. Or check out their backyard rainforest.

But instead, he saw that Tate had signed in earlier. He clicked to replay her actions.

And there was her avatar, in the kitchen, wearing heels and a dress and an apron. She stood at the stove, and Cam cocked his head, like that would make him able to see better what she was doing.

And then his avatar walked in and sat down at the kitchen table. Tate turned around and slid a plate in front of him. Cam squinted because it looked like . . .

"I made you apple fritters," Tate said.

Cam, the real one, laughed out loud, as his character in the game picked one up and said, "Mmmm."

Cam watched it one more time, and then he ordered his character to go shopping. He walked to the nearby mall and headed into a kids' store.

For one hundred and fifty virtual dollars, he bought a huge, stuffed Pinkie Pie pony.

His character couldn't fit it in his car—he had a little sports car—so he had to take a bus. And all the other passengers glared at him as he squeezed into his seat with the huge stuffed pony. Cam laughed the whole time.

And then he arrived home, where Tate's character was outside gardening.

He presented her with the gift, and she jumped up and down clapping.

"Friends truce?" Cam asked.

Tate repeated. "Friends truce."

Then he gave her a kiss on the forehead and walked into the house to eat the rest of his apple fritters.

Chapter 9

THURSDAYS WERE THE busiest nights at Deke's. It was probably a mixture of the college Thirsty Thursday mentality and the weekly dollar-twenty-five draft sale.

Either way, Cam was busy at the door checking IDs. He didn't know if it was something in the water or what, but he'd already had to turn away a group of girls and two guys for all having fakes.

The girls flirted and tried to get in anyway, but he wouldn't budge. The one guy tried to slip him money to let him in and the other guy . . . well, the other guy tried to flirt with him, too.

But Cam didn't negotiate with terrorists and turned them all away.

Tate was somewhere in the crowd with Van. He hadn't talked to her since he had lunch at the diner two days ago. He knew she'd seen the game, because she smiled shyly at him and rattled her Pinkie Pie keychain.

He'd smiled back and then tried to keep his eyes off her cleavage.

Then he wished it were winter so she had to wear turtlenecks.

Trevor was busy at the bar and gave Cam a chin lift when he turned around to check on him. Cam swung his head back to the door, but on the way, his gaze met the familiar eyes of Marcus. The guy was over in the corner of the bar with a couple of his friends, near the pool tables. They'd never been friends and Cam knew he'd just been biding his time, waiting for Cam or Tate to screw up so he could swoop in and get with her.

Bastard.

Cam didn't want to know why Marcus was sniffing around Tate now. And if he'd done more than sniff in the past.

Cam focused on a group of girls coming inside. One of them was a girl he recognized. What was her name . . . Maya? Naya? Mara? *Shit.*

She smiled at him, her tongue between her teeth in a gesture he assumed to be flirty, and handed him her ID.

Cam glanced at it as he ran it through the machine. *Kara Masters.* He snorted to himself. So he was kinda close. He'd gone to high school with her, although he thought she'd been a year younger. One check of her birth date told him she was twenty-two so his memory wasn't so bad.

"Cam Ruiz, right?" Her voice was bubbly and giggly. And he smelled perfume and makeup and a little bit of vodka. They must have pre-gamed somewhere else.

"That's me."

"How are you?" She leaned closer, and her friends whispered to each other. Then she put a hand on his biceps, right under his tattoo, and squeezed her fingers. He felt like a steak being tested for doneness.

"Good, Kara. You?"

"I'm great." Her breath coasted over him. Yep, vodka. He'd have to give Trev a heads-up on serving them.

He stood up and jerked his chin toward the bar so they'd follow him.

"You gonna buy me a drink?" she asked.

Her hand hadn't let go of his arm, and he didn't bother shrugging it off. He also ignored her question. "You ladies already drank?"

"Frozen cosmos." Her eyes glittered.

Ew, he thought. "Well, that's good. Remember, liquor before beer, you're clear. Beer before liquor, never been sicker."

She laughed and slapped his chest like that was funniest, cleverest thing she'd ever heard. "I'll have to remember that!"

He nodded. "You do that."

When they reached the bar, Cam placed his palm on the top and tugged on his earlobe, his sign to Trevor that they had some patrons who were on their way to drunk town.

"How about a pitcher of light beer on the house, ladies?" Cam asked. He didn't want them ordering shots or, heaven forbid, more cosmos.

Kara smiled huge, like he'd just given her a diamond

ring. And after extracting himself from her clutches, he resumed his post at the door. His eyes searched the bar again and this time, his gaze met Tate's.

Well, the side of Tate's head, because she was shooting a death glare at Cosmo Kara. Then she whipped her head to him. Their eyes met, and Cam waited to see Tate's reaction. She looked pissed and maybe a little hurt.

Then she shook her head, her face clearing, and turned her attention back to her pool game. Cam looked around the table and noticed Marcus was right behind her, watching as she bent over the table, lining up her shot. His eyes were on her ass. And Cam wanted to throttle him.

If Cam had any sense, he'd turn his stool around and focus on the door and his job. Forget about Tate over there laughing at something Marcus said, her hand on his waistband, stealing looks at Cam out of the corner of her eye.

Did she really want to play this game?

Because Cam had perfected this fucking game in college. If she wanted Cam "The Player" Ruiz, she'd fucking get him.

He glanced at his watch. It was break time. *Fucking perfect.*

He looked at Trevor and pointed at the clock over his head. Trev saluted back.

And it was officially game time. Cam made a beeline toward Kara, then leaned down where she sat at a table along the wall with her friend. The pitcher of beer stood on the table untouched. "Hey, wanna play some pool?"

Kara's widened, and she squealed as she bounced to her feet. And Cam sighed because if he would have said that in Tate's ear, she would have put on her game face, cracked her knuckles, and told him she'd have his balls.

He walked toward the pool table next to Tate's, her eyes on him the whole time as she stood off the side while Marcus took his shot. As he drew closer, with Kara trotting behind him, Tate narrowed her eyes.

Cam grabbed two pool sticks, handed one to Kara and then asked her to rack the balls. When she stared at him with wide blue eyes, he sighed and did it himself.

He was a dick for using Kara, who was a nice girl. But she'd caught him on a bad night, so maybe he'd tell Trevor to give her a free round of shots next time she was in or something.

Cam glanced over at Tate and caught her staring at them. He smiled to himself and focused back on the pool table and Kara's minty breath along his temple.

Game. Fucking. On.

TATE STARED AS Cam stalked toward the empty pool table beside her, Kara Masters hot on his heels, staring up at him like he hung the fucking moon.

Tate growled under her breath.

"Tate!" said an irritated voice behind her, and she whipped her head around.

Marcus stood with a hand on his hip, the other propped up on his pool stick. He made a proceed motion with his hand. "Called your name three times. Your turn."

Tate mumbled an apology and eyed the table, but her gaze kept drifting to the table next to hers, where Cam was racking the balls. Kara leaned down, chattering, her cleavage right beside his head.

Cam leaned down to break the balls, shooting Tate a glance, then he turned to Kara and said something to her with a smile.

Oh, that bastard. He wanted to play this game? She could play it right back. A thought trickled in the back of her mind, struggling to beat through the beer buzz she had, a thought that maybe this wasn't a good idea. That a friends truce didn't include jealousy. But one look at Kara's laughter and Cam's grin buried that thought under an avalanche of anger.

She tugged on the hem of her shirt to lower the neckline a little and then did a flirty turn to face Marcus. She braced her hands on the edge of the pool table and rolled her shoulders back so her chest stuck out a little. Marcus's eyes darted right where she wanted them. Out of the side of her eye, she swore she saw Cam glance over.

"So, it's been a while since I played pool, Marcus, and I'm not sure I'm holding my hands right, ya know?" She held them up and wiggled her fingers. None of that was true. She used to have a pool table in her basement until she sold it to help pay the bills.

Marcus cocked his head to the side, like he was trying to figure her out. "You want me to help you?"

"Sure!" She straightened and held up her pool stick, letting it wobble in her hands.

Marcus turned her around and showed her how to

hold her hand on the felt, so her pool stick could slide easily in the webbing between her thumb and forefinger. His technique was actually kind of bad, but Tate played along.

She stole a peek at Cam. And met his narrowed eyes.

With a sharp turn of his head, he maneuvered Kara in front of him, mimicking Tate and Marcus's positions, as he directed Kara how to shoot.

Tate arched her back so her butt snugged back up to Marcus's groin. His breath caught and his lips lowered to her ear.

Cam's face was red and he gripped Kara's hip, his face pressed intimately into the side of her neck.

"You're such a good teacher, Marcus," Tate moaned, eyes on Cam.

She heard him say to Kara, "You're a great student, babe."

"Fuck, Tate," Marcus breathed into her ear.

"Tatum Ellison," came a sharp female voice, and Tate straightened suddenly, cracking Marcus on the chin with the back of her head. He gave a grunt of pain, and Tate turned around. "Oh shit, Marcus. I'm sorry!" She held her hands up to see the damage but Van spoke up again. "Tatum, we need to have words. Go over there"—she pointed to a table in the corner—"and sit down."

"And you!" She pointed at Cam. "You go sit over there, too."

He placed a hand on his chest like *Who me?* and Kara made some noises of protest, but one look from Van had her scurrying back to her table.

Tate left Marcus's side and walked to the table with her head down. She felt like Van was going to take a ruler to her knuckles.

She sat down at the table, and Cam slid into a chair beside her.

Van stalked up and stood before them with her arms crossed over her chest. "First of all, both of you owe Marcus and Kara an apology. Because you used them in whatever little game you were playing."

Tate hung her head. Shit, that had been wrong, and she did owe Marcus an apology. She looked at Cam, and he was biting his lip.

"Now, we have a problem." Van tapped her foot. "I thought you two were friends, right? Well, friends don't act like this. They don't get jealous of the attention the other is drawing from the opposite sex. And they certainly don't put on little performances like you did just now."

Tate shifted in her chair and scratched her knee.

"Anything to say?" Van asked.

Silence. One heartbeat. Two heartbeats. Three heartbeats.

A chair scraped and Cam's deep voice was in her ear. "What the fuck, Tate? Marcus practically had you cornered in the bar the other night and now you're playing pool with him?"

Because watching you flirt with every patron was killing me, and I wanted a little attention to make me feel better. Tate turned to him. "It's not a big deal. Marcus and I have hung out before. We were just playing pool, not screwing in the bar."

Cam's jaw clenched. "Wait, are you two . . . are you together?"

Tate hesitated. "No, we're not together."

He leaned closer. "You just hesitated. Have you been together?" When she didn't answer right away, his eyes widened and then turned cold. "Wait, is that the guy—?"

"No-ooo," Tate drew out the word. "Seriously? Are you going to bring that up for the rest of our lives? No, Cam, no. If you really want honesty, I've been with Marcus once. Last year. That's it. No repeats will be happening. Are you happy now?"

The normally warm brown of his eyes swirled like a muddy river in a storm. "Well damn, girl. Glad you got someone in town when you need some."

Tate's anger reached its peak. "Oh, fuck you. What, you think I was celibate for four years? Waiting for Cam Ruiz to show up and stoop for his own leftovers? Get real."

He pointed to himself. "You have to flaunt it in my face?"

She threw her hands out to the sides. "What am I flaunting? Because I'm drinking? Because I dare to show my face in the same room as you? I mean, what the hell? Are you actually jealous?"

He made a choking sound and leaned forward, waggling his finger between them. "This. This friends bullshit. It ain't working."

She barked out a laugh. "What an Einstein you are. No shit this isn't working. Because I refuse to be a verbal punching bag. I'm not going to live my life being punished for one mistake." She stood up and leaned down.

"So you either get over it or stop bringing it up. Because I'm fucking done, Cam."

He shook his head and stood up, too. "Guess that's it then."

She'd had him. She'd had him back for about one week. She didn't know whether to laugh or cry or throw things. "Guess this truce is reversed."

He looked away, his shoulders tense. "Guess so."

She was done. She didn't want to hear any more and as she walked toward Van, who wore a devastated look on her face, she heard a "Hey, Tate."

She stopped and looked at Cam over her shoulder. "What?"

His eyes were calmer, the storm over. His voice was softer when he spoke. "I'll still be there Wednesday to drive your dad."

She wanted to refuse. She wanted to tell him to go to hell, that she'd find her dad another ride. But that would take a lot of scrambling. She didn't have the time or energy, and despite her anger and hurt, she knew she could count on Cam not to let her down. Her responsibility to her family won out. So she just nodded, and then walked to Van. Her best friend's arms encircled her, and Tate waited until she was outside the bar to break down and scream and throw things.

Because Van was there to pick up her pieces and put them back together. Then Van drove Tate home, helped her and all her pieces into bed, whispering that she'd be put back together again by morning.

But this time, Tate didn't think so.

Chapter 10

CAM SIGNED INTO Utope, biting his nail and jiggling his leg.

He'd acted like an asshole last night. He'd used Kara and he'd said some shitty things to Tate. He wanted to blame the alcohol for his actions, but he'd been sober. Stone-cold sober.

Also jealous.

And pissed off.

He signed into their game and waited for a notification to pop up letting him know that Tate had played the game. He almost wanted her character to slap him. Or yell at him.

But after five minutes of staring at the screen with no notification, he had to face the truth that she hadn't played. She didn't want to communicate with him.

His fingers ran over the smooth buttons, the controller warm in his hand. He wanted to do something. Apologize or reach out somehow. But he didn't know what to do. So instead he shut off the game and went to check on his mom.

TATE WALKED ALONGSIDE her dad in the grocery store while he rode one of those motorized chair carts. She tossed in a box of crackers on an end cap and rolled her eyes when he made a screeching sound with his mouth as he took the turn as fast as the cart would go, which was not very fast.

Years ago, when she first helped him into the chair cart, she'd thought he'd hate it, or complain that it made him feel weak.

But she should have known that he'd take every opportunity to act like a kid again. He zoomed that thing around the store like he was hot shit. He echoed the high-pitched beeping when he backed up. He practiced complicated turning maneuvers. He waved at other shoppers like he was royalty. He even had the cupped-hand wave down. She pretended to be annoyed, but she loved how happy it made him.

He grabbed a bag of white cheddar popcorn off the shelf and threw it in the cart. She glared at him. He glared back.

"It says it's healthy," he pointed out.

"Yeah, in relation to a bag of greasy chips. But that popcorn isn't exactly healthy."

"I like it."

She sighed and kept walking.

"So, Cam going to join us for doughnuts again anytime soon?" He watched her face as he asked the question.

Tate faked an extreme interest in the nutrition content of a frozen pizza. Her truce with Cam had lasted . . . not long. Before they both blew it by acting like middle schoolers at recess. Every time she thought about that night at the bar last week, her stomach churned. Because she'd used Marcus, got yelled at by Van, and still smarted from the barbs that had flown from Cam's mouth.

Why did he have to be home? And mess up her ordered life. She'd had it all figured out until Cam showed up.

"Tatum?"

She threw the box of pizza into the cart and began to walk.

"We never get sausage," her father said, leaning to the side to put it back in the freezer case.

"It was sausage?"

He nodded and nudged the cart closer to her. "What's going on?"

"Nothing."

"You want to talk about how you feel about Cam being back?"

She did not. "No, that's okay."

Tate kept walking as she heard the whir of the cart at her heels. "You want to talk about your breakup?"

No. No, no, no. She definitely did not want to do that. She'd rather rip out her eyelashes one by one. "No, Dad."

"Because I think there's a lot of things unresolved there," he pushed.

Unresolved? There wasn't a word to describe the clusterfuck that was her breakup with Cam. She whirled around. "Dad, first of all, I don't want to discuss this. And I certainly don't want to discuss this in the freaking grocery store."

He didn't back down. And those eyes didn't waver from his face. "It's hard to find time to talk to you when you aren't working or dead on your feet."

She instantly deflated. "Shit, Dad, I'm sorry, I—"

He shook his head. "That wasn't to guilt you. You're busy and I appreciate everything you do for this family. But sometimes I think you take on more responsibility than you need to."

How did he get from the Cam breakup to this? "I don't—"

"Why didn't Cam know about my cancer?"

She froze. That was a complicated answer. "I . . . um . . . I never told him because we broke up . . ."

He cocked his head. "You didn't think he'd still want to know?"

Tate looked down at her feet. She wanted to blurt out the whole sordid tale. Flop in her dad's lap and cry while he smoothed her hair and told her it would all be okay. But instead, she mumbled, "Probably."

"Baby," he said softly.

She looked up, glad that the grocery store was rather deserted for an early Monday morning. "Not trying to be hard on you, but sometimes decisions we make have a ripple effect on a lot of people. And that's okay, but you want to make sure those ripples don't turn into tidal waves, all right?"

This was weird, like he knew everything. Or maybe he suspected, but either way, all she could do was nod.

He seemed satisfied with that, and started up his cart, driving past her so she had to jog to catch up.

While loading the gallon of milk in the car, she changed the subject. "So, I think Anne's dropping off a casserole tonight."

Her father pretended not to hear her.

"I think it's that chicken spaghetti thing. Isn't that your favorite?"

He turned his head away from her and she suppressed a laugh. She teased him about Anne. About the crush the two had on each other but seemed to want to avoid. "I think she's going to stay and eat it with you."

He lifted his nose in the air, still ignoring her, and she relished getting him back for giving her a hard time earlier.

"She said she might wear her new black lace lingerie."

"What?!" he cried, whipping his head to look at her.

And she cracked up, clutching a container of a dozen eggs to her stomach as she doubled over.

His eyes narrowed. "You're full of shit."

She laughed harder. "I got you to answer me."

"Brat," he muttered.

"I'll light some candles for you and turn on some Kenny G."

"You turn on that music, and I'll smash the stereo."

"Temper," she tsked.

"How about Anne and I go out for burgers and you and Cam can share a nice intimate dinner over chicken spaghetti casserole?"

Tate sobered. "Not funny."

Her dad grinned. "Put on some Marvin Gaye?" He started swaying in his chair and snapping his fingers. "*I've been really tryin', baby*," he crooned.

"Oh God," Tate groaned and glanced up and down that empty aisle.

Her dad kept singing. "*Let's get it on . . .*"

"I'm your daughter and this is super inappropriate."

"*Let's get it on . . .*"

"I'm leaving."

She stomped off down the aisle with the sounds of her father's laughter behind her.

ALMOST A WEEK since that night at the bar, Cam still hadn't made any plays in Utope. He checked every morning and every night. He saw that Tate had signed in on her end. But neither of them seemed willing to make the first move.

It was an awkward virtual standoff. Both too stubborn to admit they'd both been out of control and immature. At least that's what Cam was telling himself.

He glanced at the clock. He had a little bit of time before he had to pick up Ted and take him to his appointment. Because no matter what happened with him and Tate, he'd never let her family down.

He peeked into his mom's bedroom and frowned when she wasn't there. Then he checked her bathroom, which was empty. Finally he found her in the basement, reaching for something on a shelf.

"Mom!"

He hadn't realized she was standing on a stool and at the sound of his voice, she started and almost fell off. "Camilo!" she said with a shaky hand to her chest. "Why on earth are you shouting?"

He was at her side in seconds to steady her so she didn't fall. "What're you doing down here? If you needed something, I couldn't have gotten it for you."

She pressed her lips together. "Yes, I realize that. But I was capable of walking down the stairs, stepping on a stool and getting a roll of paper towels."

"I didn't say you weren't capable."

She stepped down off the stool slowly, the roll of towels tucked under her arm. He followed her up in the stairs to the kitchen as she placed the paper towel roll on its silver holder by the sink. "You've been such a huge help to me already this summer. Between doing things around the house and the extra money, but I don't want to rely on you forever."

He took a step closer, leaning a hip on the counter. "Why not?"

She faced him. "Because you'll leave this fall. You'll take that job, and you'll live your life."

"Mom—"

"I'm glad you came home after graduation. It's been wonderful to wake up every day with you in the house. You can't know how much it means to me that you did this. But I can't be the reason you stay here. I just can't."

He reached for her hand. "Ma . . ."

"This where you tell me you're grateful to your single mama for raising you?"

He shook his head. "This is where I tell you again how unfair it was when I got grounded when I was six for cutting our cat's whiskers off."

She scowled. "He kept walking into walls, you hooligan."

Cam laughed. "Okay, so other than the grounding thing—"

"You were a bad boy sometimes."

"—I'm grateful, Ma. And I guess I wanted to show you that. By being here for you."

She smiled and stepped closer, gripping his forearms in her hands. "And I get that, Camilo. But the best way to repay me is for you to be happy doing what you love. If that's here, bouncing in a bar? Fine. But if it's not, and you want to take that job, then you take it. You understand?"

He lucked out with a great ma. "Yeah, I understand."

She squeezed her hands and then released him. "Good. And all I ask is that before you go, I'd like you to help look into moving somewhere cheaper. A small apartment, all on one floor. That would cut expenses so my disability check would stretch farther. I looked into a couple of places already."

Sure they rented this place, but still, they'd lived here for over ten years. "No problem, Ma."

She smiled. "You're a good man."

He hugged her and pressed a kiss to her temple.

A glance at the clock told him he needed to leave to pick up Ted.

"Need to run to get Ted. You'll be okay? Not sure if I'll be home for dinner."

She paused and did that thing where she ran her tongue over her teeth, like she was searching for the words.

He waved a hand. "Out with it. What do you need to say?"

She glared, like it annoyed her he could read her. Then she huffed. "You need to think about the long-term repercussions of getting involved in Tate's life again."

Oh great, this again. He clenched his jaw. "I'm not—"

She pointed a finger at him, "Yes, you are. You're helping her out and making her rely on you. Now, I've never been that girl's biggest fan. I'll be the first to admit I think you two were too young to be as involved as you were. But now you're adults. And you need to think about what it means to be doing what you're doing with her."

"I'm here so I should help—"

"But why you—"

"Because I should have been there this whole fucking time, Ma!" he shouted and winced when his mom jolted at the sound of his voice. "Because I left and her life went to hell and even if she made choices that contributed to that, she didn't make her dad get cancer. She deserves a break."

She raised her chin in the wake of his outburst. "I'm not saying she doesn't deserve a break. But you need to think about how that weight is going to feel like double on her shoulders when you leave again."

The guilt nearly choked him. "Well, I can't do anything about that right now. I'm here and I can't just stand by now."

She patted his shoulder. "I know. But just think about it."

He didn't. On the drive over, he blasted music and thought about getting drunk later so he didn't have to think about it.

At the Ellisons', Cam parked in the empty driveway—both Tate and Jamie appeared to be at work—and walked to the front door. He knocked once and heard a muffled "Come in."

The doorknob turned, and Cam frowned at it when he noticed the screws were a little loose. He'd have to tighten them later.

"Hello?" he called, shutting the door behind him.

"Bathroom. Be out in a minute!" Ted called back.

Cam stuck his hands in the pockets of his shorts and grabbed an apple from a basket on the kitchen counter. He bit into the crisp fruit and chewed as he walked around, checking out the pictures framed on the wall.

There were still the pictures of all the homecoming dances he'd taken Tate to. And the prom. The graduation picture where they stood laughing under the archway of their school in red and black gowns.

Some new ones had been added, but the difference was noticeable. A couple of pictures from holidays, it looked like. In them, Jamie's eyes weren't as bright. Ted was losing weight. And Tate . . . she never looked at the camera. And she wasn't smiling.

Cam walked back to their prom picture. He'd rented an all-black tux and Tate had worn an emerald dress, her whole look like something out of *Breakfast at Tiffany's*. They'd won prom king and queen their senior year. And Cam smiled sadly thinking of how they'd danced together with their plastic crowns.

"Taking a little stroll down memory lane, huh?" said a gruff voice from behind him.

Cam turned around as Ted walked slowly down the hall toward him. The older man jerked his chin toward the pictures. "Tate tried to take them all down a year or so ago. But we realized the paint had faded and none of us wanted to paint again, so we left them up. I'm glad. I like looking at 'em."

Cam resisted flinching at the thought of Tate wanting to take down all the pictures. But then, he couldn't blame her. He'd ripped them all off his walls and shoved them into a shoebox. He'd wanted to burn them, but his mom had intervened.

"Good choice," Cam mumbled, and walked into the kitchen to throw his apple core away. He washed his hands and walked back out to the living room. "How ya feeling?"

"Same shit, different day," Ted grunted. He'd said that for as long as Cam could remember, so it made him smile.

"You ready?" he asked.

Ted walked toward the front. "Already ahead of ya."

Cam ducked his head and smiled bigger.

Ted was quiet on the drive, lost in thought. Cam fretted that maybe he was in pain, or feeling sick, or a multitude of other things, but the guy was a grown man. If he wanted to talk about it, he'd start the conversation.

So Cam kept silent, fussing with the CD player. And it wasn't until twenty minutes into their forty-minute drive that Ted spoke up.

"I need you to help Tate with Jamie." Ted's voice was so low, Cam barely heard him.

"I'm sorry?"

Ted cupped his knees and then ran his hands up and down his thighs. His jaw worked. "Tate doesn't hide things as well as she thinks she does. I know Jamie's not been himself lately."

Cam tongued his cheek. Jamie was worse than just "not himself." But Cam didn't want to say too much and betray Tate's confidence, but he did think Ted had a right to know what was going on. He chose to stay silent.

Ted sighed. "I've tried to talk to him, but he avoids me. He comes home when I'm at appointments or when he knows I'm resting." He shook his head. "I got sick at a bad time. When he really needed a father who was present. I think he's angry and lost, and I wish I knew how to help him."

Cam tapped the steering wheel. "Do you want me to talk to him?"

Ted looked over and nodded. "Yes, I'd like that. He always listened to you."

Cam didn't think he had sway over Jamie anymore, but he held his tongue.

Ted continued. "I know you and Tate are . . . well . . . not what you were. So if you don't want to do it for her, then do it for me."

Cam didn't even have to think about it. "I'll do it for all of you."

Ted stared at the side of his face, and Cam resisted meeting his eyes, because he wasn't sure he wanted to see what was in those watery hazel eyes.

"You grew up into a good man, Camilo Ruiz." Ted patted his shoulder.

And Cam had to blink at the prickle in his eyes. Would Ted still think that if he'd seen how Cam treated Tate the other night? Shit, this was hard being back.

"I told Tate you'd want to know Jamie is . . . not himself," Cam muttered.

Ted licked his lips and his eyes shifted. It was minutes before he spoke again. "My girl means well, but she's going to have to learn she can't keep making decisions for everyone else."

Those eyes bored into his temple and when Cam risked a glance at him, Ted's eyes were piercing, like he was trying to convey more than just what his words meant.

But Cam couldn't read minds. And he didn't get it.

And by the time they'd reached the doctor, he hadn't gotten up the nerve to ask Ted to elaborate.

Chapter 11

"Tate?" Cam called into the house. He'd dropped off Ted at the clinic, and the doctor had said Ted would have to stay overnight. Ted told Cam he didn't need a ride home and that he'd call Anne so Tate wouldn't have to worry about it.

Cam picked up his phone to text Tate to tell her, but he hesitated. He hadn't seen her since the previous week, and this was a good excuse to check on her. He called himself a fool about fifty times on the drive to Tate's house, but that didn't stop him from pulling into her driveway, turning off his truck, and heading to her front door.

Cam knocked and listened for an answer. Instead, he heard raised voices. He turned the doorknob and found it unlocked. So he stepped inside and followed the voices until he reached the back of the house. Through the sliding glass door, he saw Tate and Jamie on the back porch, facing off to each other, bodies tense.

"You're out of control!" Tate yelled. "It took me a week to be able to corner you long enough to have a five-minute conversation with you. You think I don't have enough to deal with? I have to worry about you drinking and getting arrested now?"

Jamie fluttered his lips. "Fuck you. You act like you're so perfect but you're just as fucked up as me."

Tate threw out a hand. "What the hell is that supposed to mean?"

Cam backed away, thinking he should leave the siblings to argue in peace, but Jamie's next statement stopped him cold.

"Don't get preachy at me when everyone knows you're just a cheating slut."

Tate reared back like she'd been slapped.

And Cam was out the door. He didn't even shut it behind him as he bore down on a Jamie who looked equal parts furious and terrified.

But Cam didn't give a fuck. He hoped Jamie pissed himself.

Cam backed Jamie against the railing and leaned down so their faces were inches away. When he spoke, he kept his tone even but no less deadly. "Don't you ever, ever speak to your sister like that again. Apologize to her. Right now."

Jamie's eyes shifted beyond Cam's shoulder, but the sight of his shattered sister must not have been enough for him to grow a fucking conscience. "I don't need to apologize to her when it's the truth—"

"Jamie. Apologize right the fuck now."

The kid gathered some courage from somewhere and straightened his spine. "You of all people should be happy someone finally said to her—"

Cam leaned even closer, using all his willpower not to knock Jamie out with a fist. "No, in fact, I'm not happy. I'm not happy at all. Unless a woman is your wife or your girlfriend, it's not your concern who she gets into bed with."

"But she cheated —"

"And that's between her and me. No one else. If I hear you use that word in your sister's direction again, swear to God, you won't like the consequences. Do you hear me?"

Jamie gulped and his eyes shifted again to his sister. Cam took a step back and followed his gaze.

Tate stood in the same spot, her face white, her entire body slack, like she barely had strength to hold herself up. She stared at them, but her eyes were blank, like she wasn't really seeing anything.

"I don't want to apologize," Jamie said, and Cam whipped his head to face him again. Jamie kept his eyes on his sister as he spoke. "You did what you did and made him leave." And then Jamie whirled on Cam. "And you. You didn't fight. You didn't fight for her. You left. You just *us*." He jabbed his finger into Cam's chest on the last word and then took off into the house, slamming the door behind him.

A minute later, Cam heard the sound of Jamie's car starting up, and the squeal of tires as he took off down the street.

Cam stared at the door and then took a deep breath as he turned to Tate. She still hadn't moved. She stared at the place Jamie had been standing.

"Tate?"

Nothing.

"Tate?"

Finally she looked at him and blinked. But then her eyes went big and dark and so full of pain, he thought maybe it had been better when she had looked blank.

"How's dad?" she asked, her eyes a little unfocused.

"He's fine. He said he'd call Anne to give him a ride home tomorrow."

Tate nodded. "Good, that's good." She sucked in a shaky breath. "I have to . . ." she waved a hand and walked unsteadily into the house. Cam followed her, cursing himself for staying, for overhearing that conversation, for feeling sympathy for Tate.

When he entered her bedroom, she was perched on the end of the bed, staring at her blank TV.

"Are you going to be okay?"

Her jaw worked. "I didn't . . . I didn't think about Jamie. That he'd find out."

He sighed. "Small town. People talk."

She dropped her head and stared at her hands in her lap. "He hates me now."

"He doesn't hate you—"

"He called me a slut—"

Cam clenched his jaw and spoke through gritted teeth. "And I'll have a talk with him about that—"

"It doesn't matter," she whispered.

"It does matter. He can't talk to you like that."

"What's done is done."

The finality of her words pierced his chest. He took another step toward her even though he wanted to take a step out of the room. "Something you did four years ago doesn't define you. That's not all you are."

"It's not?" Tate looked up at him, her expression full of hope and he didn't know what the hope was for. He wanted to be in her life, but he couldn't go down that road again. He needed to get out of here.

He backed up toward the door. "Look, no offense but if you want to give an explanation just to ease your conscience, I got better things to do—"

"I'm not trying to give an explanation—"

"Good, because I don't want details—"

She slammed her fists down into the mattress and yelled, "Well that's good! There are no details, because I didn't do it!"

Cam froze, resting his weight back on the ball of one foot. "What did you just say?"

She wasn't looking at him. Instead she was staring at that damn TV again. "I didn't do it."

The words were clearer this time. Louder. And Cam knew this was one of those moments. A life-changing moment. Where he could stay and hear her out, get pulled back into her life. Or he could leave. Go back to the way he'd accepted his life. Without her.

His body rocked, back toward the door, forward. If he lowered his heel to the ground, he'd keep walking backward. He'd leave.

But his heart, his foolish heart that wanted to hear her out, pulled him forward and then he was sinking down onto the bed beside her. They sat in silence until Cam spoke. "Well, I guess I'm going to need an explanation now."

She stared ahead as she talked, and every word was like a baseball bat slamming into his gut. "Dad had just been diagnosed with cancer. And I couldn't call you at basic. And . . . all I could think about was that I was going to have to stay here. In Paradise. I couldn't leave and go to college with you. But . . . I wanted you to stay on track. I wanted you to finish school and get a great job and . . ." She took a deep breath. "I didn't know how I was going to convince you of that. I know you and I knew if I told you, you'd come home. That's the last thing I wanted. So I went to this stupid, stupid party." She shook ahead and dropped her eyes to her lap again. "And this guy was really drunk and hitting on me and I was drunk and I let him lead me to the bedroom." She twitched her lips. "I'll be honest that I thought about sleeping with him. He leaned in and kissed my neck and that's when it hit me that this was wrong. It was so wrong. So I shoved him back and told him no. And then he threw up on me, and fell on the bed and passed out. Just"—she giggled softly—"passed right the fuck out."

"That's . . . gross." Cam wasn't sure what else to say about it.

She laughed softly again. "Yeah, it was pretty gross. So I took off my clothes and I threw this T-shirt on and I walked out and that's when I saw Marcus. And he just stared at me, and then back into the room where the guy was passed out. And it looked bad. Of course it did. And he said, 'Ruiz is gonna dump your ass when he hears about this.'"

She turned to him then, with a knee on the bed. Her hazel eyes were wide, searching his. "And at the time, I was upset about my dad. And I was drunk. And I was eighteen fucking years old and my first thought was that *that* was how I could get you to stay in school. I'd let you think I cheated on you."

Cam's breath caught in his throat. His chest felt tight, like he couldn't get enough air, and he fisted his shirt over his heart. "No, Tate, you didn't."

She started crying then, softly. "I let Marcus run his mouth. And I didn't deny it. And then . . . when I was sober, it was too late to stop the rumor mill. And Dad was getting sicker and I thought, *This is for the best*." She leaned closer as the tears tracked down her cheeks. "This was the only way I could think to get you out of Paradise. You're smart and amazing and you deserve all the good things in life. I didn't want you back here with me in a dead-end job, taking care of my father. I didn't want that for you."

And then anger rose up, swift and sudden. He grabbed her shoulders and shook her. "How could you do that? How could you make that decision for both of us?"

She sobbed harder, collapsing against his chest as his hands slipped from her shoulders and his arms pressed her to him.

"That was so fucking stupid, Tatum. So fucking stupid."

"I know." The wetness from her tears seeped into his shirt.

"So fucking stupid."

She leaned back then, and he gripped her biceps as she brushed the tears from her cheeks. "I thought, or at least I convinced myself that what we had wasn't special," she said, those eyes boring into him, daring him to look away.

He didn't know where this was going. "Special?"

She bit her tongue between her teeth, then released it. "We were so young, Cam. I thought . . . I thought everyone loved like us. That strongly. That intensely. With everything they have." She looked away then, her eyes blinking rapidly and her lips trembling.

He waited, unwilling to slice into this moment, because the truth hung in a precarious vapor between them.

She faced him again, eyes wet but more composed. "But now I know better. Boy, do I ever know better. If I had known what we had was so rare, I never would have let you go."

And then that truth wrapped around them, securing them in a protective bubble, so all Cam could do was stamp this moment to make it real and true.

He pressed his lips to hers, and she sighed and shuddered beneath his hands. He nudged up with his chin and she knew what that meant, opening her mouth so he could delve inside.

That first taste of Tate was everything. Hot summers in the backseats of cars and licking drips of ice cream off her wrists and true, first real love.

She'd been everything to him. And now that he tasted her again, he knew that had never changed.

She allowed him to lick at her mouth and duel with her tongue. And she pressed into him, those full breasts rubbing against his damp shirt.

He pulled her into his lap so her legs straddled his hips. She gripped his shoulders and rocked her body into him, her lips parted, her eyes now full of need. For him.

CAM'S EYES WERE big and dark, his full lips begging her to taste them again. She never thought she'd be here in his lap. She never thought she'd get to see Cam like this again. She gripped tighter with her knees. "Please, Cam . . ."

"Please what?" His voice was pure gravel.

She moaned, because he was torturing her. She scooted closer, until she felt his arousal snugged up where she wanted it most.

"Tell me, Tate. Tell me what you want, and I'll give it to you."

"Make me come," she whispered.

His answer was a hissed yes and her eyes closed under the weight of her desire for him.

There'd been so many times, late at night, under the protection of darkness and her twisted sheets when she'd imagined Cam's fingers, while her own had been a poor substitute.

But now . . . now this was better than she remembered and better that she'd dreamed of. Because this was an older, more mature Cam. A Cam with experience that she didn't want to think about. All she knew, as his hand slid into her underwear and cupped her, was that she was benefiting from this experience.

Because she shamelessly rode his fingers as they slid through her wetness and inside her. She moaned as he whispered into her ear that he missed her, that she was beautiful.

He pressed harder inside, searching for that spot he'd always known, and she whimpered, bucking her hips. The heel of his palm pressed against her clit as he twisted his wrist.

"Why?" he whispered against her neck, his lips burning into her skin.

"Why what?" She dug her fingers into his shoulder and kept her rhythm, searching for it because she was so close . . .

"Why would you throw this away? When everything about you and me is so right?"

She turned her head and kissed his jaw, the stubble rasping over her lips. "Please," she begged, her voice hoarse.

His hand stilled and he pulsed the heel of his hand once. "Tell me this is right. Tell me we're special, that we'll never have this with anyone else."

Her voice broke on a sob. "We're special. This is right. It's always been you, Cam. It's always been us."

And then his fingers pressed and twisted, and she was flying. There was a deep voice murmuring to her and another high voice gasping in pleasure, but Tate heard everything in echo. Because her focus was on that feeling in her belly, the warmth that spread out to every limb until even the tips of her toes and fingers tingled.

Cam talked to her through it, cupping the back of her head while her face was pressed into his neck so all she smelled was him, all she felt was his hands and his very presence surrounded her.

When she came back into her body, she couldn't feel her legs and her eyelids drooped. Cam's fingers were still inside her, and he drew them out slowly. She winced and shuddered as they slipped over her sensitive skin. If only she could just sleep, right here, in Cam's lap.

"That was fucking beautiful," he said against her ear, his teeth catching an earlobe, and her eyes popped open.

She smiled against his neck and reached down between them, feeling for what she hoped was still an alive and eager erection. Her grin widened when her hands closed around his hard shaft through his shorts. He hissed when she stroked him.

Even though her legs were jelly, she managed to slide to the floor without falling on her ass. And she watched his face as she slowly undid the button and zip fly of his shorts. He leaned back, bracing his weight on his arms on the bed, his face flushed, his eyelids lowered, lashes brushing his cheeks when he blinked.

And then she lowered the waistband of his boxers under his balls, so he was fully exposed in front of her. She touched the tip of his cock where it had leaked a little and then brought her finger to her mouth.

"Fuck, Tate."

She gripped him and stroked up once, twisting at the top like she knew he liked it, muscle memory kicking in. Who knew a hand job was like riding a bike?

"Tate . . ." His voice was strained.

She stuck out her tongue and licked once, right under the head. Then she leaned back on her heels with a wicked smile and stroked again. "Tell me. Tell me this is right."

His chest heaved. "You tease."

"Payback's a bitch."

His eyes narrowed and his nostrils flared. He breathed once, twice. And then his face softened. He leaned onto one hand and reached out with the other. He ran his fingers over her cheekbone, through the ends of her hair, and then cupped her chin. "It's always been you, Tate. It's always been us."

The sincerity in his voice cracked her heart wide open, and she parted her lips to suck him in. He kept his hand on her chin, his thumb on the corner of her lips, where he glided in and out and of her mouth.

His breath came out in gasps as she gripped the base and pumped with the same motion as her mouth. Her other hand reach down and rolled his balls, making him hiss out, "Fuck, baby."

When his legs began to tremble against her shoulders, she knew she had him and she kept up her rhythm. His hand slid down her neck to her shoulder and he squeezed with his fingers. "I'm gonna come."

She glanced up, met his eyes, and then he threw back his head on a gasp and came.

It'd been a long time since she'd had a dick in her

mouth, but apparently blow jobs were like riding a bike, too, because she easily swallowed all he had to give her. When she felt the last of his orgasm pulse, she let him slip out of her mouth and then she rested her head on his thigh.

He'd collapsed onto the bed on his back, his chest rising and falling as he took in gulps of air. His hand ghosted over her hair, like he wanted her to know he was still here, in the moment. He was still with her.

Then his fingers twisted in a lock of hair. "Come up here."

She rose to her feet with a groan and crawled on top of him. He shifted them so they were lying lengthwise on her bed, her head on his chest.

His hand slipped under her shirt and his fingers played with the knobs in her spine. His other hand was behind his head, elbow cocked, which made his shirt rise. So she ran her fingers through the trail of hair leading down into the waistband of his boxers, which he'd pulled up.

"I'm sorry about what I said. About Marcus."

She sighed. "It's okay. He's a source of a lot of regret for me. And that night at the bar . . . God, we were dumb."

His chuckle shook her head where it rested on his chest. "So dumb."

"You were totally flirting with that Kara girl, though."

"Only because you were flirting with Marcus."

She bit her lip. "I wanted to be flirting with you."

He laughed again. "Well, so much for only being friends."

She caressed his skin with her fingers. "I like this better."

The feel of his firm muscles beneath her head, the beat of his heart, his smell, was like slipping back into her skin.

"I want to be mad at you." His words were a contradiction to the soft kiss he placed on top of her head.

"It's okay, I'm mad at me, too." She flattened her hand against his stomach, marveling at the changes in his body. From the boy she'd once known to the man he was now.

"I said I want to be. Not that I am."

Tate gathered her hands under her and lifted off the bed. Cam tugged to get her to stay lying down, but she smiled. "Hold on. I have to do something."

He turned on his side and propped his head on his hand as she sat cross-legged on front of her TV. She looked back and saw he watched her with dark eyes.

She pulled up Utope and went into their saved game. And then she arranged Avatar Cam and Avatar Tate in bed. She had them "copulate with protection," which used to always make them laugh. She turned around and Cam watched her with a smile on her face. She smiled back.

And then she pulled up the speech bubble and Tate's avatar said, "I'm sorry."

Tate paused until she felt Cam behind her. He grabbed the controller and sank down behind her, his legs on either side of her body, and leaned her back onto his chest. She melted into him. And smiled as he pulled up the speech bubble on his character. "I'm sorry I didn't fight for us."

She grabbed the controller back. Tate's avatar said, "I love you."

Cam's avatar said, "I love you, too. Always."

And then a kiss was pressed into her temple. On the screen and in real life.

"I want to hate eighteen-year-old Tate," she said. "But if she hadn't made that dumb decision, I wonder if we'd be here today. If we'd realize how important this is. What we have."

Strong arms circled her. "Eighteen-year-old Tate did something pretty dumb. But, as cliché as it sounds, it happened for a reason, I guess."

She ran her hands down his arm and linked their fingers. "We still have a lot to figure out."

"I know," he said. "But that's for another day."

Chapter 12

LATER THAT NIGHT, they sat cross-legged on the bed, an almost-empty pizza box between them. She'd thrown on a T-shirt and a pair of underwear and he wore his boxer briefs.

Tate checked her phone and growled under her breath when she saw Jamie hadn't returned her calls or texts. She'd called his friends (who didn't know where he was) and obtained his girlfriend's number from them and called her (who didn't answer her phone). At this point, Tate was out of options other than getting in her car and tracking him down herself. Which Cam had agreed would be a waste of time.

"I can't tell you the last time I had Hawaiian pizza." Cam swallowed a bite.

"Really?" Tate picked off a piece of bacon and dropped it in her mouth.

"Only one place at Bowler had it. Tried it freshman year and it sucked."

Tate smiled. "Guess that's one reason to stay in Paradise—Georgina's Hawaiian pizza."

He reached over and grabbed her hand. "Hey, that's not the only reason."

His thumb rubbed circles on her wrist, and she shuddered at the touch. "You weren't saying that a couple of weeks ago."

He shoved the pizza box to the side and tugged her toward him. She crawled into his lap and he wrapped his arms around her, kissing the top of her head. A gesture he'd always done. She wasn't sure if he realized he used to do it, or that he was doing it again, but it all added up to her finally feeling like she was where she belonged.

"I might not have wanted to come home, but I'm here now. And I'm glad I'm here."

She ran her hands over his thighs, over a groove in the muscles of his quads. "What about the fall?"

His chin rubbed along the top of her head. "What about it?"

She turned around so she could see his face, because this was an important conversation. She didn't want him to get by with evasion. He spread his legs and she sat between them cross-legged. "You know what I mean."

He let his head fall back and he stared up at her ceiling. A heavy weight settled in her gut. This was what she'd been avoiding four years ago. This decision. Would Cam choose his future or her?

He lowered his head to look at her, then bent his legs, resting his wrists on his knees, caging her in. "I don't know yet."

"But it's a good job, right?"

His lips scrunched to the side and after a pause, he said, "Yes, it is."

"So you should take it."

His brows lowered. "You think I'm going to start something up with you and then disappear?"

She flopped her arms out to the side, then gripped his ankles hear her hips. "I don't know! It's not like we planned this. One minute, Jamie and I were fighting, then we were fighting, then your hand was down my pants."

"I think everyone would be much happier if all fights ended like that."

"Cam," she growled.

He leaned forward and tangled a hand in her hair, curling his fingers around the back of her neck. "Stop, you're overthinking everything. I don't have to take the job. I can find something else. Like reenlist in the guard or sign up for active duty."

Oh God, no no no no. She knew his dreams, and they were never to be in the military full-time. He planned to serve in the guard for four years, get his college paid for, and get out. Did he think she wouldn't remember? She shook her head slowly, then gained speed until her hair was flying around her face. "I can't . . . I can't handle that. You always said you'd never get deployed. And you haven't. But if you did, I couldn't handle that . . . I just . . . no."

His fingers tightened. "Tate—"

"That was never what you wanted," she whispered.

His shoulders lowered and his eyes softened. "Plans change, Tatum."

She searched for what to say, to make him understand. She'd suffered four years and for what? So he stayed home anyway? Signed up to the service of his country for another four years?

"I—"

And then whatever she had planned to say went out the window when she heard the ringtone for her brother.

"Jamie!" she yelled, completely unnecessarily, launching herself out of Cam's lap and scrambling across the bed to where her phone was chirping and vibrating on her nightstand.

She picked up her phone, swiping her hand over the screen to answer. "Jamie?"

There was no answer, just deep voices in the background. Tate's stomach dipped. "Jamie?"

More deep voices, then, in a broken voice that shattered her heart, she heard, "Tate?"

She shot up to sitting position. "Jamie? What's going on? Where are you? Are you okay?"

She registered Cam moving behind her, pulling on his clothes, and gathering hers and laying them in her lap.

"Tate," Jamie said. "I . . . I need you to come pick me up."

More deep voices, then . . . a siren? Shuffling over the speaker.

"Jamie?"

"Can"—muffled voice—"pick me up?"

"Jamie, of course I can pick you up, but where the hell are you?"

"—pital."

"What?" She jerked onto her knees and pressed the phone harder onto her ear. "You're at the hospital?"

"Car's probably totaled."

"Totaled? What? Why?" Her voice sounded shrill in her ears.

"Can you stop yelling?" Jamie's voice gained strength.

"Then tell me what's going on!" Tate hollered into the phone.

The phone was no longer in her hand. Cam had it, and he was speaking into it in low tones while she stared at him, frozen. Then he was off the phone and helping her into her clothes, fixing her hair, kissing her forehead.

He led her out to his truck and helped her in the passenger seat.

As he started the car, she said, "I should have called more friends or something. I should have tracked him down."

"He's okay, Tate."

"But—"

"He's banged up a little and from what it sounded like, his car's a wreck. But he's alive and he's okay."

She stopped talking then, until they got to the hospital. Cam dropped her off at the entrance to the emergency room and she rushed in. Jamie was already being seen, so she sat in a cold metal chair, jiggling her leg and chewing on a thumbnail.

When Cam strolled in, he sat beside her and put his arm around her shoulders. "He's being seen already?"

Tate glanced around the sparsely populated waiting room. "Yep."

He patted her shoulder in reply.

"Did he say what was wrong? Why he had to be here?"

"It was hard to hear him on the phone, but something about his wrist."

She bent her head and rubbed her hands on her jeans. "He needed that car and that job. Damn it. We needed that paycheck."

He moved his hand to cup the side of her head and laid it on his shoulder. "We'll figure something out."

There was that *we* again. Like they were a team. A family. And she was letting it happen, like it was no big thing to believe that Cam would be around forever. But it was hard. Because that big job in New York beckoned and how could he stay in this town with her?

And she couldn't leave with him. Not when her dad was sick and Jamie was a mess. She was needed here. And the sooner she remembered that she was better off not relying on someone else, the better. But Cam's fingers rubbed soothing circles on her scalp. And his shoulder warmed her cheek. And he smelled good. And maybe she could enjoy this now, while it lasted. As long as she kept in mind there was an expiration date.

They sat in silence, Cam's fingers doing their magic. And Tate wondered if she could fall asleep here. But then a throat cleared, and she raised her head.

Jamie stood before them, his face dark, a cast on his left wrist. His clothes were wrinkled and his shoes untied. He looked like shit.

But damn, was she glad to see him in one piece.

She stood up and walked to him, throwing her arms

around his stiff form. "I'm so glad you're okay." She felt fingers flutter over her hips, but his arms didn't return her embrace. And when she stepped back, Jamie's eyes were over her head, his glare fixed on Cam. "What are you doing here?"

"I think you don't need to worry about that. I gave your sister a ride."

"She can't fucking drive herself now?"

"Watch your mouth."

"Don't tell me what to do."

Cam's jaw clenched, and Tate figured this was when she needed to step in. "Look, you two can argue all you want when we get home. Can we please leave the hospital?"

Jamie grunted and turned on his heel, walking out of the doors of the emergency room with a slight limp. Tate trotted to his side. "What's wrong with your leg?"

"Just twisted my ankle a little. It's fine."

She motioned to Jamie toward where Cam's truck was parked in the visitor parking garage. She glanced over her shoulder at Cam, who was walking behind them, staring holes in the back of Jamie's head.

She turned again to face her brother. "What happened?"

He shrugged jerkily. "Took a corner too tight. Hit a tree."

She gasped. "Jesus. You hit a tree?"

"It wasn't a big tree."

"I don't really care how big the tree was."

Jamie fell silent and he asked the question she was dreading. "How's the car?"

Another shrug. "The front is kinda in a V-shape, what do you think?"

She narrowed her eyes. "I don't think it's funny."

"I'm not laughing," he shot back.

"How did you wreck?"

"Took a corner too fast, car slid. I overcorrected and the tree got in my way."

"Again, not funny."

"Again, not laughing."

Tate stopped asking questions.

The car ride was tense. Jamie sat in the cab of the truck behind Tate and Cam. Tate could feel the waves of frustration rolling off him and she turned the air conditioner up full blast.

She'd planned to corner Jamie tomorrow, talk to him and find out what was going on. But then this thing had happened with Cam and this accident and all she wanted to do was crawl under her covers and stay there for days.

But she couldn't.

Because no matter what, Jamie needed her. And no matter how much of a teenage dickhead he was being, she loved him.

She turned around in her seat. "Your wrist hurt?"

He stared at her like she was an idiot, and held up his injured hand. "It's in a cast."

"I know that, I—"

"And there are these pills you can take to help with pain—"

"If you can't carry on a civil conversation, Jamie, then don't fucking talk at all," Cam growled from the front seat.

And that was the end of any sort of talking until they pulled into the driveway of their house.

Tate was grateful that her father wasn't home to see this. She didn't want him to have to deal with Jamie's mess.

As soon as they walked into the house, Cam whirled on Jamie. He grabbed his chin and leaned in, checking his eyes. "Are you drunk?"

Jamie jerked his head back to get out of Cam's grip, but Cam held firm. "No," Jamie said through clenched teeth.

"High?"

Jamie jerked back again and this time, Cam dropped his hand. "No," Jamie spat at him. "Cops already checked that shit after the accident, but thanks for implying I'm a loser."

Cam held out his palms and responded with a voice dripping with sarcasm. "Oh, hey, I'm sorry. Must have been some other brother of Tate's sitting drunk in a yard recently. My bad."

"Jamie—" Tate started, but when his brother's head whipped to her, she snapped her jaw shut.

"Thanks for picking me up, but if you think I'm going to stand here and get ganged up on by you two, then you're wrong. Neither of you have your shit together any more than I do."

"Why don't you can the angry teenager act? For fuck's sake, Jamie," Cam said.

"What's going on?" said a voice, and all three of them turned their heads to see Tate's father standing at the entrance of the hallway.

"Dad?" Tate took a step toward him. "What are you doing here? I thought you were spending the night?"

He waved his hand. "Turns out they didn't need to keep me. I called Anne and she came to get me."

"Why did you call Anne? I could have—"

"Frankly I'm much more concerned about what I just overheard." He took several steps forward, his eyes shifting from Tate to Jamie. "Because I heard something about drinking and an accident. And I'd really like to know why this is the first I'm hearing about any of it."

Tate's heart plummeted into her stomach. "Maybe you should sit down, Dad. I can get your oxygen tank and—"

"Tatum Frances Ellison." Her dad's voice had deepened into a low growl. "You and your brother take a seat on that couch over there, and I better start hearing some explanations."

Tate slumped her shoulders and trudged to the couch, footsteps behind her. She flopped down in a corner of the couch and watched as her brother sat in the opposite corner, face sullen.

Cam stood off to the side, arms crossed over his chest, eyes on her. Her dad followed, perching himself on the edge of his recliner. "First, I want to know what Jamie's been up to."

Tate started at her hands in her lap. Why did she feel guilty for what Jamie had done? "Last week, he was drinking at a party and got in trouble. The cops let him off with a warning and I had to pick him up. And tonight, we got in a fight and then he drove and wrecked his car."

Silence. Tate looked up at her father through her

lashes. His eyes were on Jamie, who stared straight ahead at the wall in front of him. "What's going on with you, Jamie?"

"Nothing."

"Nothing?"

He shrugged. "Just having a little fun."

"Wrecking your car is fun?"

Jamie started to lose some of the surliness in his expression, as his anger began to fade and embarrassment crept in. "Well, that wasn't so fun."

"What did you and your sister fight about?"

Jamie clenched his jaw.

Her father sighed and rubbed the bridge of his nose. Tate could tell he was tired. It was late. "Dad, why don't you—"

"Why didn't you tell me his behavior was this bad?" Those hazel eyes were locked on her now and she felt the heat of the stare.

She flicked her eyes to Cam. His gaze was steady, but there was encouragement in his expression. She took a deep breath. "I didn't want to worry you."

"You didn't want to worry me."

"I was worried the stress would be bad for your health and—"

"I love you, baby. But the fact that my son almost got arrested for underage drinking is something I need to be aware of. Even if I'm on my deathbed—"

Tate sucked in a breath. "Please don't say that—"

"— he is still my son and what happens to him is my business."

"I know that but—"

"Tatum." His voice softened. "You can't keep doing this. You can't keep making decisions for other people, thinking it's the best for them. You just can't."

Tate's eyes blurred. She was making this a habit, wasn't she? First keeping Cam in the dark, and now her father, because she thought it was best for them. "I thought I was doing the right thing." She sniffed.

"I know that," he said quietly. "But you get what I'm saying to you?"

Tate looked up and smiled at Cam through her tears. He returned her smile, and she turned her head to her father. "I get you."

Tate's father's gaze shifted to Cam. "I'm getting the sense you're gonna be around more now?"

Cam swallowed. "Your senses are accurate."

"Wait, what?" Jamie sat up, his head turning to Cam and then back to Tate.

"You don't worry about them right now." Their father pointed at him. "You and I are going to talk here in a minute." He held his arms out to Tate. "Give your old man a hug and then leave us be."

Tate jumped up and ran to her father, squeezing him until he grunted. "I love you, Daddy."

"Love you, too, baby," he said, smoothing her hair. "Now git so I can talk to your brother."

Tate walked to Cam and grabbed his hand, eyeing Jamie over her shoulder. His eyes were on their clasped hands, his brows furrowed. She knew they still needed to talk, but right now, he was in for a father-son chat.

She led Cam down the hallway and into her bedroom, shutting the door behind them. She flopped onto the bed on her back, her legs off the edge. "So, this was a day."

The bed dipped as Cam sank down beside her. "Sure was."

She closed her eyes until she felt a hand on her arm, and then Cam linked his fingers with hers. She rolled her head to the side and opened her eyes. He was watching their hands as he rotated them.

"You think Jamie will be okay?" she asked.

His eyes rose to hers. "Yeah, yeah I do."

"Why do you think so?"

"Because he has a sister who watches out for him and a dad who loves him. And . . ." Cam licked his lips, and then brought their hands up. He kissed their thumbs. "And now I'm back."

"For how long?" she whispered.

His brows lowered. "You see me going anywhere?"

"No, but—"

He leaned closer and pressed a kiss to her lips, swiping his tongue along the seam until she opened for him. And then any lingering questions she had vanished as his arms came around her, cradling her head, thumb rubbing that sensitive spot behind her ear. And when he pulled back, all she could do was return his smile. "We'll figure it out," he said softly. "For now, let's get used to each other again. All right?"

She bit her lip and nodded. "Okay."

And that earned her another kiss.

Chapter 13

CAM WATCHED TATE as she wiped down the counter of the diner. Her brows were furrowed, and every time the bell rang over the door, her eyes darted to see who it was.

And every time it *wasn't* Jamie, her posture relaxed slightly until the next time the bell rang. Cam had let Jamie borrow his mom's car so he could keep working, even though it wasn't easy for him to deliver pizzas with a cast. It'd been a couple of weeks since the accident.

Cam took a gulp of his water and crushed an ice cube between his teeth. He'd thought meeting Jamie on neutral turf was a good idea, but now he wasn't so sure. Hell, he was tempted to set parameters for which weapons to bring.

The bell rang and from Cam's booth in the corner, he heard Tate's intake of breath. He took another sip of water and waited.

Jamie's heavy footsteps came up behind him, and

then the old booth creaked and leather squeaked as Jamie slid in across from him.

Cam pointed to a cup in front of Jamie. "Got you some water."

Jamie's eyes flicked down to it, then back to Cam. He didn't say anything.

"You're welcome," Cam said.

Jamie's eyes narrowed.

Cam sighed. He knew this wasn't going to be easy. But Tate and her dad had asked him to talk to Jamie. At one time, they'd been close. Jamie had looked at him with hero worship in his eyes and although it had made Cam a little uncomfortable, he hadn't wanted to disappoint the kid.

But then shit hit the fan, and Cam had been too angry and selfish to check in with Jamie. He should have known that Tate and his breakup would be close to a divorce to Jamie. And with no mom and a sick dad, he must have been lost.

The guilt pushed down on Cam's shoulders, but he took a deep breath. He was back now. He could try to get the kid back on track.

Cam clasped his hands on the table in front of him. "Okay, so I owe you an apology."

No movement from Jamie. In fact, it looked like he wasn't breathing.

Cam continued. "I should have checked in with you when Tate and I broke up. And that's on me. I can bet you felt pretty abandoned. And with your dad getting sick and . . . well, I'm sorry." He looked Jamie dead in the eye.

"That's on me. You didn't do anything wrong. And I'll always regret not being there for you."

Jamie didn't move. But he held Cam's gaze, so Cam figured that was a good thing. At least the kid hadn't gotten up and walked away.

"Why?" Jamie's voice was almost a whisper when he finally spoke.

"Why what?"

"Why didn't you keep in contact with me?"

Cam shook his head. "I was so wrapped up in myself, man. I was so focused on being pissed at your sister. So I cut everything out of my life that reminded me of her. And that was wrong. So wrong. I didn't think about how that would impact you. I was a selfish kid at the time. I see that now."

Jamie's jaw worked, and his eyes shifted, like his brain had to shift a couple of gears. Then he finally dropped his eyes to the table in front of him.

When Jamie spoke, he kept his eyes on the table. "You were just . . . gone. No word. Nothing. And Tate was always crying. And Dad was so sick. He just slept all the time." Jamie raised his eyes. "I hated you. I kept thinking you'd be back and you'd take care of us. But you never came back. And then you finally show up now. And acted like you could boss me around and tell me what to do. And I hated you even more."

Cam felt flayed alive. Like his skin was peeling off his bones and every nerve was raw, exposed. The fuck had he been doing in college? Fucking off, playing video games. Drinking and screwing girls. While Tate's family was back here struggling. He couldn't even blame Tate for this. He'd dropped the ball with Jamie. "I realize I can't make up for when I was gone. I wish I could."

Jamie's eyes flicked to Tate behind the diner counter. Cam followed his eyes as Tate stood there, face pale, wringing a towel in her hands.

"It's her fault," Jamie said.

"No it's not."

"But—"

"Jamie, she was eighteen. You don't need details but it didn't go down the way everyone thought it did. But she did make a bad decision. And we're trying to get past it now."

There was still wariness in his eyes. Hesitation. Mistrust. Jamie fiddled with the wrapper to his straw, his eyes on his fingers. "How long you gonna be around this time?"

That was a million-dollar question but Cam answered as honestly as he could. "Tate and I are doing everything we can to make it last this time. We're in it for the long haul." He reached over and stilled Jamie's fingers, and the younger man's eyes shot up to his. "But Jamie, no matter what, I promise you, I'll keep in touch with you. Always. Our relationship is independent of my relationship with Tate."

Jamie stared, and his Adam's apple bobbed as he swallowed.

"Do you believe me?" Cam asked quietly.

Jamie bit his lip, then nodded jerkily.

Cam let go of his fingers and leaned back in his seat.

He let a grin stretch his lips, and when an answering grin passed over Jamie's face, Cam let out a breath.

He jerked his chin toward the counter. "You think you could spare some time and have a chat with your sister?"

Jamie ducked his head and the blush staining his cheeks showed Cam he knew he had been an ass.

"Sure, but uh, can we talk sometime about joining up?"

Cam cocked his head with brows furrowed.

Jamie fidgeted. "Was thinking about the military. To help for school. And to . . . get my head on straight, I guess."

Cam nodded. "Of course we can talk. I'll tell you everything I know."

Jamie smiled. "Thanks."

Cam knew the next topic was going to be uncomfortable but he brought it up anyway. "Hey, we also need to talk about what you said to your sister."

Jamie ducked his head as his ears reddened. He was embarrassed. Good. Recalling that he hurled "slut" at his sister should embarrass him. "I'm sorry," Jamie mumbled.

Cam licked his lips. "Yeah, I'm sure you are. First of all, you need to tell her that. And second of all, you need to understand why that's not okay."

Jamie looked up. "Because she's my sister?"

"Well . . ." Cam tilted his head as he thought of how he wanted to word this. "Yeah, because she's your sister, but you also don't treat any woman like that. Would you call me a slut if I started talking about girls I slept with?"

Jamie shook his head slowly.

"Yeah, so don't say that shit to your sister or another woman. Got it?"

Jamie's face was red, but he nodded.

Cam patted the table and stood up. "Gonna get your sister. Sit tight, all right?"

As he took a step away, Jamie called his name. Cam turned around. "Get me a burger, will ya?" Jamie asked, his eyes bright again.

Cam rolled his eyes. "Sure, man. Gotta put some meat on your bones, right?"

Jamie flexed. "Hey, nothing wrong with my guns."

Cam turned back around, laughing, and walked toward Tate. Her face lit up and she sprinted out from around the counter. He met her at the end as she launched herself into his arms. "Thank you," she whispered.

"Of course."

She pulled back. "You guys had a good talk?"

"Yep."

"About what?"

Cam ran his tongue over his teeth. "That's between us. But I think we're on our way to getting our relationship back."

Tate's smile was worth all the anxiety. "I'm so glad."

He patted her ass. "Now you're up. He's got some things to say to you, I think."

"Yeah?"

"Can you take your break now?"

"I think so."

"Then go talk to your brother."

She blinked, then pressed her lips to his in a quick

kiss. With a squeeze to his hip and a wink, she was off to Jamie. "Oh, and he wants a burger!" Cam called after her.

"Great, can you order us two?" she said over her shoulder.

Cam huffed and she laughed.

TATE SLIPPED INTO the booth across from her brother. He looked chagrined.

"Hi," she said.

"Hey," he answered.

And that was pretty much the extent of the conversation aside from the awkward meeting of gazes until Anne came over and plopped their burgers in front of them. "If I don't see lips moving soon—and I don't mean for eating—I'm going to come take these burgers away. Am I clear?"

"Yes," Tate said.

"Crystal," Jamie answered.

Anne nodded and then walked away. Tate met Cam's eyes where he was perched at the counter on a stool. He winked at her with a laugh, and she glared at him before focusing on her brother.

Tate poked around her fries, looking for the perfect one that wasn't too crunchy or too soft.

"You're doing that weird fry thing," Jamie said.

Oooh, that one looked good. She picked it up and dunked it in ketchup. "What weird fry thing?"

He pointed to her with a fry that looked soggy and limp. "Where you spend five hours picking out the perfect fry, which makes no sense, because you always eat the whole basket anyway."

"I do not spend five hours."

"Well, it sure seems like it."

"Why do you care how I eat my fries?"

"I don't care. I was just pointing out—"

All of a sudden, Tate's basket was no longer in front of her. And Jamie's wasn't in front of him. And Anne was standing at the end of their booth, her lips pressed in a thin line, her eyes flashing. "What did I say?"

"I want to point out that our lips were moving," Jamie explained.

Anne's head whipped to face him and he shrank in his seat.

"I hand these both over to that Hispanic hunk over there to eat unless I hear some real conversation."

"Quit pressuring us," Tate huffed.

"Quit stalling," Anne snapped back.

Tate slumped down and crossed her arms over her chest.

She started to count to ten to get her blood pressure down, when she heard across from her a mumbled "I'm sorry."

She looked at Jamie, who was tugging on his ear and eyeing her through his lashes. "I've been a dick lately, huh?"

Tate softened her posture and leaned forward. "It's not all your fault. I haven't been there for you."

He shook his head. "No, you have. But I took it for granted and didn't take into consideration how much stress you've been under."

She reached out and laid her hand over the top of his. "It's been stressful for both of us."

Tate's nose twitched and she glanced over to see their plates at the end of the table. Anne was gone, having left sometime when they weren't paying attention, leaving the food behind.

Tate turned back to her brother. "I made some mistakes, and when Cam and I broke up, I hadn't thought about how that affected you. And I'm so sorry about that."

Jamie flipped his hand over so their palms met. "He said the same thing."

"But we're older now and—"

"You were the same age as me when you guys broke up, though. And you keep talking about how you were so young then." He squinted at her.

Tate bit her lip. "I hate saying, 'You just wait,' but in a way that's the only thing I know to say. When I was eighteen, I thought I knew everything. I thought I was such a grown-up." She laughed sadly. "The thing is, now I'm not any closer to being a grown-up. I think that's how I know that I have grown up a little bit. Because now I realize I might not ever feel grown-up." She cocked her head. "Does that make sense?"

"You're a grown-up when you realize you'll never feel like a grown-up?"

Tate nodded as sagely as she could. "Pretty much."

"That . . . shouldn't make sense, but it kinda does."

Tate reached over and rummaged through her fries. Jamie did the same, and then a fry was under her nose. "Why are you giving me a fry?"

"It's a good one, right?"

She eyed it, checking for crispness and oil content. "Yeah, it does look pretty good."

He dropped it in her open hand.

"Are you calling a truce with a fry?" she asked.

"Does your highness need filet mignon or something?"

Tate answered by tossing the fry in her mouth. "Fine, truce."

They dug into their burgers, while Tate told him a story about how Anne thought an upright mop was an intruder and called 911 before she realized cleaning supplies weren't going to steal the register money.

Jamie laughed, and Tate saw the younger boy in the almost-a-man's face.

They fell silent until Tate spoke up. "I tried, you know. I tried to keep us together."

Jamie tore apart a napkin and dropped the bits on his plate. "I know. I thought a little bit about it, because I'm close to the age you were when you found out and . . . I'm not sure I would have handled it all like you have. You kept the bills paid and you worked your ass off. And you took care of Dad and me. I just didn't appreciate it."

Tate tried to swallow her gulp of water around the lump in her throat. "Thanks for saying that."

Jamie met her eyes. "You deserved to hear it." Then his gaze shifted over her shoulder and his face lit up. Tate turned around. She hadn't heard the door to the diner open. She blocked it out when she wasn't on duty, so she hadn't realized someone had walked inside.

A girl stood inside the door, scanning the diner. She stood about Tate's height and had long brown hair she pulled into a ponytail. She wore glasses and a simple pair of jeans with a plain red T-shirt. Nothing about her stuck out, but when her gaze found Jamie, her face cracked into a huge smile and Tate raised her eyebrows.

She looked at Jamie like he held the Earth on his shoulders. *Hell*, Tate thought, *if someone looked at me like that, I'd be smitten, too.*

"I, uh," Jamie began, drawing Tate's attention away from the girl who was making her way toward their table. "I invited Ashley to meet you. I hope that's okay."

Tate looked down at her stained T-shirt and fraying apron.

"You look fine." He chuckled.

She shot him a glare as the girl took a seat in the booth beside Jamie. Her big brown eyes focused on his face and she had a pretty, soft voice. "Hi."

"Hey." Jamie's face was softer than Tate had ever seen it. She liked the look. Ashley seemed to calm him, and she wondered where Ashley had been when he was getting drunk. "Tate, this is my girlfriend, Ashley. Ashley, this is my sister, Tate."

Tate was a hugger but it was awkward to reach across the table so she stuck out her hand to shake. Which also felt awkward but she'd already made the movement, so she went with it. The girl shook Tate's hand with a nervous smile on her face. "Hello, Jamie talks about you all the time."

"About how I'm a pain-in-the-ass dictator?"

Ashley shook her head, her ponytail swishing along her shoulders. "No, he loves you."

Tate glanced at Jamie, but his eyes were on his girlfriend. They'd had sex. Tate knew it with every bone in her body. Teenagers weren't that attentive with each other unless they'd taken that step. She needed to make that birds-and-bees convo top priority.

"And thank you," Ashley said, drawing Tate's attention.

"For what?"

Ashley glanced at Jamie before shoring up her shoulders and continuing. "For getting him back on track. For a while there . . ." She waved her hand, and Jamie cut in. "We broke up."

Tate frowned. "Oh, I didn't know . . ."

Jamie sighed. "I didn't tell you."

"But," Ashley cut in, "things have been better since the accident. He's promised to get his act together and I know it's because of you."

Tate didn't think she did much other than piss Jamie off, but she'd take the thanks. "He's my brother and I love him, so you're welcome."

Ashley smiled.

"You hungry?" Jamie asked her.

"Burger and fries?"

Jamie called over to Cam. "We need another burger and fries."

"What, do I look like I work here?" Cam called back.

Tate laughed as she stood up to put the order in. "Nice to meet you, Ashley. I hope to see you around a lot more."

Ashley grinned. "Me too."

Chapter 14

CAM RAN HIS fingertips down Tate's arm and watched as goose bumps rose on her skin in the wake of his touch. He pressed a kiss to her bare shoulder and felt her shudder under his lips.

They were in her bedroom and he needed to leave for work in approximately thirty-five minutes. They'd just finished playing Utope and all he wanted to do was get her naked and get inside her. But her father was right outside in the living room, and Tate had never been good at being quiet.

She rolled onto her side and propped her head on her palm. "It's not nice to get me all worked up and then jet off to work in your tight black T-shirt."

He laughed and leaned in, pressing a kiss to her neck, adding a little tongue and teeth. When another shudder ran through her body, he grinned.

"Come out tonight." He cupped the back of her neck

and ran a thumb along the hinge of her jaw. "When I get a break, we can hang out."

She scrunched her lips to the side. "I'll text Van. If she's going to be there, then I'll come. How's that?"

"That's acceptable."

She dropped her eyes to the comforter between them. "Thanks a lot for talking to Jamie."

He scooted closer. "Of course."

Her eyes met his. "When are we going to talk about . . . the future?"

Cam knew she was uneasy about what was going to happen in the fall. She hadn't fully let herself enjoy this time with him. He could tell sometimes by the way she zoned out or hesitated before full leaning into his touch.

It killed him, but at that point, he didn't have answers yet. The job prospects in Paradise sucked. And unless something better came along than what he had now, he didn't know if he had any options but to take the job. And if he didn't leave, his mom might toss him out.

He had a couple ideas swarming in his head, and he decided to test the waters with the first one. "So, your dad is doing well, right? And he's got Anne here. And your brother still has another year of school. Would . . ." He took a deep breath and plunged in. "Would you consider moving to New York with me?"

Her eyes widened, and then blinked. Once. Twice. Her chest rose with deep breaths, and her hand was limp in his. He tugged on it. "You don't have to answer now, but . . ."

"Go with you?" she whispered.

He nodded. "Yeah, go with me."

She blinked again. "Live in New York with you?"

He kept nodding. "Yes, live with me. In sin. Until we can afford a wedding or make an appointment at the justice of the peace."

Her head jerked, and then her hair whipped his face as she threw her head back and burst out laughing.

He didn't know if that was a good or bad sign. His body tensed. "What the hell are you laughing at?"

She lowered her head with watery eyes. "Oh, Camilo Ruiz, you blew me away with that romantic proposition, so—"

"Do you want romance? Because—"

"I didn't say I wanted romance, ya idiot." She chuckled. Then her face softened. "I'd live in sin with you anywhere. You know that."

He relaxed and shoved her onto her back, then he covered her with his body and nudged her chin with his nose. She angled her head so he could focus his attention on the pale skin of her neck. "Freaking me out, laughing at me like that." He followed the tendon with his tongue and teeth. "Is that a yes?"

Her body tensed for a second below him and there was a pause before she answered. "I want to. Please know that."

He pulled back to look in her eyes. "But . . ."

She shook her head. "There's no *but* coming. I was going to say that I want to make it work, and I need some time to think about it. Okay?"

"Okay." He fingered a lock of her hair spread out on the pillow. "You know I'd stay here with you, too."

She gripped his face in her hands. "I love you, Camilo. But I don't want that for you."

"But what about what I want for me?"

Those hazel eyes bored into his. "Can you honestly tell me right now that you'd be happy living in Paradise, knowing you had an amazing job off in New York?"

He hesitated because, fuck, did he ever want that job. But that job didn't come with Tate. And he wanted her more than anything. But that hesitation was a mistake because Tate pounced on it. "See? That's what I thought."

Cam pulled his head out of her grasp and sat at the end of the bed to pull on his boots. "So you get to think about moving to New York with me, but I don't have thirty fucking seconds to answer a big life question?"

"Because I know the answer—"

"Do you?" He turned his head to face where she sat up on the bed. "Do you really?"

She bit her lip, uncertainty crossing her face, but she plowed on. "If I would have told you about my dad back when we were eighteen, what would you have done?"

"I would have come home," he answered immediately.

"Aha!" she said, rising onto her knees and pointing at him. "But you'd regret it. And then you'd resent me. And then where would we be?"

He snatched up his T-shirt and pulled it on, then walked toward the door to her bedroom. He opened it, then turned around to face her. "That's where I think you're wrong. You act like you can tell the future, and that's utter bullshit. Time to grow up and realize adults compromise on decisions, Tatum."

Her mouth fell open on a gasp, and Cam walked out.

But his Tate never could let him have the last word. He heard a thump behind him as she jumped off the bed, and then bare feet thudding down the hall behind him.

Tate's father was watching TV in his recliner and stared at them with wide eyes as they both stomped by.

"Don't you dare walk away from me," she growled after him and he turned around, finding her wicked hot all pissed off. No one did angry female like Tatum Ellison.

"I have to go to work, Tatum," he growled back.

"This conversation isn't over." She pointed at him with narrowed eyes.

"You bet your ass it isn't."

She crossed her arms over her chest, and he had to suppress a grin, fighting the twitching muscles at the corner of his mouth.

"You're doing that thing where you're trying not to smile."

"No, I'm not."

She cocked her head. "Your lips are twitching, you liar."

He reached out and grabbed her hand and hauled her to him. He leaned down to kiss her but stopped when his lips were an inch from hers. "Think about what I said?"

She heaved a sigh. "I will. Think about what I said?"

He nodded. "I will."

She rose up on her toes until her lips met his. Then she backed away with a smile. "See you later tonight."

He raised his chin to her, gave her dad a salute, and then walked out.

TATE SIPPED HER light beer and watched as Cam checked IDs at the door. He sat in an alcove, and the lighting cast odd shadows over his face, which only made his dimples more noticeable when he smiled at some forty-year-old cougar.

Tate glared at the woman's back as she made her way to the bar and then focused again on Cam.

He turned his head, met her gaze. And then winked.

That smug, sexy bastard.

Van plopped down across from her with a pink drink in a martini glass. Tate eyed it. "What's that?"

"Cosmo."

Tate raised her eyebrows and looked around the bar like it was the first time she'd seen it. "A cosmo? I'm sorry, are we in Manhattan dining on lobster and wearing our good diamonds?"

Van shoved Tate's shoulder with a laugh. "Shut up. A cosmo isn't that fancy."

"You're just practicing for L.A., huh?" Tate lifted up her beer and tipped the neck toward Van before taking a swig. "I'll be over here enjoying my Miller High Life like that classy gal I am."

Van rubbed her finger over the rim of the glass. "Maaaybeee this winter you will be in Manhattan, sipping cosmos, dripping in jewels."

Tate plunked her beer down on the table and glared at her best friend. She'd told Van as soon as she got to the bar about her conversation with Cam, spewing it all out in one long stream of breath before they could even get their first drink.

"Van . . ."

Her friend leaned forward. "You're thinking about it right?"

Tate blew out a breath. "I am, okay? I'm thinking about it very seriously. But Jamie will still have another year of school and Dad . . ." She let her voice trail off. Why was she wishing doom on their heads? He'd been doing well.

Van took a sip her drink and made a face. "Gonna have to talk to Trev about this. Anyway, I think you need to realize they would want you to live your life."

"But we just got Jamie speaking to us again and he seems to be getting back on track but—"

"Your father is aware of Jamie's behavior now, so he can help get him back on track. This isn't all on you anymore. It never should have been."

Tate scrunched her lips back and forth, mulling it over. She wondered if part of her was scared to take that leap, to travel to an unknown city when all she'd known all her life was Paradise. Was she making excuses now? She looked up at Cam as he sat on his stool at the bar. His head was turned, shouting something to Trevor behind the bar. Then Cam threw back his head and laughed. And the sound was like a warm blanket, wrapping around her, promising her safety. How could she leave that?

"I think I want to," she said quietly.

"And I think you should," Van said back, just as quietly.

A chair scraped beside her and she looked up as Marcus took a seat at their table. "Hey, Tate."

She hadn't talked to him since that awkward night at

the bar. She darted her gaze to Cam, who was no longer laughing, his eyes dark and piercing into Marcus's back.

She cleared her throat. "Hey."

"Haven't seen you around for a while." Marcus's jaw was tight, and she didn't like the glazed look in his eyes, like he'd already had a couple of drinks.

"Uh, just been busy, you know. Working. Helping the family."

Marcus chuckled, a weird, choked sound. "Right, just working and helping the family and crawling into Ruiz's bed again. Really fucking busy, Tate."

Tate was stunned. Utterly stunned. Marcus might not be her best friend, but he'd never been nasty.

"Marcus," Van spoke up, her voice low. "If you don't get up right now and leave us be, I'll be forced to call Trevor and Cam over here, and no one wants that."

But it was like Marcus didn't hear her, because his gaze never wavered from Tate.

She put her hand on the table, palm down, in front of Van and met Marcus's gaze. "First of all, there's no crawling being done, Marcus. What I do and who I do it with is none of your business."

He snorted and his lip curled. "You think you're hot shit again, don't you? Ruiz is back so you get to relive your popular prom queen days. Well, news flash, Tate. You're just a high school graduate working at a diner. Cam's gonna hightail it out of here and away from your white trash ass as soon as he can. You're nothing but filler."

Tate's mouth dropped open. "Wow."

"Holy shit," Van said with raised eyebrows. "You practice that filth in the mirror before you came out, Marcus? Damn."

Marcus pointed in Van's face, and then at Tate. "Laugh it up, both of you. You'll see."

Tate heard his boots first and knew what was coming. She shrank back in her seat, wishing she could hide away in the bathroom.

"Outside, Marcus," Cam said once he reached their table. His arms hung at his sides, loose, like he was the picture of relaxation, but the veins in his forearms stood out, revealing the tenseness of his muscles.

Marcus's eyes widened and he smirked. "Oh, you even got your own bodyguard now, Tate. Good for you." He leaned closer. "But he's not going to be around forever."

Cam grabbed Marcus around the biceps to haul him to his feet. "Leave her alone."

Marcus tried to shrug him off, but Cam held firm. "Fuck you, Ruiz. Just go on and get the fuck out of town already. Looking forward to catching Tate on the rebound again."

Cam's face didn't move, not even a muscle twitch, and it was a little freaky. He stepped up to Marcus, toe to toe, their noses almost touching. "I'm going to kick you out of this bar in thirty seconds but before I do, I'm going to make it clear that Tate will never be on the rebound. Ever. Because she's with me. And I'm with her. And if I do leave this town, she's coming with me."

Now Marcus was the one with an open mouth, speechless. And so was Tate, and so was Van.

Because that was it. Cam had spoken.

And then he was leading Marcus to the front door of the bar and out the door, before Tate could react. "Wow."

"Holy shit," Van said.

Tate turned to Van and blinked. Van blinked back. And then they dissolved into giggles. Tate straightened and wiped her eyes. "Am I supposed to be upset about what Marcus said? I mean, it was just kind of mean and weird, right?"

Van plopped down in her chair and sipped her drink as Tate took her seat across from her. "No, you're not supposed to be upset. He's jealous and drunk."

"That was kinda hot. Cam going all 'Imma tell it like it is.' " Tate started giggling again.

Van tilted her head. "I'm glad you're not getting all weird and letting some asshole get to you."

Tate wiped the condensation off the bottle in front of her. "Marcus is . . . Marcus. And Cam is . . . well . . . *Cam*. He says what he means and he means what he says and he doesn't lie."

Van's eyes softened. "And he loves you."

Tate nodded. "He does. He loves me, and I believe it. I know he hooked up with all kinds of girls in college. I used to stalk his Facebook page when I was feeling pathetic about myself. In his pictures . . . so many girls." She straightened and leaned forward. "He could have stayed with any of them. Smart, pretty girls who want to be teachers or doctors or whatever. But he didn't. He came home. And he chose me. Again." She swirled her bottle on the table. "And I'm going to try really hard not to fuck it up again."

"What do you want to do?" Van asked. "Cam wants to work in security research but what do you want to do? Weren't you going to go to college for software developing?"

Tate snorted. She'd had such big dreams in high school. She thought she could do anything. And then life knocked her on her ass and she still hadn't gotten up. "God, that was a silly dream, and no, I don't want to do that anymore."

"So what do you want?" she pressed.

Tate glanced at Cam, who had walked back inside after tossing Marcus out and stopped to talk to Trevor at the bar. "I want to spend time with my family, and I want to be with Cam. Do I have to have huge career ambitions?"

She glanced at Van, who wore a small smile. "No, no you don't."

"I feel very anti-feminist. Rosie the Riveter would be disappointed."

Van laughed. "It isn't anti-feminist not to have big career ambitions. You just have to agree women deserve equality if they want a career. We fought so we'd have this choice, to have a career or not, you know?"

Tate sighed. "I want to be a mom."

Van blinked and brushed her hand under her eye. "You'd make a great one."

Cam's boots clomped on the floor as he stepped toward them. He leaned down with one arm braced on the table and the other cupping her neck. "You all right? Dude's an asshole."

She smiled. "I'm fine."

Cam stared into her eyes, like he didn't believe her. "I heard what he said. You sure?"

She shrugged. "What would that make me if I believe things he said to me over what you say to me?"

Cam frowned. "Uh . . ."

"An idiot," Tate said decisively. "It would make me a pretty big idiot."

Cam's smile started at one corner of his mouth and spread to the other side, until the whites of his teeth showed and his dimples popped. "And my Tatum's not an idiot," he whispered.

"Not this time," she whispered back.

He pressed his lips to hers and stood. "Need to get back to work. You gonna hang out for a little?"

"Yep."

He gave her another smile, nodded to Van and then walked back to his post at the door.

Van took a sip of her drink. "You lucky bitch."

TATE YAWNED AS she wiped down the tables early one morning at the diner. She'd stayed up late with Jamie last night, talking about his grades and possibly joining Junior ROTC next year at school. She'd been going to the bar more often than usual last week to see Cam at work, so she'd stayed home last night with Jamie and her dad.

They'd watched baseball and ate ice cream—moose tracks—and yelled "steeeerike!" at the television. She had to start making sure she spent as much time with them as she could, especially if she planned to leave this fall . . .

Her stomach dipped and a bead of sweat dripped down her lower back. Her hands shook as she straightened a ketchup bottle. She blamed it on caffeine but really, she knew it was the thought of moving. God, what would she even do in New York? She couldn't picture herself in a big city. Being a "New Yawkah." Cam always had that attitude, that look, like you knew he wasn't long for Paradise. But her? No one ever thought she'd leave. She never thought she'd leave. She'd avoided talking to Cam about it. If he brought it up, she told him she was still thinking about it. At first he just smiled, but then the frowns started and now he hadn't brought it up for a couple of days. She wondered if he was starting to give up on her.

"Damn it," she muttered to herself. She could leave if it meant keeping Cam, right?

She hadn't told her dad yet. And there was a reason for that. Because part of her knew he'd tell her to go. And she wasn't sure she wanted the permission.

"Tate," Anne's voice said from behind her, and she straightened up from the table she'd been cleaning. "Yeah?"

Anne gestured the back room with her head. "We got a frozen shipment in the back. Would you help me put it away?"

"Sure," she answered. She checked with the one table she had, a trucker eating breakfast, and dropped him his check. After filling his coffee again, she told him he could leave the cash on the table when he was finished and to holler if he needed anything.

She and Anne loaded bags of chicken nuggets and fries in the freezer in the back room, throwing out anything that had expired.

"Spoke to your father." Anne nudged a bag of Tater Tots with her toe.

"Oh yeah? What about?" Tate lifted the bag.

"You moving to New York."

Tate dropped the bag of Tater Tots on her feet and

then howled as hard rocks of frozen potatoes crushed her toes. She kicked the bag off and glared at Anne. "What're you talking about?"

Anne smiled. "How are your feet?"

Tate glared. "Don't you worry about my feet. What do you know about me moving to New York?"

"I overhead you talking to Cam—"

"So you were eavesdropping like a weirdo—"

"— and he mentioned you moving to New York with him in the fall. I didn't realize it was this big secret. I said something to your dad in passing and . . . well . . . he was surprised."

The blood drained from Tate's face. "When was this?"

Anne leaned on the steel counter behind her. "A couple of days ago?"

"Why hasn't he said anything to me?"

Anne sighed. "I think he's waiting for you to tell him yourself. I'm sorry I spilled it. I didn't realize it was classified information." She looked chagrined enough that Tate couldn't be mad at her. She hadn't done anything malicious on purpose. And Tate should have told her father all of this sooner. Her own fault really. She wiggled her toes and kicked the bag of Tater Tots. "It's okay." She looked up. "What did he say?"

Anne smiled. "I think you need to talk to him about that."

Tate clasped her hands under her chin and batted her eyelashes. "Pretty please? May I at least have a hint?"

Anne pursed her lips and rolled her eyes. "He wants you to be happy and live your life."

Tate squinted. "Here or in New York?"

Anne cupped her cheek. "That's up to you. You have to make a decision for yourself now. It's time, don't you think?"

Tate bit her lip and nodded.

BY THE END of her workday, Tate was dead on her feet. Cam had texted about coming over for dinner but she told him she needed to talk to her dad.

His reply text:

Why?

You know.

His next text came five minutes later.

I love you.

Love you, too.

She pulled into her driveway and parked her car. She didn't see Jamie's car. Or . . . rather . . . Mrs. Ruiz's car that Jamie was borrowing until he found something else cheap. She didn't think he was working tonight. As she stepped out of her car in her bare feet, Jamie pulled in behind her.

He smiled at her as he got out of his car, and then reached back in to pull out a pizza box. "Hungry?"

"Famished."

"Come on then."

Jamie called out, "Pizza's here" when they walked into the house, which was unnecessary because their dad sat on the recliner in front of them, an amused smile on his face. "I see that."

They set the pizza box on the coffee table and ate their pizza slices off paper plates on their laps. It was Tate's favorite type of family dinner, sitting around the TV, eating and laughing. Forgetting about everything else that was going on and just enjoying each other's company. With Jamie's issues and her stress, they hadn't done this enough.

She looked over at her dad, and he must have felt her eyes on him, because he winked at her before looking back at the TV.

She smiled and looked down at her pizza, picking off a pepperoni slice and dropping it in her mouth. She mulled in her head how to bring it up, because Jamie was in the room so she had to break it gently to him . . .

The footrest of her dad's recliner jolted back, and he placed his feet on the floor, leaning forward, eyes on her. "I was waiting you out, baby, but we need to talk."

Tate's eyes darted to Jamie and then back to her father. "Um . . . well . . ."

Jamie waved his hand. "It's cool, I know already."

Tate threw up her hands. "What the hell? Everyone's stealing my news!"

Her dad clasped his hands in his lap. "Why didn't you talk to me about this sooner?"

Tate relaxed her arms and picked at her fingernails. "I dunno."

"I think you do."

She bit the inside of her cheek. "Because I wasn't ready to make the decision yet myself."

"And why's that?"

"This feels like therapy," Tate grumbled.

"Seriously, join the club," Jamie muttered.

Their father shot them both a stern glance, then focused again on Tate. She felt like there was a bull's-eye on her forehead. "And why weren't you ready to make the decision?"

"I had to make sure it's what I wanted. That this time I'm making the decision for me."

He raised an eyebrow. "And is it?"

She nodded. "I'm scared and freaked and nervous, but it's what I want."

He nodded and brought down his fist on the arm of his chair like he held a gavel. "Then you go."

Tate sat up. "But Dad—"

He held up a hand. "I'm doing fine. And even if I wasn't, you need to live your life. This isn't what I want for you."

"But I'm not miserable here."

"Of course not, now that Cam's back," Jamie interjected.

Her father nodded. "Right, he's back, and you're happy. I can't imagine how you'd be if he left without you. Now that you both know what it's like to be together again, as adults. Don't you think?"

Damn man. Always so insightful. Like he could read her mind. "Yes," she said grudgingly.

"So, again," he said, his voice softer. "You go. We'll miss you. We'll miss you so much. But you aren't far. And I'll be so happy knowing you're happy and you're with the man you're supposed to be with. You two take care of each other. And that's the way it should be."

Tate's eyes prickled as she turned to her brother. "Jamie?"

His smile was sad. "It's okay. I only have another year of school."

"I'll be at your graduation."

"I know you will." But his tone was less than reassuring.

Tate tried harder. "And homecoming. And prom. And the holidays—"

Jamie launched himself across the couch and hugged her. His big hand rubbed her back and she buried her face in his neck. "I know, Tate. I know."

She pulled out of the hug and wiped her eyes, then stood up and walked over to her father. She bent down and wrapped her arms around his shoulders, kissing his whiskered cheek. "I love you, Dad."

His voice cracked when he spoke, but she pretended not to notice. "I love you, too, baby."

IT WAS TWO a.m. when Cam got off work and all he could think about was Tate. He was itching to know how her conversation with her father went. He got into his truck and started it up, then tapped on the dashboard and stared at the clock. It was really late, and he knew she'd be asleep.

He sighed and pulled his phone out of the glove box. He could just let her sleep. Nothing was changing overnight, right?

Oh God, what if she changed her mind?

He thunked his forehead on the steering wheel and groaned. There was no missed call, no text message. Nothing. So she was either torturing him on purpose or it was bad news.

By the time he got home, he was fuming and assumed she was torturing him. Because he'd rather be pissed off than depressed.

He didn't shower like he always did when he got off work. He signed right into Utope, planning to leave a flaming bag of shit on her door or a severed horse head in her bed. Go big or go home on the revenge, right?

But when he signed into Utope, he saw Tate had been in several hours ago. In the game, there was a note on the kitchen table. He clicked on it.

I know you're mad I didn't call. Probably want to put a bag of flaming shit on my doorstep, don't you? Well, before you get the lighter, check out the bedroom.
    Love, T

He'd actually already grabbed the lighter so he put that back in a kitchen drawer and walked his little avatar body to the bedroom.

And when he opened the door, he swore his eyes in real life got misty, or maybe that was from staring so hard at the television screen. Because Tate had found posters in the game and plastered the walls of the bedroom of their house with them. The Empire State Building. Central Park. A *Lion King* Broadway advertisement. *30 Rock*. Macy's. And more iconic New York City landmarks.

He spun his avatar in a circle, checking out all the posters.

And then Tate sauntered out of the adjoining bathroom, wearing an I <3 NY shirt. And Cam started laughing. He clicked for his avatar to laugh, and then the room filled with two deep chuckles.

Chapter 16

CAM TONGUED THE corner of his mouth as he filled in his spreadsheet on the computer. He loved spreadsheets. Everything all nice and orderly and color-coded. His roommate in college, Alec Stone, had shown him the genius of spreadsheets and Cam had been hooked ever since.

This spreadsheet was organized with possible apartments for his mom. He had columns for security deposit, estimated utilities cost, insurance and on and on. If he was out of state, he wanted to make sure she was in a place she felt comfortable and could afford. Of course, he'd be sending her money. Every month. Like clockwork. She was Ma.

He liked the complex called Nichol Way Estates. An available apartment was on the first floor and she could look out her kitchen window every day and see a small flower garden courtyard. She loved flowers, especially peonies, so he'd make sure they had a peony tree or bush or whatever the hell those things were.

He'd officially accepted the job that morning. With a fancy e-mail to his new boss. That was still a weird word to say. Boss. Every time he thought about, his stomach flipped with nervous excitement. He had a future, doing what he loved, with the girl he loved. He wondered how the hell he got so lucky.

His phone rang and he picked it up with one hand while typing with the other, because he had one more column to fill. He jammed the phone in between his ear and shoulder so he could still type with two hands. "Hello?"

The first sounds on the other end of the line were breathless, like the person was breathing hard, then, "Cam." It was Jamie's voice.

Cam reached up and grabbed the phone, pressing it to his ear. "Yeah, what's up? Why are you out of breath?"

"I need your help, man."

"Of course, whatever you need."

"It's . . . it's Dad."

Only three words. But they were said with an unmistakable tone of dread. The oxygen sucked out of the room like a vacuum and Cam's lungs gasped. He braced himself on the desk in front of him. "What happened?"

Jamie's voice was a little muffled, like he was looking around him. "He said he had chest pains and then collapsed. I don't know what's going on. We're waiting for the ambulance right now."

"Is he conscious?"

Jamie sounded like he sucked in a breath, and when he spoke, his voice was almost a squeak. "Sort of?"

"Where's your sister?"

"I can't get ahold of her."

Cam squeezed his eyes shut, because Jamie must be completely freaked, dealing with this all on his own. How he was holding it together this well was a mystery to Cam.

"Okay, buddy. I'm on my way over, okay? Just—"

"Oh, the ambulance just pulled up outside so—"

"I'll meet you at the hospital, and I'll keep trying to get ahold of your sister."

When Jamie spoke again, his voice was steadier. "Great, great. Thanks, Cam."

"Glad you called me. Hang in there. See ya soon."

There was a muffled "Bye" and then the call disconnected.

Cam called Trevor and told him he wouldn't be in to work. Then Cam called Tate. Her phone went right to voice mail. He called the diner, and Margo said Tate and Anne had run a quick errand. It was unlike Tate not to have her phone with her, but he figured her guard was down now. This was a blow none of them had expected.

He made it to the hospital in half the time it normally did, because he ran a couple of lights, and found Jamie in the emergency room waiting area. "Any news?" He slid into the seat beside Tate's brother.

"Last I heard, they're admitting him. They told me they'd come out and tell me when I could see him." Jamie's eyes were huge, a little boy in a man's face. "That's not good. That they're admitting him."

"I don't know."

Jamie hung his head. "Thanks for coming."

" 'Course."

Jamie's phone rang, and he fumbled in his pocket before pulling it out. He glanced at the caller ID, his eyes shooting to Cam's when he answered. "Tate."

Cam could hear her voice on the other end, firing off questions. She must have listened to their voice mails.

Jamie muttered a couple of words and then hung up. "She'll be here soon."

Cam squeezed Jamie's shoulder. "We all gotta be strong for your dad, all right? We can do this."

Jamie bit his lip and then nodded. "Okay."

WHEN TATE BURST into the waiting room, she saw Cam sitting with her brother. His arm was around Jamie's shoulders as Jamie slumped forward, his clasped hands smashed against his forehead between his legs.

Cam was talking in low tones, his fingers rubbing slow circles on her brother's shoulder.

She filed that away in the back of her mind, Cam's attention to her family. How he'd make an amazing father.

But today was about her father.

Cam looked up and saw her, then he patted Jamie's back. Her brother nodded and raised his head, giving Tate a watery smile.

She couldn't return it. Not now. When she didn't know if her dad was okay.

Cam stood up and held his arms out. And all she could do was run into those arms and burrow into Cam, as deep as she could go.

He squeezed her tightly and pressed kisses on the top of her head. "We'll figure this out, Tate. It'll be okay."

Cam pulled back and brushed his thumbs over her cheeks, marring the tear tracks she could feel on her skin. "A nurse came out a little bit ago, letting us know the doctor will be out soon to give us an update, okay?"

She nodded and turned to Jamie, who'd stood up beside Cam. She grasped him in a hug and he squeezed back, his breath hot along her temple.

When the diagnosis had come, Jamie had been a few inches shorter than her. He'd clung to her as she smoothed his shaggy hair off his thirteen-year-old face.

But now the stubble along her jaw rubbed her forehead as he stood above her. His arms were longer, his chest broader.

When had he grown in to a man? How had she missed this?

"No ice cream in the bathtub this time," he said quietly.

"I even had moose tracks in the freezer for you."

He chuckled softly as her head bounced off his chest. "When we get home. I think we still have some of that chocolate that hardens when it gets cold."

"And waffle cones."

"And rainbow sprinkles."

She started crying again then, wishing they were back at home, arguing over the umpire's strike calls. Tate curled up on Cam's lap. Jamie in the corner of the sofa so he could reach his dad in the armchair for good-natured shoulder punches.

Jamie's grip tightened and she was jostled as a solid

heat warmed her back. She took a shuddering breath as the tears slowed, and she relaxed in a cocoon of the two most important men in her life other than her father.

Eventually, they migrated to the chairs, Cam and Jamie beside each other, Tate sitting on Cam with her legs over Jamie's lap. She wasn't sure how long they sat there. At one point, someone force-fed her a granola bar and poured water down her throat. But the food tasted like cardboard and the water did nothing to settle her stomach.

Eventually a doctor came out and explained that her father had recently been put on a new medication and he'd had a negative reaction.

"So what does that mean?" Tate stood on wobbly legs. A strong arm rested on her lower back, supporting her more than she wanted to admit.

"Well," the doctor said, brushing her hands over her white coat. "We need to keep him for a little and run some tests. Make sure this isn't a symptom of a larger problem."

"Did you do a blood test yet? How are his white blood cells?" Jamie asked.

"We're waiting for the results."

"Can we see him?" Tate reached for Cam's hand and exhaled when he linked his fingers with hers. The doctor nodded and motioned them back. She eyed Cam, who clearly wasn't family, but Tate set her face and plastered herself to his side. The doctor tipped up her lips and didn't object.

Hospitals were always described by smell and while

Tate hated the smell, it was the sounds that she despised the most. The squeak of the nurses' shoes, the swish of paperwork, the beep of machines, the soft voices. All of it grated on her nerves until every one felt raw and exposed. She wanted to yell, or blast music, or something. Anything to get rid of the weird faux silence that surrounded her.

And this reminded her of when her father was first diagnosed. When she gripped the hand of a thirteen-year-old Jamie and felt like she was on an out-of-control roller coaster.

Part of her didn't want to admit it, but her hand in Cam's steadied her. She finally felt like she could maybe make it through whatever life tossed at her next.

Hospital beds always had a way of making the person in them seem pale and small. She hated that. Plus she was tired of seeing IVs in her dad's arms. He bruised so badly now.

"Hey guys." He smiled at them. "Sorry for the scare."

"You better apologize." Jamie sat at the foot of the bed. "I'm going to let your ice cream melt just for freaking us out."

Their dad smiled at them and then turned to Tate. "Hey baby."

Tate scrunched her lips to the side, resisting the urge to wail at seeing her father in a hospital bed again. "Hey Daddy."

"I'm okay."

"I know."

He reached his hand out, the one that wasn't attached to the IV, to shake Cam's hand. "Glad you're here."

Cam smiled. "Me too."

He leaned his head back on the pillow. "Lunch was a cold chicken sandwich."

"Ew." Jamie wrinkled his nose.

"Get me a burger?"

"No." Tate pointed a finger at both the men in her family. "Dad, you'll eat what they tell you to while you're here. When you get out, I'm sure Anne will make you something fancy and calorie-laden."

"I feel fine. I can go home now."

"Nice try, Dad."

He snorted. "It was a weak effort."

Jamie picked at the sheet. "They think it's just the medication, though. You should be fine."

The "should be" hung in the air between them. Hovering. Waiting. They all saw it but no one wanted to acknowledge it. Cancer had knocked her dad down several pegs but it'd never once dimmed his light. Not when his hair thinned and not when chemo made him puke up water.

Tate sat on the edge of the bed near her father's hip and leaned down, wrapped her arms around his shoulders.

He hugged her back, and she could feel slight tremors in his arms. She hugged tighter.

They stayed with him for another hour or so, leaving the room occasionally to get snacks at one of the hospital's many delis.

Her father was in good spirits, making jokes. Although sometimes a tenseness would pass over his face, and his lips would tighten, which made Tate nervous. But then in an instant it'd be gone.

But when the doctor walked in, her shoes barely making a sound on the tile floor, and announced the results of the blood test were back, her face was carefully blank. Tate's stomach slammed into her shoes.

There were numbers and words coming from the doctor's mouth, which Tate at one time had studied like crazy so she knew every bit of her father's illness.

She thought they were done with those. That the last round of chemo had been it. She'd happily wiped that area of her brain clean so it was ready for some other type of information.

Which she shouldn't have done. Because these numbers were back, and Jamie was crying. And her dad's face was pale. And Cam looked like he'd been punched in the gut.

And Tate? Tate felt . . . numb. Like she was floating above the room, listening to someone else hearing that their father's cancer was back.

This wasn't her life. In her life, her father had beaten cancer, and Jamie was maturing and she was off to start a life with her soul mate in New York.

But then she made eye contact with Cam, and the devastation was written all over his face. He didn't even try to hide it. And that's when her bubble popped, and she slammed back into her body.

Because this, right here in the hospital room, this was her life.

She raised her chin and straightened her spine. This

time, damn it, this time she wouldn't let it defeat her. She wouldn't crumble in this sanitary prison. She'd stay strong for her dad and she'd meet this head-on. And she'd break down and mourn her selfish thoughts in private.

Because she couldn't leave her dad. There was no way around it. She didn't want to leave him, no matter if he had six months or six years left. The doctor was talking treatment again, but he seemed less confident this time around. She wanted as much time with her dad as she could get. She wanted to soak in his presence and learn all the lessons she still needed to learn.

There'd be no New York for her.

She stood up and walked to her father's bedside, then leaned down and pressed a kiss to his forehead. "I'm so sorry, Dad."

His face was turned away, toward the window, as if he could lessen the blow of the doctor's words if he didn't meet them head-on. And then he met her eyes, and all she saw was defeat.

"So it's back," he said quietly.

She smoothed his thinning hair off his forehead. "It is, but we've been here all along. And we'll always be here."

He must have known then what she was saying. Because his eyes welled up. Then Tate's vision blurred and she turned around to allow herself to be wrapped into Cam's arms.

Jamie's voice murmured behind her to their father.

She clung to Cam, burrowing his face in his chest while one of his hands glided up and down her back.

They didn't stay the night. Her dad insisted they go

home. Mostly, Tate was glad. She needed to be home and have the time to process the news.

Cam stopped her with a loose grip on her biceps before she walked out of the doors of the hospital. "Do you want me to come home with you?"

She looked at Jamie, who shuffled his feet, eyes on the glass doors of the hospital to the night sky outside. She wasn't sure how much time she had left with Cam. And the news hurt him too. She could read it all over his face. If she really thought about it, all she wanted was to go home and fall asleep in Cam's arms.

She looked up into his dark eyes. "Could you?"

Relief softened his features as he nodded. "I'll follow you in my truck."

She drove home with Jamie in the passenger seat in silence. No radio or anything. Like they both needed time to clear their heads.

When she turned onto their street, she felt a light touch on her arm. She looked over at Jamie. In the dark light, his expression was hard to read. Then that light touch migrated toward her hand. She took it off the steering wheel, and he linked his fingers with hers. He squeezed, and she squeezed back.

"You're not leaving anymore, are you?" His question wasn't a plea. It was more of a statement than anything.

She didn't dare speak, just shook her head.

Jamie made a sound, like a small sob. "I'm sorry."

She squeezed his hand again. "We'll do it right this time. Spend as much time together as we can. Okay?"

Jamie nodded. And she let go of his hand so she could put her truck in park.

Cam's headlights cut across the front of her house as he pulled into her driveway. Jamie stepped out but she sat at the steering wheel, staring at her house until Cam opened her door for her, unbuckled her seat belt and led her into the house.

She wasn't sure what came next. He helped her out of her clothes and shoved a toothpaste-laden toothbrush into her mouth. Slipped a pair of pajama cotton shorts up to her hips and a big T-shirt over her head. Then she was in bed, wrapped in Cam's arms. She hadn't shed a tear yet. Not one.

She rolled into Cam, who wore only a pair of boxers, and ran the tip of her nose along the side of his neck. She walked her fingers up each rib, along the grooves of his stomach, tracing the cut muscles at his hips.

He made a sound in the back of this throat, gripping her arm. She felt a slight push, but she wouldn't let him dislodge her. She wouldn't let him turn her down. She opened her mouth and latched on to his neck, sucking the smooth skin and humming. The pressure on his arm eased and when she added a nip of teeth, he relented, his motion switching directions, and now he was pulling her tighter to his body.

His lips brushed along her temple as a hand rose up into her hair. "Tate." She released the skin at his neck and nibbled at his earlobe, tonguing and tugging at the small earring. "Are you sure?"

She rose above him, her hands on either side of his head, straddling his hips so his hardness nestled between her legs. They hadn't had sex yet since they got back together, like neither wanted to take that final step again, that last big commitment. She knew once they came together again, they'd be soldered together, the melting parts of themselves hardening into one. It would take a sharp, hot knife to separate.

But she didn't care anymore. Because their future was burning up before them, that dream turning to dust. This time, when it was over, she wanted to take a part of him with her. She wanted to leave a part of herself with him.

"I've never been more sure. I need you." And then she lowered herself above him, pressing her lips to his, and he opened for her, angling her head so he could get deeper inside her. She rocked her hips and he moaned into his mouth.

She hurt. Everywhere. And she ached for Cam so badly. Ached to forget about everything crumbling around her and lose herself in the one man she ever loved.

With a small growl, he rolled her onto her back. He tucked his face into her neck, licking and biting, kissing and sucking to the dip in her throat and along her collarbone. He gripped her leg above the knee with a strong hand and propped it up on his hip, opening her up to him. She bent her other knee, planting her foot on the bed, and squeezed it to him.

And then she surrendered. She let him strip her of her shirt and she writhed under him as he sucked one nipple into his mouth. She gasped at the sharp sting of teeth. God, she'd always loved that. Cam knew just how to play her, when to give her that edge of pain and when to soothe it with a lick. He knew just how hard to suck that it hurt and then when to back off.

It had always been Cam. And it always would be.

He slipped off her shorts and underwear, taking his boxers off at the same time, then resumed his position between her legs. All she could do was grip his hair and run her hands over his back. Her muscles felt like jelly and she hadn't even come yet. But Cam had rendered her drugged with his hands and lips and teeth. That hard arousal pressing against her nakedness.

He reached down between her legs, running his fingers through the wetness, dipping inside and then rubbing her clit. "You're crazy ready for me." His lips and tongue traced the shell of her ear and his fingers were doing crazy things. All she could gasp out was "Always."

"Fuck, Tate," he moaned.

"Missed your mouth."

"Yeah? The things I do with it or the words that come out of it?"

She gasped out a laugh. "Both."

He grinned then, a wicked grin along with a twist of his fingers. And then she wasn't laughing. Because her hips were churning, grinding against his hand. But that wasn't what she wanted. Somehow she got the muscles of her arm and hand to work as she reached down and gripped him, and stroked from root to tip. He grunted.

"I want this," she said, and bit his shoulder.

"Fuck."

"That's the idea."

She squeezed and pumped her hand. His hips rocked against her and his mouth crashed down on hers. "Condoms?" he mumbled against her lips.

"Nightstand."

He leaned back and raised an eyebrow.

She rolled her eyes. "I just bought them, stud. Chill out."

He smirked and pulled out the top drawer, fumbling in the box before pulling out a foil packet. He ripped it open with his teeth, then rolled it on with one hand. The ease of it stung.

"We're going to have to talk about how you have this one-handed condom act down to a science," she said.

He shook his head and braced himself on his forearms over her. He nudged her nose with his. "How about we not talk about that right now?"

And then he kissed her again, and all thoughts of other girls fled as his tongue proved she was the only one on his mind.

She felt him at her entrance, nudging. And then his hips canted, and he slid inside.

Tate hugged him to her chest and wrapped her legs around him as they both gasped. When every inch of him was inside her heat, he didn't move. One hand cupped her neck and the other lightly gripped her hair. His forehead pressed into her temple and his breath rushed hot over her face. "Tate. God. I fucking missed you."

And that was when the first tears threatened. When the magnitude of the day caught up with her. She tucked her head into his neck and urged him to move with a rock of her hips. "Missed you, too."

But he didn't let her get away with hiding. He pulled back slightly and raised her head to meet her eyes. "No one's ever come close to meaning to me what you mean to me. You know that, right?"

She bit the inside of her cheek, hard.

He gripped her chin and circled his hips, once. She gasped.

"Tate, you know that, right? I love you."

She couldn't speak, because the sobs were starting in her throat. So she just nodded.

But again, Cam didn't relent. "Please say the word," he whispered.

A sob escaped. "Yes."

And then he moved. In that lazy, rolling motion that only Cam had. He started slow, watching her face, kissing the corners of her eyes and mouth.

She gripped his hips harder with her legs and met his thrusts. And that was when his lazy rolls turned into powerful thrusts. He rose up on his palms and watched their connection. She admired the shifting muscles in his thighs and shoulders and biceps. The straining veins in his neck and forearms.

There was no sight like Cam during sex.

The angle wasn't hitting her right, so she lowered a hand just where she needed it, pressing and rolling, circling. Cam's breath was coming faster now, his movements a little erratic as he lost control. "Fuck, that's hot, Tate. Come for me."

And it didn't take much longer, as the orgasm started in her spine and then radiated into the rest of her body and out to her limbs. She bit down on her other hand to hold in the cries, and Cam shoved his face into her shoulder, his grunts and muttered curses bleeding into her skin.

He didn't pull out right away, instead he stayed inside her, nudging her sensitive skin with shallow, gentle rocks.

She'd forgotten about this. Or maybe she'd blocked it out of her mind. Because this was always the best part of sex with Cam. The way he kept them together as they both came down, as the aftershocks of their orgasms faded. Like he didn't want to leave her yet. Like he wanted to crawl inside her and stay there.

She rubbed his back with her hands and up into his hair, sliding her cheek against his. Her skin would probably show the evidence of the contact with his stubble tomorrow, but she didn't care.

Finally, he pulled out, got rid of the condom, and then crawled back beneath the sheets. He enclosed her in his arms, her head resting on the hot skin of his chest over his heart.

"You break me, Tate," his rocky voice said.

She kissed his skin. "And you put me back together."

He squeezed her shoulders and as she was falling asleep, she realized she hadn't shed a tear.

CAM BLINKED IN the darkened light of Tate's bedroom, sensing an odd light in the room. He could hear something clicking, like nails on tile, and something else . . .

He reached a hand out for Tate but she wasn't in the bed with him. A roll of his head showed the time was three a.m. What the hell?

He rubbed his eyes, and the other sounds became clearer. Heavy breathing. And muffled sobs. He shot up straight in bed and looked over to the TV. Utope was on, and he could see the back of Tate's head, her hair pulled up into a messy ponytail.

Another sob ripped from her throat, and he scooted across the bed as the scene on the TV became clear in his head.

Tate's avatar was in their bedroom. And she was screaming while she ripped down every New York City poster off their walls, and then she hauled them into the fireplace and screamed and stomped her feet some more as they ignited. Until all that remained were the blank walls.

Louder sobs from Tate on the floor and then she reared back her arm, like she planned to toss the controller through the TV. It had been weeks ago when he prevented her from throwing her phone and he would prevent this, too.

He stretched out an arm and gripped her wrist. She gasped in surprise, struggling a bit until she whipped her head around to face him.

And then she crumbled. Like a puppet with the strings cut. Her whole body slumped to the floor, and Cam had to slide off the bed to catch her so she wouldn't hit her head.

She lay sprawled in his lap, crying, sobbing, falling

apart like he'd never seen her before. His chest tightened and if he hadn't felt the overriding need to prop her up, he would have been right there on the floor sobbing with her.

Because Ted's cancer was back. And Tate wasn't coming with him.

He cradled her and rocked her and made soothing noises he didn't know he was capable of. He didn't tell her it was going to be all right. He didn't make one single promise except to tell her he loved her.

He hoped it was enough.

When her sobs had died, and her breath was interrupted with intermittent hitching, she leaned back and cupped his face. He raised his hands and swiped her cheeks with his thumbs.

Her gaze searched his face before resting again on his eyes. "No lies this time. No smokescreens. Just me in front of you with my heart splitting open telling you that I can't go."

It hurt. Those words. He didn't trust himself so all he said was "I know."

"And you might be thinking I'm doing the same thing. That I'm making a decision for someone else but I'm not. This is a decision for me. A selfish decision, because I want to be with my dad for as long as he has left." Her laugh was sad. "But it's a sadistic and masochistic decision at the same time, isn't it? And I guess it's no different than the last time. I'm breaking both our hearts again."

Cam's head was spinning, because there was so much to say.

"But you're keeping the job."

He jerked back. "What?"

Her face was set. "You'll keep the job. And you'll go and do what you've always wanted to do. That's the way it's going to be."

He didn't want to get into it now. He had his own decisions to make. But they weren't decisions to be made at three in the morning while he sat on the floor with a devastated Tatum, while a fire fueled by tourist posters raged on the TV behind them.

So he ignored her command. "Well, I didn't see it coming, what happened to your dad. But this news? I saw it coming as soon as I got the call from Jamie. So maybe that's why I'm not losing my shit right now. Or maybe it's because I'm tired. Or maybe it's because your avatar looks like a nut job stomping her feet."

On the TV, Tate's avatar continued to wave her arms and holler. Tate turned back to him, a smile starting to creep onto her face. "I was pretty upset so I dialed up her emotions."

"I can tell." Cam pulled out the ponytail holder holding up her mass of hair and finger-combed it into some order, then pulled it back up into a neater ponytail. Tate sat passively in his lap, her eyes half closed. He used to comb her hair for her sometimes in high school. Of course, he never would have admitted it to his friends, but there was something about touching the strands and massaging her scalp that calmed him as much as her.

He gestured toward the TV. "Can we douse the fire so you don't burn our house down, and go back to sleep?"

She glanced at the TV. "I think the dogs are upset."

He huffed out a laugh. "Come on, Tate."

She grabbed a fire extinguisher and put out the fire, then turned off the game and crawled back into bed, where Cam waited with open arms.

She nestled into his chest. "My head's killing me now."

"Crying?"

She nodded.

He remembered. She hated crying. Sometimes the headache even turned into a migraine. "You want to take a couple of pills?"

"Nah, that's okay." She yawned. "Just need to sleep, I guess. And worry about everything else tomorrow."

He smoothed his hand down her back. "Yeah, guess so."

He waited until Tate's breaths evened out, her face slackened as she slept. But Cam was wide awake now, seeing that fire like a ghost image in front of his eyes. Because no matter what Tate thought, he still had a decision to make. At the moment, it was black and white, but Cam wanted to scratch and claw below the surface, to see if there was a gray area he was missing.

He was still digging when he felt himself drift into sleep along with Tate.

Chapter 17

CAM SHOVED AN extra shirt into his book bag and then put his hands on his hips, surveying his room, making sure he didn't forget anything.

His mom sat on the bed, smoothing the comforter with her hands. "Camilo, I know once you make a decision, that's it. That's final. But—"

"Mom, we talked about this. Over and over again. But it's done. I made the call already."

She pursed her lips. "I wasn't talking about that. I was talking about not telling Tate."

He clenched his jaw and stared at his book bag. Yeah, that was the one rare decision he wasn't so sure about. Looking back, he should have talked to Tate first.

He had two options. Tell her and discuss his decision with her while she went off the rails and yelled at him.

Or say fuck it, make the call himself and then spend this night showing her how good they were together before telling her what he'd done.

_ He went with the latter. And he still wasn't sure it was the right decision. But what was done was done. Because his hands were bloody from digging, and he hadn't found any gray.

He shook his head. "I'm not sure. But it's done."

His mother's gaze roamed to his stuffed book bag. "What did you tell her about tonight?"

Cam remembered his battery-operated radio. He pulled it down from the top shelf of his closet and stuffed it in a side pocket of his bag. "I told her I want to take her camping, like we used to do. Just the two of us away from all the stress."

His mom wasn't happy with him. He knew that. But this was his life now. So all she did was sigh. "What did she say to that?"

Cam winced. Because Tate had smiled and acted excited but the whole thing had felt forced and false. Didn't she know he could see through all that? But he didn't call her on it. She had a lot on her mind. Her dad was home from the hospital now, and she'd spent a lot of time making sure he was comfortable. Jamie took off tonight to stay home with him so Cam could take Tate out. So maybe she was nervous about leaving her dad. Cam was going to go with that, because it made me feel better than to think Tate didn't want to be with him.

It'd been a week and he hadn't seen her or talked to her much. There was a huge river between them, and Cam wasn't strong enough to swim through the current.

"Camilo?" his mom asked.

"What?" Had she asked him a question?

She smiled tightly. "Nothing."

"You doing okay?"

Her smile was genuine this time. "You know I am."

"You don't mind that I won't be home until morning?"

She shook her head. "Of course not." Her eyes narrowed a little. "But be safe."

"We get cell service out there—"

She raised her eyebrows. "I wasn't talking about that kind of safe."

He rolled his eyes. "For God's sake, Ma, I'm twenty-three. I know to use condoms."

She laughed. "Hey, I'm your mother. And it's my job to tell you that."

He waved her off. "Right, right." She probably didn't want him to get Tate pregnant. That would just be a cherry on top of this sundae.

She stood up slowly. "You need any more help with dinner?"

"Nah, I packed everything we need. Thanks for making the chicken salad."

She patted his shoulder. "I know how much Tate likes it."

"Yeah, she does." He fidgeted with the strap of his bag and then hauled it over his shoulder. "Wish me luck."

She wrapped her arms around him and kissed his cheek. "Good luck, sweetie."

On the way out the door, he grabbed the cooler with their dinner. His mom's special chicken salad with kaiser rolls, cut fruit, sweet potato chips, and turtle brownies.

All Tate's favorites.

When he pulled into her driveway, a curtain moved

to the left of the door, so he knew he'd been spotted. He waited a minute and was about to get out of his truck when Tate stepped out of the front door and closed it behind her.

She stood on the porch, bag clutched in her hands, staring at him while biting her lip. He wanted to rush to her and grab her in his arms, but this had to be her decision, to come to him. To want to be with him.

She swayed on her feet and then with a jolt, like she'd made her decision suddenly, she jogged down the stairs and to his truck. She threw her bag in the bed along with the rest of the camping gear and then hopped up into the passenger side.

After she was buckled in, she looked at him. Her eyes were clear for the first time in a week. And he began to feel hopeful.

She smiled at him. "Okay, I'm ready."

He returned her smile. "Bug spray?"

"Check."

"Toilet paper?"

"Check."

"Bear Mace?"

"Ch—" Her eyes narrowed and she glared at him.

He laughed. "You know bears are rare where we camp."

She pointed a finger at him. "See, silly me, but I'm hung up on this word *rare*."

He began to back out of her driveway. "I got my gun in the glove box."

She looked horrified. "You can't shoot a bear!"

He peeled off down her street. "Tatum, if there is a choice between being mauled by a bear, or shooting it, I'm going to fucking shoot it."

"What if it's a mommy or something?"

"So you want me to let it maul me?"

She wrinkled her nose. "Maybe it'll just give you a warning scratch."

He laughed. "A warning scratch? A warning would be severing my heard or some other vital limb."

Tate crossed her arms in a huff. "I don't want to talk about this anymore."

He reached over and tugged until she dropped her arms, then he laced his hand with hers. "I won't shoot any bears. We're going to eat my mom's chicken salad and make a fire and cook dessert moon pies and then sleep in the tent in the bed of my truck."

She squeezed his hand. "I bet we could sacrifice some chicken salad to the bear and make our getaway."

"Shut up about this damn hypothetical bear."

She giggled, and the sound trickled over his skin like a blast of hot air.

The last time Cam had visited Ehrhart Park, it'd been shortly before he left for basic training. He and Tate had done this very thing—camped out in the bed of a truck. Although at that time, it'd been a rusted-out Ford that didn't like to start about seventy-five percent of the time.

He pulled into the parking lot and waited while Tate hopped out and shoved aside the gate, which had a big sign notifying them no vehicles were to travel down it. Everyone in town ignored it, taking off down the road farther into the park. It was the popular teenage make-out spot, and Cam felt a little old, but he was trying to do this right. And he knew how much Tate liked to sleep outside.

She climbed back inside the truck, her skin showing a pink blush of excitement. "Buckle up," he said, as he took off down the road, the truck's shocks getting a workout on the uneven road.

He remembered the route they'd always taken, even though it'd been years, and finally came to a stop at a clearing next to a small stream.

Cam looked over at Tate, her face taking on a pretty glow in the light of the setting sun. "Here we are."

She turned to him with a smile. "Haven't been here since . . ." Her voice trailed off, her expression sobering.

"Yeah, me either." He grabbed her hand and kissed it. "Let's get set up and then we can eat, all right?"

She nodded, and they both hopped out of the truck. Setting up the tent together was like riding a bike. They each knew their role and the two-man tent was up in less than ten minutes.

They gathered sticks for the fire, starting with a pile of small kindling. Cam struck a piece of flint and lit a spark into a clump of lint he'd pulled out of the dryer that morning.

By the time the sun was half gone over the horizon, they had a decent fire and sat cuddled together, eating sandwiches and crunching chips.

Up in the mountains where they were, along the edge of the Appalachian Trail, the temperature dropped quickly once the sun set, so Cam spread a blanket over them, placing Tate between his legs so she reclined on his chest while he braced himself on the trunk of a tree. He picked up a grape and popped it into his mouth, then did the same for Tate.

He wrapped his arms around her and dropped his chin on the top of her head as they stared at the fire.

Tell her now, a voice whispered in his head. But damn, he was so comfortable. And he didn't want to fight. He wanted to have this night with Tate. He wanted to prove to her that what they had was worth fighting for. It was worth sacrificing things.

She had to see that, didn't she?

"Did you date a lot in college?"

The question surprised him. It wasn't accusatory or meek. She tilted her head back a little with a small smile, which eased him somewhat.

"Uh, no, not really. I didn't date."

"No?"

He shrugged. "College was . . . fun. I had a nice time. But I wasn't looking for anything serious and most girls I . . . spent time with . . . weren't looking for anything serious either."

She chuckled and squeezed his hands. "So you didn't leave broken hearts in your wake back at Bowler?"

He kissed her temple. "Nah, I don't think so."

She fell silent and it was several minutes before she spoke again. "I'm sorry."

He didn't know what for, so he didn't speak and waited her out.

She took a deep breath. "I was looking forward to being with you at Bowler second semester, you know? Then Dad got sick and I messed up."

"And you didn't try to go to community college?"

"I didn't have the same goals anymore. What I thought I wanted in high school . . . well, it wasn't what I wanted anymore."

He squeezed his eyes shut and drew her closer to his body. The fire was hot on his face and her body was warm and soft against him. Her hair smelled like flowers, and he wanted to stay in this moment forever. "What do you want now?"

She broke from his grip and turned in his arms. She sat between his legs on her knees, her hands on his thighs. The fire burned bright behind her, backlighting her body so she was a sexy silhouette of big hair and curvy woman. He clenched his fists so he didn't grab her.

Those hands on his thighs crept higher, higher, until they reached where his legs met his body. And that was when he reached out and wrapped his fingers around her wrists. "What're you doing?"

She shifted closer. On all fours in front of him, knees on the ground and hands on his thighs. Her face was so close, he felt the lightest brush of her lips on his. "I'm answering your question."

His mind scrambled. "What question was that?"

Another brush of her lips, a swipe of her tongue along his jaw and back to his ear. He shut his eyes when she sucked his earlobe into his mouth and tongued his earring. She released it and her voice was steam and heat and promise. "You asked me what I want. And I want you."

He moaned. "I meant—"

"I know what you meant, but I don't know. All I know is what I want. Right now. And that's you, Camilo Ruiz."

CAM SMELLED AMAZING. Like campfire and chocolate moon pies and man. Every muscle in her body, every cell was drawn to him.

She brushed her lips over his jaw and back to this mouth, teasing the corners of his lips before she swiped out her tongue for a taste.

Because she wanted Cam tonight. She wanted to remember this when he was off being the successful man she always knew he'd be. She'd said good-bye once already when she saw him off to basic training. And that would be the last time she uttered those words to him. This time, she'd say good-bye with her body. Because come morning, she'd tell him she was letting him go. Off the hook. Too bad, his hook was in her too, so when he pulled it out, it'd leave her bloody and gouged and broken. She wasn't going to think about that yet.

Because right now, Cam's tongue was slipping in between her lips, and his hands were gripping her face. And then all she could think about were the sensations that were racing through her body.

He pulled away with a growl. "Tent."

She blinked. "What?"

"Go in the tent. I'm putting the fire out, then I'm coming to show you how badly I want you, too."

Okay then, that worked for her. She rose on wobbly

legs and walked backward to the tent as Cam poured water on the fire. Thick plumes of gray smoke billowed above them. Then his dark eyes turned to her, a wicked grin on her lips. She squealed a laugh, turned and ran, the cracking of branches letting her know Cam was on her heels.

She dove into the tent and Cam was a second after her, careful not to crush her as his body covered hers.

He gripped her head hard, his thumb on the underside of her jaw, directing her right where he wanted her. And she gripped his wrist and gave in, succumbing to him.

He covered her face and neck in openmouthed kisses, and somehow she pulled his shirt off. She ran her fingers up his sides and he shivered when she hit where he was ticklish. He huffed into her neck, his stubble rasping her skin.

Her top came off. Then her bra. And his mouth moved lower. Sucking her nipples, nuzzling her ribs, dipping a tongue in her belly button.

When she was naked before him, he sat back on his heels, the top button of his jeans undone so she could see where that happy trail led.

He gazed down at her body, one hand caressing her calf.

"So beautiful, Tatum," he murmured.

She felt it, when he looked at her like that. She could have lain there forever with his hot eyes on her body. She spread her legs wider in invitation. "So are you, Camilo."

He kicked off his boots and pants, then bent and

pressed a kiss on each hip. He dipped his head between her legs, his nose brushing her clit as he began to lick.

And lick he did. And suck. And hum, like she was an instrument and he the only one with the musical pick. She raised her arms over her head and arched her back and made all the sounds she wanted. Whimpers and shouts. Because no one could hear them in the middle of nowhere under the star-filled sky.

When she came, it wasn't a thunderclap, but a slow-moving storm. She moaned and rode it out and let it linger until she was dried out and boneless.

Then Cam was above her again, his breath hot in her ear, his hand cradling her head, telling her he loved her, telling her they were right. And she was too tired to cry. So she kissed his biceps beside her head, waiting while he rolled on a condom, then entered her slowly on a hissed-out breath.

She raised her lips and wrapped her legs around his waist. But Cam had other ideas. He rolled onto his back, taking her with him. She rose above him, bracing herself on his chest.

He gripped her hips, hard. "Ride me, Tatum."

She liked being on top. It hit all the right spots. But she didn't want this to end. And she wondered if she kept him from coming, kept him inside her, would she never have to say good-bye?

But his fingers gripped hard, and he clenched his jaw. "You gotta move."

She didn't want to. Because once she started, there would be an end. To this night. To them.

But she wanted to feel him one last time more than she wanted to delay the end. So she squeezed her thighs and moved. First she rose up, until all but the tip of him remained inside. She swirled her hips a little while Cam went ballistic beneath her, swearing and arching his neck.

And then she lowered herself. And rode Cam hard.

He cursed more and so did she. Because there was something desperate about this time. About the way he looked at her with eyes on fire and the way her face burned from it.

When he came, his eyes, those dark, hot eyes, stayed on her the whole time and she wondered if a strong wind came, would she blow away like ash?

She slowly lowered herself on top of him, as he churned his hips so his sated length slid in and out of her. He pressed kisses to her face and told her he loved her.

She was too tired and drained to say it back.

He made her turn to look at him and his brows dipped. "You okay?"

Nope. She went for honesty. "Not really."

Concern crossed over his face, his eyes perusing her body. But he must have known it wasn't physical. "Let me go take a leak. I'll come back and we'll talk, all right?"

She didn't want to do that, but for now, she just nodded.

Another kiss, to each of her eyelids, then he pulled on his pants and shoved his feet into his unlaced boots. With one look back at her, tangled among the sleeping bag, he walked out.

She fell back onto the pillow, wondering how they didn't put a hole in the air mattress below them. Sex with Cam had always been good. But never that good.

She wished she could leave now. Before he got back. Leave him a note that she couldn't do the good-bye this time. But that was the coward's way out. And she had to be a big girl now.

Cam's phone pinged somewhere beneath the rumpled sleeping bags. Tate rummaged around until she found it and noticed it was lit with a missed call from his mom and a voice mail.

She craned her neck out of the tent but didn't see Cam. She didn't know why he had to go so far to take a piss. It wasn't like she hadn't seen him without his pants on.

She bit her lip and then swiped to listen to the voice mail. If it was an emergency, she'd go hunt Cam down. But as she put the phone up to her ear, it wasn't Mrs. Ruiz's voice in her ear. It was a male voice. With a slight New York accent.

"Hello, Mr. Ruiz. We're sorry to hear you won't be joining us at Marino Security this fall. We were really impressed with you when you interned . . ."

And that's when her arm gave out. The phone fell with a muffled thud onto the bedding below, the voice still droning on in low, indecipherable tones.

Tate's chest tightened, constricting her breathing, and her toes went numb because of her kneeling position.

He'd done it. That asshole had turned down the job. To stay in Paradise. To stay in motherfucking Paradise.

She pulled on her clothes and then crawled out of the tent. She knelt in the truck, staring at the phone like it was her worst enemy.

She heard the crunching of boots but she was in a tunnel. A tunnel that held her pinned in place as the oxygen was slowly sucked out. She didn't want this. This wasn't how this was supposed to go. They were supposed to be saying good-bye.

The toes of his boots stopped in front of her and then his warm brown eyes were looking into hers as he knelt in front of her. A hand caressed the side of her head. "Tate? What's wrong?"

She squeezed her eyes shut.

"Tate? You're freaking me out. What's going on?"

Her eyes popped open. "I didn't mean to but I listened to your voice mail."

"Okay . . ."

"You did it," she whispered.

He frowned. "Did what?"

"You turned down the job."

For a beat, he didn't move, and then he sucked in a sharp breath and stood up, running a hand through his hair. "Shit."

She stumbled to her feet, her legs screaming as blood rushed into them. "Shit? Shit? That's all you're going to say for making this decision without me?"

He reached out for her waist. "It wasn't like that—"

She took a step away from him and his hand hung there between them before he dropped it to his side. "Tate."

She shook her head. "This was supposed to be good-bye. That's what this date was. And I was okay with that and I loved every single minute of it. And you were keeping this secret—"

He pointed at her. "I wasn't keeping this a secret. I planned to tell you tonight. But first I wanted to show you why this"—he waggled his finger between them—"matters. Why this time, we can make it last." He waved the hand at her. "But nope. You're still being Tatum fuck-ing stubborn Ellison, thinking you know what's best."

The words flew at her, some digging into her heart, others glancing off her thickened skin. "But that's what you're doing, isn't it? You made the decision not to take that job without me, and it affects us both!"

"There's a difference. I'm making this decision be-cause it benefits you and me."

She shook her head. "How does this benefit you? You're giving up your dream job. Your future!"

He took a step forward, his face like thunder. "I'm not a martyr, Tatum. I'm being selfish, too. Because I want you. And I'm not giving up my future, because my future is with you."

She stumbled back and had to grip the tent to keep herself upright. The force of his words and the meaning behind them was like an electric shock to her heart. Her mouth opened and closed, no sound escaping, because how was she supposed to respond to that?

But it didn't matter that for once, she didn't have a comeback.

Because Cam wasn't done. "Fuck it, though. Just fuck

it. Because I'm finally fighting for this relationship, and you want to be pissed and dream up supposed resentment ten years from now. What about now, Tatum?" He slammed his fist into his chest, his voice rising. "I'm supposed to deny what I want and who I love because you're worried about feelings years from now?"

He closed his eyes and hung his head between his shoulders, shaking it back and forth, hands on his hips. When he spoke again, he didn't look as angry. He looked disappointed and wrung out. "If I'm the only one fighting for us, then it's never going to work. Let's head back."

It was like his words entered her brain on delay. And it wasn't until he began throwing his stuff in his pack that she realized what her outburst had done. She scrambled toward him. "Cam, I'm sorry. Let's stay here and . . ."

But he wasn't listening, collapsing the tent in seconds and pointing her in the direction of the passenger side door of the cab. "Get in."

What had she done? "No, Camilo, I'm sorry—"

He held up a hand, silencing her, and his jaw flexed once. "Please don't use that name. Now get in the car, because I'm taking you home."

After she buckled herself into the truck, and Cam began driving, she let the tears flow. She sat in the passenger side of his truck and cried to herself as softly as she could. She wanted to ask if she'd completely ruined them. She wanted to ask if they were beyond repair. How many times could a couple fuck up before they split for good?

And why the hell did she think she could ever live without him now that she'd had him again?

When they pulled into her driveway, her tears had dried. She unbuckled her seat belt and sat in the car, refusing to leave.

"You gotta get out, Tate."

She turned to him, knowing she looked a hot mess. "Is this it?"

He hesitated, and every second was a hammer blow to her heart. "I think we both need to think about what we really want."

The tears threatened again. She opened up the passenger side door and slid out. Right before she shut it behind her, she whispered, "I want you."

She didn't know if he heard her. But she felt his eyes on her back as she walked into her house.

Chapter 18

CAM WOKE UP the next morning, smelling like campfire
smoke and regret.

He should have showered last night when he got
home, but it only would have washed away the smoke.
The regret was here to stay.

He'd planned to tell Tate he'd turned down the job. In
fact, she heard the voice mail about one minute before his
planned speech. And fuck if that surprise didn't blow up
in his face. He didn't know why Mr. Marino left a voice
mail anyway. He'd already spoken to him, so why he
called was weird.

But it didn't matter now, because Tate threw it all in
his face.

Cam had done it this time, put himself on the line to
fight for this relationship, and he was tired of it. Tate had
to want it as bad as he did.

He closed his eyes as he remembered the time in the

tent before she listened to that stupid voice mail. When she told him she wanted him. When she came apart in his arms. When she acted like there was nowhere else she'd rather be. Ever.

How could she so easily give it up? Even now, he felt like his heart was splitting open.

There was a knock at the door.

"Come in."

His door creaked open and he turned to see his mom walk inside. She looked good. The pain lines no longer dug into her face. Thank God she'd finally found a pill cocktail that worked. "How you doing, Ma?"

She folded her arms over her chest. "Since you slept here last night, alone, I think you're the one we need to be talking about."

He groaned and held a pillow over his head.

The bed dipped beside him and then his fingers were pried loose from his protective plush covering.

"Camilo." She shoved the pillow back under his cheek when he raised his head. "What happened?"

He lay on his side, facing her. He wasn't sure where to start. "Why'd you call my cell?"

She waved a hand. "It wasn't important. Just something I saw on the news. I wasn't thinking and called to tell you, then hung up when I figured you were a little busy on your date."

Cam groaned. "Yeah, and things were going great until it all went to shit."

She stayed silent, waiting for him to continue.

He sighed. "I love her, Ma. More than anything. Why

can't she accept that I'm not giving up my future when I can't see my future without her in it?"

"Did you tell her that?"

"Yeah, and I could tell she regretted reacting like she did, but it pisses me off that that's her reaction. And she should feel that strongly, too. She should be fighting this out with me, trying to make this work."

"You don't think she wants to?"

He shrugged. "I don't know. I know she's got a lot going on, but damn it, we're not kids." He looked up into his mom's brown eyes. "I want to marry her someday. Have kids. Why can't she see that me staying in Paradise is the only option for us? That it's the only option for *me*."

"You talked like that about her in high school. And I thought . . . I'm not sure anymore. But I guess I finally see now that she makes you happy." She ran her hands over his hair. "Did you tell all of this to her?"

Did he? He wasn't even sure. God, their whole conversation last night felt like a blur. "Well, things got a little messed up. Because she accidentally listened to a voice mail Mr. Marino left me earlier."

His mom cocked her head. "Why'd he leave you a voice mail if you already talked to him and turned down the job?"

"I don't know. I haven't listened to it yet."

She stood up with her hands on her hips. "Where's your bag?"

He shifted his arm out from under the covers and pointed to the floor of the closet. "There."

She went over, unzipped it and began digging around.

Her arms stopped moving and then she pulled out a box of condoms with a raised eyebrow.

"Hey, you told me to be safe," he smirked.

She rolled her eyes and went back to digging in his bag. And he sobered up to realize he probably wouldn't be using any of those condoms for a long, long time.

His mom pulled out his phone and walked over to the bed. She held it out to him. "How do I work this thing?"

"What do want to do?"

She sat down on the bed again. "I want to listen to the voice mail."

"Oh." He swiped his thumb across the screen and pulled up the voice mail app. "Here you go. Just press that little arrow there."

She did and then held the phone to her ear. She listened to it, her face placid at first. Then her eyes slowly widened and her mouth dropped as she turned to look at Cam.

"What?"

She didn't answer him yet, still listening to the voice mail, then held the phone out to him. "You didn't listen to this voice mail?"

"No, not yet."

She shook the phone at him and then whacked him in the nose with it. "Ow, Ma!"

"Listen to this voice mail right this minute!"

"Okay, okay, keep your pants on," he grumbled.

He pressed PLAY and listened to it. And then his eyes widened. And his jaw dropped. And by the time Mr. Marino was done talking, Cam wondering if he was having a heart attack. Because his heart was beating out of his chest and his hands were sweating.

"Holy shit," he said, staring at the now-silent phone.

"You need to call him back!" his mom screeched.

"I know!" Cam yelled back.

"Camilo, this is huge—"

"Big."

"Important."

"Life changing."

And then an idea began to form in his head. He complained about Tate not fighting for their relationship? Well, he still had some weapons. He could still fight.

And damn it, fight he would. For the future he wanted with the girl he wanted.

Now all he needed was to get to New York.

EVERYTHING SMELLED LIKE campfire smoke. She'd forgotten how that scent seeped into clothes and hair and every fabric within a mile vicinity. Three days later and it was still lingering despite four showers and two loads of laundry.

Normally, she didn't mind it. She loved camping and loved the smell. But now it reminded her of so many things she didn't want to remember. Like being in Cam's arms. Like that voice mail. Like that epic fight.

And she still hadn't gotten up the nerve to call him. Because calling him meant admitting she was okay with his decision. That she was okay with him placing his life on hold for her. And maybe other girls would love that.

Maybe other girls would be charmed. But Tate wasn't other girls. And this rankled and dug under her skin.

Between the two of them, how many dumb decisions had they made for each other?

Maybe there wasn't hope for them. How could they have a relationship when they kept fucking up this badly? Maybe the world had other plans for them. She wished she could look ten years into the future. She liked to read romance books, and they were all about the journey. Because romances always ended in happily-ever-afters for the couple. So she knew to root for them the whole way through the book.

But her own life? Who were the hero and heroine? Whom was she supposed to root for?

Cam's words swirled over and over in her head. *If I'm the only one fighting for us, then it's never going to work.*

She had to leave for work soon, but for now, she turned on her TV and picked up her controller. She hadn't checked Utope since camping and when she signed in, she saw that Cam hadn't been on since their fight. Which made her stomach hurt.

With her avatar, she walked through the house, running her little pixel hands over the walls and petting their dog. She walked out into their backyard and stared at the rain forest full of poison dart frogs. And then she headed up to the bedroom. In the corner sat the stuffed pony Cam had bought her. She patted its head. Then she went out the front door and sat on the porch swing, where Cam's avatar sat.

This was what they dreamed of, but in real life. A

home with the two of them and a dog, minus the deadly rain forest. She tried to imagine her life years in the future, with Cam and without. And as the tears burned hot in her eyes, she couldn't deny that to be truly happy, she wanted Cam there.

She turned to him and said, "If I promise to fight, can we still have this?"

Her finger hovered over Cam's avatar, prepared to bring up the speech bubble so he'd answer. But then she paused the game. Right there. With that question hovering in the air above their heads.

And she hoped Cam signed in to the game to see it. Because her heart felt like it was in a vise and she knew his answer held the key to freeing it.

ANNE HAD BEEN in a somber, pissy mood all morning. By the time the breakfast rush had slowed, Tate knew she had to talk to her. Maybe if they commiserated together about her father's cancer returning, it might not be so hard on each of them.

She left Margo out front to deal with the counter and stomped her way to the back room, where Anne was shelving cans in storage.

She was grumbling to herself and slamming cans so that the whole metal shelf rattled. Tate shut the door behind her and leaned back against it, arms over her shoulders. "I know, the whole thing sucks."

Anne didn't turn around. "Damn right it does."

Tate scuffled her feet on the floor and looked down. "But we're all together, and that's what matters."

Anne didn't answer. Another slam of a can.

"I know you're upset but—"

"Upset?" Anne whirled around, a can of diced fruit in her hand. "Oh Tate, I'm not upset, I'm pissed."

Tate took a step forward. "Well, you can be pissed. I'm pissed, too."

Anne's eyes narrowed, and a weird sensation crept up Tate's spine when Anne answered. "Well, then you should have done something about it. But now he's gone."

Tate's head spun. She put out a hand to brace herself on the shelf and waved the other in front of her face. "Whoa whoa whoa. What could I have done? He's not gone, he's at home watching baseball!"

Anne's eyebrows rose. "He's most certainly not at home. He left yesterday."

Tate stared at Anne. "I saw him this morning!"

Anne opened her mouth, but then her mouth flapped open soundlessly as her face paled. "Wait, who are you talking about?"

Tate threw up her hands. "My dad. Who else?" But as soon as the words left her mouth, a sick feeling churned in her gut. "Oh no. You're talking about . . ."

"Cam," Anne finished on a whisper.

"Cam." Tate rolled the name on her tongue. "What . . . what do you mean he's gone? Where'd he go?"

Anne's entire posture oozed sympathy, in the way

her eyes focused on Tate's face, in the way her arms hung loose at her sides. "He left for New York."

And that sick feeling in Tate's stomach gained strength. Rolling and bubbling and threatening to toss out her breakfast. "What?"

Anne shifted and scrunched her lips. "You didn't know?"

Tate shook her head. "I haven't talked to him in a couple of days. Not after . . . well, you know about our fight. But he . . . he left? Without saying anything?"

Anne looked horrified. "I wouldn't have said all that if I didn't know—"

Tate blinked, barely keeping herself together. "How do you know he left?"

Anne reached out and grabbed Tate's wrist. "Tate . . ."

She shook her head. "How did you find out?"

Anne bit her lip. "I ran into Mrs. Ruiz at the grocery story this yesterday."

Yep, breakfast was going to come up. Any second now. "Was she smugly victorious?"

Anne stepped closer. "Oh, Tate—"

"Was she? Was she happy that the white trash was out of her son's life?" This hurt. Her stomach, her heart, her head. Everything hurt so bad. Because she'd fucked everything up and Cam. Was. Gone.

"Don't say that." Anne's hands gripped her shoulders and shook her gently. "She did seem happy. Hopeful. But I doubt it has anything to do with you."

Tate snorted. "Sure. Right."

Anne was silent for a beat. "What're you going to do?"

Tate shrugged and tried to step away from Anne's touch. She didn't want anyone near her. She wanted to go to the bathroom and curl up in a stall and cry until there weren't any tears left. "He made his choice."

But Anne didn't let go. "Yeah? And what's your choice?"

Tate scanned the room, eyeing the shelves of cans. The cat yoga calendar that still said it was May. Her frayed apron. Anne's concerned eyes. What was her choice? If Cam answered yes to her question in Utope, what would she do?

The easy decision would be to collapse into Anne's arms. Let her hold Tate as she cried. Then wipe her face and keep working. She'd go home to her dad and her brother and she'd throw out Utope once and for all and find another hero to root for.

Or she could make the hard decision. She could hold her chin up. And step out of Anne's arms. And she could fight and be the heroine of her own story.

So that was what she did. She took a deliberate step back. Anne's arms fell away along with her face. But Tate raised her chin and clenched her fists. When she spoke, her voice was steady. "My choice? I'm going to fight for him. For us."

Anne made a sound somewhere between a laugh and a sob. She hauled Tate against her body for one quick hug and smoothed a hand down her hair. "You need help?"

Tate shook her head. "I'm doing what I should have done weeks ago. I'm going to have a visit with Teresa Ruiz."

Anne patted her cheek. "Good luck, baby."

By the time Tate finished her shift, she was steel determination. She'd called her dad to check in and told him everything. She'd been avoiding him since her fight with Cam, making excuses about why her boyfriend hadn't been around. And now that her dad knew, she could hear his strong voice in her ear, letting her know he supported her in whatever she wanted to do.

Tate wasn't sure what solution would allow her and Cam to be together. She still wasn't willing to leave her dad to move to another state. But she was willing to compromise.

She hadn't been to Cam's home since he'd been home. As she hopped out of Cecil and walked to the house, the front door opened.

Mrs. Ruiz stood in the opening, watching Tate with an unreadable expression on her face. When Tate stood before her, Mrs. Ruiz cocked her head. "I was wondering if you'd come to see me."

"Hello, Mrs. Ruiz." Tate kept her voice firm. "I'm here to talk about Camilo."

The women's lips pressed together, making Tate think she was about to get chewed out, but then Mrs. Ruiz gestured to one of the chairs on the covered front porch. "It's not too hot out, why don't you sit down. I'll get us some lemonade."

Already, this was going better than Tate imagined. Unless Mrs. Ruiz slipped rat poison into the lemonade. "Okay."

The older woman returned a minute later, her long

skirt swishing around her legs, her bare feet padding on the wooden boards. On a table between the two chairs, she placed a tray that held a pitcher of pink lemonade, two glasses and a plate of cookies.

Mrs. Ruiz made the best cookies, chocolate chip ones with a hint of cayenne. Cam used to sneak them for her all the time.

Tate eyed them as Mrs. Ruiz lowered herself into her seat. She chuckled at the look on Tate's face. "Go ahead."

Tate grabbed a cookie and bit off half of it as Mrs. Ruiz poured the lemonade.

Tate picked up the glass, already coated with condensation, and took a sip. With a jolt, she spit out the lemonade and some of her chewed-up cookie. "What the hell is in this?"

Mrs. Ruiz grinned at her with the devil in her eyes. "A little vodka."

"A little vodka?" It tasted like a little lemonade with a lot of vodka.

"Okay, so maybe more than a little." Mrs. Ruiz held up her thumb and forefinger an inch apart.

Tate huffed in the back of her throat. "Warn a gal next time, would ya?"

Mrs. Ruiz smiled, her dimples popping out, and all Tate saw was Cam. She ducked her head and took a deep breath. "So—"

"I'm sorry."

Tate jerked her head up. "Excuse me?"

Mrs. Ruiz braced an elbow on the arm of her chair and ran a finger down her own cheek. "I always wanted so much for Camilo. His father has never been in his life. And he was a Hispanic in a white, often prejudiced town. I wanted him to rise above and be great and follow his dreams."

"Mrs. Ruiz—"

"Teresa. Please."

Tate swallowed her tongue. She'd known the woman since she was a kid and never once had the woman asked Tate to call her by her first name. Tate kept quiet.

Teresa chuckled sadly. "But I forgot what it was like to fall in love. Especially young love. It's deep and consuming. But it often fades, yes?" She turned to Tate now and eyed her. Waiting for an answer.

Which Tate couldn't give. Because her young love with this woman's son never faded. Not once.

So she answered honestly. "It often does. But not always." Her voice dropped. "Not for me."

Teresa shut her eyes and then looked back at the street before opening them again. "So I supported him when he enlisted, and I cheered when he went to college. I thought you'd hold him back, but you didn't, did you?"

"No." The word was a croak in Tate's throat.

Teresa faced her again. "He told me what happened. What you did."

Tate didn't know what to say about that. "Okay."

"It was stupid, but it had the outcome you wanted, right? What I wanted? Cam stayed in school?"

Tate nodded.

Teresa's eyes burned into Tate's. "But this time, it's not working how you want it to, is it?"

Tate shook her head.

"He loves you, Tate Ellison. He loves you so much, he's miserable right now. And that makes me miserable."

Tate bit her lip to keep herself from crying.

"So, this altruistic act needs to stop. Your decisions send ripple effects to a lot of people. And what I care about most, what I want most for my son is to be happy. What I want most is a woman who will fight for him."

Tate bit her lip harder until she tasted blood.

Those brown eyes burned into her. "Is that you? Are you that woman for him?"

It took a minute for Tate to be able to speak. For her to release her abused lip, open up her mouth, and say, "Yes. That's why I'm here. I'm fighting."

Teresa's eyes finally softened and the burning in Tate's skull eased. "Good girl. I'm guessing you need an address in New York?"

This was it. *Be your own heroine.* "Yes, please. I'd love that address."

This was a

Chapter 19

AT HOME, TATE threw clothes in a duffel bag that still smelled like campfire smoke. She wasn't taking the time to pick out anything nice. She might end up wearing something horrid and unmatched, but this was New York City, right? She'd probably fit right in.

Actually, shit, she had no idea what NYC was even like. Or how she was getting there.

She sat down on the bed and deep breathed. No way would Cecil make it. She could take a train, maybe. A train? She had no idea where the closest station was.

Oh God, how was she going to do this? But she had to. This was her grand gesture. This was her moment, to show Cam how she felt. To prove to him that she could fight for them.

Tate frowned and tapped her chin. How much was a plane ticket to New York?

She picked up her phone and began searching for

flights. Which was confusing as all hell. Where was the Easy Button that she could click that automatically knew what she wanted? Stupid phone and technology.

She was about to throw her cell across the room when there was a knock at her door.

"Come in," she muttered.

Her dad walked into the room first, then Jamie, followed by Anne.

Tate frowned. "Hey, what's going on?"

Anne stepped forward and held out a sheet of paper. "Your plane ticket."

Tate blinked at her and then stuck a finger in her ear, wiggled it, then pulled it back out. "I'm sorry, what did you say?"

Anne shook the paper in Tate's face. "I bought you a plane ticket."

Tate's eyes landed on the paper. And there it was, in black ink on a crinkled piece of white computer paper. A flight number and time and bar code and everything.

Departure: BWI

Destination: LaGuardia Airport

"But—"

"We all talked, baby." Her dad sat down on the bed beside her. "We know you were in here wracking your brain about how to get to New York. Anne said she wanted to buy your ticket. So, here we are."

Tate plunked her head down on her father's shoulder and looked up at Anne. "You didn't have to do that."

Anne patted her cheek. "I wanted to."

Jamie smiled reassuringly, and Tate imagined the

picture they all made. She groaned. "This is so Hallmark right now."

Her dad jiggled his shoulder so her head bounced. "Jamie said he'd drive you to the airport. To make your flight, you need to leave now."

Tate snatched the paper from Anne's hand and checked the departure time. "Oh shit!" She jumped up and began throwing more random clothes in her bag. Then she ran out into the hallway to grab toiletries.

She ran back into her room, brandishing her toothbrush. "Wait a minute. How long am I going to be there? When's my return flight?"

Anne rolled her lips between her teeth. Jamie rocked on his heels, and only her dad met her eyes. "We didn't get you a return flight."

Tate's hand with her toothbrush dropped to her side. "What?"

He stood up slowly and walked toward her, placed a hand on the side of her neck. "It's not that we think you're staying there. But we don't know how long and we're hoping . . . that you come back with someone. And you two can decide when and how. Maybe stay for a little? Take some time off. We can hold down the fort here."

"But—"

Her father squeezed his fingers, silencing her. "Please, baby, do as I ask. Go fight for Cam."

Tate's eyes pricked with tears. "This is the best pep talk of all pep talks."

He kissed her forehead. "Have a safe flight."

She turned to grab her bag, then turned around, gesturing with a finger between her father and Anne. "Well, we'll be discussing this, by the way. You two."

Her father reached out and clutched Anne's hand. "This is something we probably should have done years ago."

"Aw damn, I'm going to cry again," Tate muttered as she hugged them.

On the ride to the airport, Tate and Jamie didn't do much talking. She was nervous as hell and couldn't deal with conversation. But music and dancing? Well, Jamie knew her, and so he cranked up the radio and they sang along to Billy Joel and Bruce Springsteen and all the legendary songwriters their dad raised them on.

Jamie hugged her after he helped unload her bag from the car in the drop-off area at Baltimore-Washington International Airport. "Be safe," he said.

She nodded and kissed his cheek. With a wave, he got in the car and drove away, leaving her on the sidewalk with "Tiny Dancer" in her head.

Tate turned to face the doors of the airport. She could see the security line through the glass, and that's when it hit her that she'd never flown alone. Hell, she'd never traveled alone. And the only time she'd been in a plane, she'd been eight and flew to see her father's now-deceased parents in Colorado.

What if they strip-searched her? She didn't even like removing her shoes.

She'd called Cam on the way, but he hadn't answered. She didn't leave him a voice mail because she didn't know what to say, other than, *I'm coming.* Teresa had said he was staying for at least three days.

So Tate took a deep breath, straightened her shoulders, and walked into the airport.

Luckily she didn't even have to remove her shoes, being one of the fortunate ones to be waved into the express security line. She dumped her bag on the conveyor belt and then picked it up after it passed muster.

Once past security, she checked her ticket and began to make her way to her gate.

She'd been a little girl last time she was an airport. Everything had seemed larger than life. Everything moved so fast. She'd wanted to be one of those people, on their way to bigger and better things. And now she was one of those adults, flying to their dreams.

She self-consciously hitched her tattered bag onto her shoulder. As she passed several restaurants, her stomach growled, reminding her she hadn't eaten since Teresa's spiked lemonade and half a cookie.

And now it was past lunch. Damn, she'd arrive in New York around dinner.

She bought a chicken Caesar salad at a small café in the airport. But as she sat down to eat, she began to panic. What if Cam rejected her? What if she couldn't find him?

She wasn't this person who took off on a whim after a boy.

But then she took a deep breath. And sipped the rum and Coke she'd ordered for courage.

This wasn't a whim. And Cam wasn't some boy.

She finished up her late lunch and walked to her gate, proud of herself that she'd found it all on her own.

She checked her phone. No call from Cam. She texted

her dad and let him know she'd made it to her gate and was waiting for boarding.

He texted back.

Proud of you.

She smiled.

Proud of me, too.

Chapter 20

I'm in New York City and I was going to make this grand gesture but I don't know where I am and there is some naked guy beside me drawing a mural of the apocalypse on the sidewalk.

You're in NYC?

Yep.

You're in NYC.

I already confirmed this.

Where are you?

I love you.

Tate . . .

I'm fighting for us this time.

Tate, where are you?

I want you.

TATE GODDAMN IT WHERE ARE YOU?

Will you fight with me this time?

Fuck it, I tracked your phone. Stay where you are.

OK.

Tate?

Yeah?

I'm fighting, too.

Chapter 21

NEW YORK CITY was huge. Population of over eight million people in five boroughs.

It made Cam twitchy but he'd traveled a bit.

He couldn't imagine how Tate was feeling. You could take the girl out of the small town but you couldn't take the small town out of the girl.

But yet, despite the size of NYC, she'd found him, or at least came pretty close. So either his mom had a hand in this, or Tate had done some digging.

And if the app on his phone was correct, which he used to track her location, she was about a block away. He'd excused himself from the tour to go to the bathroom after receiving her first text. And now he was still getting a tour of the office. He didn't know why. It's not like he planned to work here any time soon.

By he smiled at his soon-to-be-boss anyway, nodding at the appropriate times even though his feet hurt in his shoes, his tie felt like a noose and sweat was dripping down his back.

It was only another fifteen minutes, but it felt like fifteen hours when he burst out of the front doors of the office building.

He walked toward her location, peering through the pedestrians on the sidewalk before he spotted her. Her hair was up in that hairstyle with the bump he loved. Her eye shadow was dark on her hazel cat eyes. She wore a simple blue dress and a pair of sandals and stood out like a million bucks among every else around her.

Tate was in front of a street vendor with a table full of sunglasses, trying them on one by one, while the guy's mouth moved a mile a minute.

She'd pose and laugh and the guy would talk more, surely buttering her up to make a sale. Although Cam was sure he was smitten.

You couldn't not be smitten by Tate.

She was here. In New York. She'd come for him, not knowing he was moving mountains for her.

He took a deep breath and let out the exhale slowly. It'd been worth it, this trip. It'd been worth it to find a way to be with Tate. Now that he knew she was fighting, too.

She took that moment to look up, a pair of large, round, forties-style sunglasses over her eyes. Her lips parted and then she smiled.

In seconds, Cam was in front of her, bending her back over his arm as he kissed her, pouring everything he felt into that connection. She was hot under his hands and her lips were soft and she made tiny moans in the back of her throat.

He pulled back and helped steady her on her feet. She gripped his shoulders and bit her lip. He reached out and pushed the sunglasses onto the top of her head. Tears leaked out of her eyes as she gave a little sob-laugh. "Surprise," she said softly.

Cam shook his head. "You're crazy."

She swiped her eyes and laughed louder. "Crazy for you."

A throat cleared and they both looked over at the street vendor. He appraised them with squinted eyes and a cocked head. Then he waved at the sunglasses on Tate's head. "Free for the lovebirds."

Cam opened his mouth, because the card on the table said they were only ten dollars, but the man waved again. "No. I said free. Yesterday, a woman tore a wig off another one in front of me. This"—he gestured to their embrace—"is much happier. Now go, and enjoy the rest of the evening."

Cam glanced at the sky, darkening as the sun dipped below a tall building. "Thanks, man."

The vendor gave him a two-fingered salute and then directed his attention to a customer.

Cam took Tate's duffel bag and slung it over her shoulder, then grabbed her hand to lead her down the sidewalk. He wasn't sure where to start with all the questions forming in his head. He went with an easy one. "How did you get here?"

Tate's eyes were wide as she took in the scenery. "I flew."

"You flew?"

She focused on him. "Yeah, Anne bought me a ticket so I could get here as soon as I could."

He stared at their clasped hands, listening to the click-clack of his shoes and the slap of her sandals on the sidewalk. "And why did you want to get here as soon as you could?"

She swung their hands a bit. "To . . . to prove to you that I'm fighting. That I want this. Us." Their eyes met. "That this time I believe, want, need to make it last."

He'd planned to stop at a deli or restaurant, take her out on the town. But fuck it. Not when she said those words. Those words that he'd been dying to hear.

He pulled on her arm so she followed him in to the hotel. He strode right for the elevators, walking so fast that Tate had to jog to keep up. Her head was whipping around as she took in the lobby. "Is that a Starbucks?"

He shoved her into the open elevator doors, thanking everything holy they were the only ones, then backed her against the doors after they shut. He jabbed his finger on the number five, and then cupped her face. "The nice, gentlemanly thing to do right now would be to take you out on the town. Wine and dine you or whatever." He kissed the corner of her lips, then the other side. "But Tatum, I really need you alone right now. In a bed. Preferably naked."

Her soft chuckle washed over his skin as her hands rose and slipped under his suit jacket. "You know me. I'd much rather be alone with you. In a bed. Preferably naked. Than in some stupid restaurant wasting money on some food I'll forget about in an hour."

He laughed and kissed her jaw. She angled her head so he could feast on her neck. "Fuck, I love you," he mumbled against her skin.

Her fingers began to pull his shirt from the waist of his pants. "Love you, too."

The elevator doors opened behind Tate, and she stumbled backward into the hallway, giggling as Cam wrapped an arm around her waist to keep them upright.

Luckily, his room was right by the elevator bays, so he swiped his card and then tugged her inside, pushing her up against the wall beside the door to resume what they had been doing in the elevator.

Tate's fingers returned to his waist to continue to pull up his shirt when her hands stilled.

"Cam?"

He was busy kissing her neck, running his hands along the edge of her panties under her dress, and didn't want to stop to talk. "What?"

"Why are you wearing a suit? Are you . . . are you taking the job?"

He couldn't stop his fingers, as they caressed the soft skin of her ass. His brain was on that, not on her line of questioning. What did she want to know again? He dipped his head to her collarbone and ran kisses along the skin there. "The job? Oh yeah, I'm taking it."

Her body froze beneath his.

She pushed on his shoulders so he had to raise his head. "You're . . . you're taking the job? Here in New York? I thought—"

Oh, that's what he said. "No, no, but I'm not working in New York."

Her brows knitted. "I'm really confused."

He groaned and dropped his forehead onto her shoulder. "Damn it, you wanna talk and all I can think about is that I got you alone in a hotel room with a minibar and room service on the company dime."

She pursed her lips, but the ends tipped up so he knew she was trying to hide a smile. "Camilo, please explain."

He backed away with a muffled curse and began removing his suit piece by piece, starting with those awful shoes that hurt his feet. Tate followed him as he left a trail of clothing to the bedroom. The hotel room was a suite, with a living area separate from the bedroom.

"Okay, so you didn't listen to the whole voice mail, did you?"

Tate sat down on the end of the bed. "I . . . I don't remember. I just heard that you turned down the job and—"

Cam waved a hand as he loosened his tie with the other. "Yeah, let's not rehash. Anyway, I listened to the whole voice mail, which apparently, you hadn't done. They said they had a new research job come up that they thought would be perfect for me based on my skill set and military experience. And the best part is that I could do the job remotely. But they wanted to talk to me in person about it. So I got my ass up here as fast as I could."

Tate's eyes were wide as he kicked off his pants and it wasn't because he stood there in boxer briefs and a tight white T-shirt. "Wait, remotely?"

He was done talking. They had things to do before digging into the minibar and calling room service. Things that involved Tate naked in million-thread-count sheets. He put a knee to the bed beside her legs and a hand at her shoulder so she had to lie back on the bed. Although she protested along the way. "Damn it, Cam, explain this to me before I'm naked, please!"

He reached under her and hauled her up toward the head of the bed, then braced himself above her. He pulled out her hair clip and raised the skirt of her dress up to her waist.

She shifted her legs and made a small sound in the back of her throat. He groaned at the sight of the pink cotton fabric darkened with her wetness between her legs. He ran his fingers along the top edge of her underwear, watching his hands. "I can do all the research and work I need to do from Paradise. So I can stay there. And we can live in sin, for as long as we want. The door is open in the future for me to move here."

He pulled down the side of her underwear and kissed her hip, then finally raised his gaze to hers. She was up on her elbows, staring down at him with wild hair, smeared mascara and wet lips. "Are you serious?"

"As a heart attack."

She sucked in a breath. "So . . . you . . . we . . . this can work."

He pulled her underwear down her legs and tossed it over his shoulder. "You bet your ass it'll work."

Lowering himself between her legs, he pushed on her thighs so she opened wider. The soft thump above him let him know she'd collapsed onto the bed, but her body was strung tight so that when he applied that first, long lick, she snapped.

Tate had never been quiet during sex and now she whimpered and moaned and begged and cried as he spread her with his thumbs and indulged on Tate.

He remembered how she liked it, and how a swirling suck on her clit sent her over the edge.

It did this time, and when he rose above her, her eyes were glazed. He helped her out of her dress while he pulled his shirt over his head and slipped off his boxers.

He settled his hips between her legs and kissed her face and neck and nuzzled below her ear. "Just think. We can sleep in on weekends and do this all day."

Her body shook with laughter below him. "I think people will start to talk if we hole ourselves up in our bedroom every weekend."

He lowered his head and sucked a nipple into his mouth. He let it go with a pop. "Let them talk."

She twirled her finger over her head. "Wherever you put my bag, it has condoms in it."

He shot her a grin as he rolled off her in search of her bag. "How many?"

"Don't get too cocky, Cam!" she called after him as he left the bedroom, laughing.

He rolled the condom on as he walked back to Tate lounging in the bed. She was running her hands along the comforter. "Damn, this bed is nice."

He put his hands on his hips. "I'm standing in front of you naked and you're talking about soft sheets?"

She giggled and held her arms out. "Come here. I'm sure I can make up for it by stroking your fragile ego."

He crawled onto the bed over her. "There's something else I want you to stroke."

She reached down and did just that. "I set you up for that one on purpose."

"I know you did." He kissed her as he entered her slowly. She moaned into his mouth as he began to rock his hips.

Last time they'd had sex, it had felt desperate, like they both had agendas.

But this . . . this was how could they could be together, in sync with matching breaths and heartbeats. He pulled her hands above her head and linked their fingers together as he continued to thrust slowly, not willing for this moment to end anytime soon.

Tate's eyes were at half mast, her lips slightly parted and tilted into a small smile.

His orgasm built deliciously slow, and when he came, he did on an openmouthed groan below her ear.

He let go of her hands, so she wrapped them around his shoulders and he cradled her head, stroking her hair. He stayed connected with her, shifting his hips as he enjoyed the feel of her around him.

Tate heaved a long, contented sigh beneath him and he rolled off her. With a kiss to her forehead, he disposed of the condom, then came back to bed, tucking them both beneath the covers.

They lay on their sides facing each other, holding hands. Cam's arm was over her head, fingers stroking the hair at her temples. Her makeup was smudged, but her cheeks were a rosy pink, her lips wet and swollen. She'd never looked more beautiful.

"So, you came up here to learn more about the remote position?" she asked.

He nodded. "And to accept it."

She shifted closer. "Even though I acted like a shit."

"You didn't act like a shit. But you pissed me off."

She looked down at their hands. "I'm sorry."

He tapped her head so she lifted it to meet his gaze. "What did you think was going to happen when you got here?"

She snorted. "God, it could have gone bad, huh? I didn't let myself think about it. All I knew was that I needed to prove something to you. That I was worth it."

"I always knew you were worth it. I needed you to believe you were worth it."

She bit her lip. "Okay, well, I believe it now."

He kissed her and then rolled onto his back to grab the room service menu. Tate propped her chin on his shoulder so she could look at it, too. "Were you serious when you said the company paid for this?"

It'd surprised him, that they were willing to put him up in this fancy place. But he wasn't going to argue. "Yep, so what do you want?"

"Aren't they going to notice if they get a charge for two dinners?"

She had a point, but he shrugged. "I'm a big boy. I eat a lot."

Tate laughed and pointed to the mushroom Swiss

burger with pommes frites. "I want that. What's pommes frites though?"

He squinted. "Aren't they French fries?"

"Why don't they just say fries then?"

"Because they wanna be fancy?"

Tate rolled her eyes. "They're fried strips of potatoes. There's really no need to dress them up."

Cam laughed. "You tell 'em, Tatum."

"I want dessert too. Ooooh, Death by Chocolate cake. I want that. How long do you have this room?"

"Tonight's the last night."

"Oh." She looked disappointed.

He dropped the menu on his chest and turned to her. "Hey, we'll take a train home tomorrow night. So we'll wake up and do some sightseeing before that, okay?"

She tapped her chin.

"What's there to think about?" He laughed.

"That means we have to get out of bed."

He rolled his eyes. "You decide then. Stay in bed all day or sightsee."

She flicked his nose. "Just kidding. I'd like to check out the city."

"Good answer."

Chapter 22

TATE GROANED WHEN the phone in their hotel room rang. She picked her head up as she heard Cam's sleep-roughened voice say, "Hello?"

They'd set their cell phones and scheduled a wake-up call with the front desk. Which was a good thing. Because Tate had thrown hers when it went off. Cam had hit the snooze on his twice and now maybe the third time would be a charm.

She blinked her eyes and tried to lull herself into consciousness as the phone rattled back onto the receiver. After eating themselves silly last night, they'd rented action movies and bad porn. Then Cam had woken her up once to have sex, while she'd returned the favor with a sunrise blow job.

She lay on her stomach and rolled her head so she was facing Cam. He lay on his back, rubbing his eyes with the heels of his palms. He dropped them at his sides with a thud, then turned to her. "Damn it, I'm tired."

"Me too."

He sat up and rolled his neck. "Okay, game plan. We take showers and then find somewhere to eat breakfast. If we order room service, we'll probably never leave."

Tate pushed herself up onto her elbows. "I need coffee first."

"Me, shower. You, coffee."

Tate nodded.

Cam clapped his hands together and hopped out of bed. As he walked toward the bathroom, he called over his shoulder. "Now, Tatum!"

"Bossy drill sergeant," she muttered.

It took them forty-five minutes, but eventually they were out the door. Tate hadn't packed much, so they'd managed to fit everything inside Cam's bag, which he carried on his back.

They stopped at a coffee shop for more caffeine and bagels.

"Where do you want to go first?" Cam asked, squinting into the sun.

Tate took a sip of coffee from her to-go cup and pulled her new (free) glasses down over her eyes. "You need sunglasses."

He pulled a pair of mirrored aviators out of a cargo pocket in his camo shorts and slipped them over his eyes. His eyebrows rose above the lenses. "Happy?"

She nodded. "Those are hot."

"My sunglasses?"

"Way hot."

"Since when do you have a thing for sunglasses?"

She chewed her bite of bagel and swallowed. "Since they're on your face."

He laughed and slung an arm around her shoulders.

They spent their morning doing all the touristy things New York offered. They walked around Central Park and sprayed perfume at Macy's and ate vendor hot dogs.

"You want to check out Rockefeller Center?" Cam asked as he tossed his napkin in a trash can.

Tate slipped her hand into his. "That's where they do the big tree at Christmas and ice rink, right?"

Cam nodded. "I mean, it's the summer, but it's still cool. They film the *Today Show* near there."

The day was gorgeous, not too hot, but sunny with a slight breeze. Cam could have led her anywhere and she wouldn't have cared. "Sounds perfect."

As they walked, Cam chuckled to himself.

"What's that for?"

He watched his feet eat up the sidewalk with a small smile on his face. "I haven't told you much about my roommates in college, have I?"

He'd mentioned them once or twice. A guy named Alec who looked like Elvis and a big, lovable asshole named Max. Alec's girlfriend, Kat, a firecracker who used to date Max. And Max's girlfriend, Lea, a girl who finally put him in his place. "A little."

He swung their arms. "Did I tell you about Max's first date with Lea?"

She shook her head.

"So, she always wanted to skate at Rockefeller Center at Christmas when she was a kid. Ended up getting hurt in a car accident and wasn't able to go. Max found out and rented out a skating rink. Decorated it like crazy with Christmas stuff and took her skating."

Tate's heart melted. "That's incredibly sweet."

Cam smiled. "Yeah, he did good."

"Do you miss them?"

Cam squeezed her hand. "Yeah, I do. Max and Lea visited me at in Paradise at the beginning of the summer. Alec and Kat are a trip. She makes me laugh. So yeah, I miss them." He ran his thumb along the inside of her wrist. "So, uh, I didn't tell you earlier because I didn't want to make you nervous, but you're going to meet them."

Tate stopped and tugged on her hand in his hold but he didn't let go. "What?" she screeched.

"Calm down. See? This is why I didn't tell you back in the room."

She ran her hands over her hair. "Damn it, you don't spring something like that on a girl." These were his friends. His smart college friends from a world she had never been a part of.

"Come on," he said, forcing her to walk again. "They'll love you."

In the summer, the area that usually held an ice rink was a patio with umbrella-covered tables. They stood at the balcony off to one side, looking down at the golden Prometheus fountain. She put the future meeting out of her mind and enjoyed this time with Cam.

Tate looped her arm in Cam's and laid her head on his shoulder. This moment was everything, with the breeze in her hair and the contentment of having Cam at her side. The knowledge that he'd stay at her side.

She opened her mouth to tell him that when a voice shouted, "There's Ruiz!"

They spun around to the source of the voice as a muscular man in a tight T-shirt, khaki shorts and brown leather flip-flops strode toward them. He had a crooked grin, and his eyes were a warm brown when he pushed his sunglasses into his short dark hair.

He was also über attractive, in that arrogant jock kind of way.

Cam extended his hand. "Hey Max." They did that bro hand-clasp, back-slap hug thing and then Max reached back, pulling forward a petite girl Tate hadn't even seen behind him.

The girl had long brown hair with bangs and stood a little oddly, like she was keeping her weight off one of her legs. She hugged Cam and then stepped back, eyeing Tate.

Cam cleared his throat. "Uh . . ."

"Cam!" came a squeal, and then a flurry of dark blond hair, wide blue eyes and tan skin came flying into Cam's arms.

Tate took a step back, unsure if this was some ex-girlfriend who still had a thing for Cam. Because . . . totally awkward. But Cam's face showed no concern, so Tate held her tongue on judgment. "Alec!" the blonde yelled. "You're so slow, hurry up, it's Cam!"

A man walked up and placed a hand on the blonde's shoulder. So this was Alec. He had a pompadour hairstyle and a pair of thick-framed glasses. He wore cutoff jean shorts, which normally would look horrid on a guy, but he seemed to pull them off with his worn chucks and V-neck T-shirt. In fact, he looked like a modern-day Elvis.

"Cam," the blonde was saying, and Tate guessed she was Kat, Alec's girlfriend. "I think I made it on the *Today Show*. I'm not sure. But I was waving behind Matt Lauer—"

"She looked crazy," Alec piped in.

Kat ignored him and kept talking. "And Lea said she saw me on the TV. I wasn't thrilled about my makeup today but thank God I wasn't wearing yellow or some awful color, right?"

Cam laughed. "You're famous now, Kat."

She flipped her hair over her shoulder and stuck out a hip. "That's what I said. Alec is being a party pooper."

Alec rolled his eyes, hauling his girlfriend back against his body and kissing the top of her head. She looked at him over her shoulder with bright eyes and a smile. The obvious affection between them made Tate grin.

Cam opened his mouth, probably to introduce her, when a woman walked up to them. About Tate's height, with dark pink hair cut in a short bob with bangs. She wore a cream-colored, tight dress with gold trim, gold gladiator sandals, and a sort of gold-snake headband. She looked like a funky Cleopatra.

Tate wondered if she was some sort of street performer until she opened her mouth. "Is Kat still talking about being on TV again? I think the camera was just trying to get away from me."

Tate didn't know why, because the girl was stunning.

"Danica, you made it on, too, I saw it," Kat said.

Danica rolled her eyes and then spotted Cam. "Hey Cam."

Cam hugged her and Tate watched closely for any extra touching. But Danica seemed about as interested in Cam as a piece of dry toast.

Cam spoke up again. "So, I need to introduce you guys to someone." He grabbed Tate's hand and hauled her beside him. He pointed out Max and Lea, who were a couple, along with Kat and Alec. Danica, the pink Cleopatra, was another friend. "And guys, this is Tatum. Tatum Ellison. My girlfriend."

Danica was the first to greet her with a chin lift to her face. "Nice makeup."

Tate fluttered her hand near her cheek. "Oh. Uh, thanks."

Max was next. "Nice to meet you. Damn Cam, you move fast. I just saw you a month or two ago."

"Yeah, well, she was my girlfriend from . . . before."

Five smiles wiped off five faces. The girls blinked at Tate and the guys scowled. Tate felt two inches tall. Cam must have told them about her.

"Hey," he spoke up. "I know . . . I said some things. But there's much more to the story. And let's just say, it's in the past now. We're moving forward. I swear, she didn't do me wrong, okay?"

Alec stepped forward. "Sorry, kind of attached to the guy. Nice to meet you, Tate." He shook her hand, his smile warm, and Tate began to relax.

"So thanks for meeting me, guys."

Max shrugged. "Kind of cool we were passing through when you were here. What's this about an interview?"

Cam waved his hand. "Long story, but I'm taking the New York job . . . just not in New York. I'll be working for them remotely back home."

Max raised an eyebrow. "And that's cool with you?"

Cam glanced at Tate and smiled at his friend. "Yeah, it's perfect for me. So what do you guys want to do?"

"We were just about to grab some lunch." Kat shaded her eyes from the sun. "Want to join?"

Cam looked at Tate and she smiled. "Sure." She wanted the opportunity to get to know Cam's friends better. He looked genuinely happy to see them. Kat was a little different, but fun to be around, and Lea's sarcastic remarks and Max's return quips were entertaining.

Alec . . . seemed quiet. And a little fidgety. Tate hadn't figured him out yet.

They sat at table in front of the fountain and ate lunch. Kat sipped her iced tea and stared rapt at the fountain.

Cam eyed Alec. "You okay, man?"

Tate was glad this was unusual for Alec and not his normal behavior. His leg bounced and sweat dripped down his temples. "Yeah, sure."

"Dude, you're sweating." Max slid a glass of water over to him. "How about you hydrate."

Danica patted Alec on the shoulder and whispered something in his ear, then pressed the water into his hand.

Alec composed himself a little based on whatever

Danica told him. Then he gulped down the water and crushed a piece of ice before turning to his girlfriend. "Hey, you wanna go closer to the fountain?"

Kat turned and looked at him with her brows furrowed. "What do you mean?"

"Do you want to walk up there? Get closer?"

She wrinkled her nose. "I don't know. I'm having a good hair day and that mist from the water will frizz it right up."

Alec took a deep breath. "Kat, please walk with me to the fountain."

She opened her mouth, looking like she was going to protest again, but then she stopped and cocked her head, studying her boyfriend's face. "Um, okay."

"Great," Alec muttered under his breath and grabbed her hands as they rose from the table. She shot him a big smile, but that didn't seem to relax him any.

Their table was relatively close to the fountain already, so Kat and Alec had to walk only about ten feet to the edge.

Tate watched their backs and thought what an attractive couple they made, with Kat's looks and Alec's style.

And then Alec turned to Kat, licking his lips. When he gripped both her hands in his, they were trembling.

And Tate knew what was next. She clapped her hand over her mouth and said through her fingers, "Oh my God."

"What?" Cam asked. And Tate pointed at Kat and Alec.

She was staring at him as he dropped to one knee in

front of the fountain. Lea whipped out her cell phone and began to snap pictures. Danica watched, a huge smile on her previously controlled face.

"*Meu coração*, my heart," Alec said. "I love you. I love your laugh and your wit and your heart. And I want that in my life every day. For the rest of my days. Will you marry me?"

He pulled a ring out of his pocket and held it up to Kat. Tate's eyes watered even though she'd just met these people.

Kat was crying. And Tate noticed the girl even cried beautifully. Kat nodded and let Alec slip the ring on her finger and then she wrapped her arms around his shoulders and kissed him.

The crowd on the patio began to clap. And Cam whistled while Max hollered.

When they came back to the table, Alec no longer looked nervous. He looked like he just won the lottery. Kat dropped into her seat, eyes on her ring. The round diamond sat on a yellow gold band. "It's so beautiful."

Alec leaned over. "The gold is actually from my father's ring. My mom let me have it and the jeweler melted it down for you."

Kat looked up at him with wide eyes and started crying harder. Alec wrapped her in his arms while she sobbed on his shoulder.

Tate looked at Cam questioningly. "His father died when he was a kid."

Tate nodded and smiled knowingly at Alec over Kat's head. He returned the smile.

Max cleared his throat. "So, uh, I don't wanna be a dick or anything—"

"So that means you're gonna be a dick," Cam growled.

"—but you kinda stole my thunder, man," Max said with narrowed eyes.

Kat leaned back and wiped her eyes while Alec stared at his friend. "What?"

Max waved his hand. "Rockefeller Center. Hello, this is my romantic gesture."

Alec rolled his eyes. "You own fucking Rockefeller Center now?"

"Just saying, this is kind of my thing. This is where I thought I'd get engaged."

Lea smacked Max on the head. "Will you shut up? Let them have their moment." She leaned in closer to her boyfriend. "And what do you mean this is where you thought you'd get engaged? Who says I'll say yes?"

Max threw back his head and laughed. "Oh, doll, don't even act like you'd turn me down."

"I might," Lea said, her eyes all fire.

Max's hardened with determination. "You challenging me? Because I *will* plan the best engagement in the history of engagements."

"Yeah? What if I said I want to get engaged while listening to the London Philharmonic Orchestra and drinking South African wine?"

"Done."

Lea's chin tilted up. "On top of an elephant."

"I'll bring the whole fucking circus, doll."

Alec reached over and waved a hand between them. "Shit, you two. Give it a rest."

Max leaned back but mouthed, *This isn't over* to Lea.

She smirked back.

Tate decided she needed Lea to be her best friend.

Alec smiled at Cam. "You gonna get the marriage fever now."

Cam laughed. "I think we're just gonna live in sin for a little bit."

Max turned to Danica. "What about you? Going to make an honest woman out of somebody when you move out to California?"

Tate raised her eyebrows at "woman." Danica eyed Max over her glasses. "I don't think marriage is my thing."

Alec shoved her shoulder gently. "Even if you don't decide to get married, you'll find someone that you want to spend the rest of your life with."

Danica shrugged, and her gaze wandered to the fountain. "Maybe."

After chatting for another hour or so, and getting interrupted by strangers wishing Kat and Alec good luck, they all parted ways.

Tate was sad to see Cam's friends go and told him so as they began the walk to the train station. "Can we all get together again?"

Cam smiled. "Sure, and hey, we have a wedding to attend now."

Tate frowned. "I need a dress."

Cam bumped her with his hip. "I think you got some time."

They bought Tate's train ticket at the terminal and then took a seat at the station so they were ready when their train departed. Cam rolled his head on the back of his seat to face her and laced his fingers with hers. "When I propose, it's not going to be in Rockefeller Center."

Tate laughed. "That's quite all right."

He stared at their hands and rubbed his thumb in circles on her skin. "You know I wanna marry you though, right?"

"With the house and dog and rain forest with the poison dart frogs?"

He pressed a kiss to her lips. "Wouldn't want it any other way."

Chapter 23

In Utope:

CAM STOOD OUTSIDE their house with his hands on his hips. Months ago, they had razed the deadly rain forest in the backyard, donating the poison dart frogs to the zoo. Now, their backyard was fenced while a live Pinkie Pie grazed. He waved to the pony, and she grinned back. It was weird that a horse could grin. And it'd been one heck of a hack on the game to do it.

He walked inside the house, his anxiety meter bordering on red.

Everything had to be perfect. He had all their bags packed by the door. He called for Tate and she ran down the stairs with an extra backpack on her shoulder.

He rolled his eyes and ushered her out of the house.

They hopped in their yellow Jeep with the top down

and cruised to a secluded spot to set up camp. They made s'mores over a fire and told ghost stories.

And then, as Tate's figure was silhouetted against the back of the fire, Cam got down on one knee and held up a huge diamond ring. He'd had to hack the fuck out of the game for this, too.

Tate's hands flew to her cheeks, and then she flapped her arms as little pixel tears streamed down her face. "Yes," she screamed. She tackled him, and then their bodies blurred out because their clothes were no longer on. That was on the next hack list.

CAM COCKED HIS head, listening for the footsteps. And there they were, flying up from the basement of the house he and Tate shared.

He'd told her to open up the game console down in the basement, while he used the one upstairs in their bedroom. It might not be the most epic proposal. It might not be Rockefeller Center, but it was he and Tate.

The door flew open and Tate stood there, her hair wild and wet around her head from her recent shower.

"Are you fucking serious right now?"

He pulled a box out from under his pillow on the bed. "As a fucking heart attack."

And then she tackled him in real life, and nothing was blurred when their clothes came off. And in the end, Tate wore nothing but a diamond ring and a smile and Cam thought it was the best she'd ever looked.

The End

Don't miss any of Megan Erickson's
Bowler University series! Read on for
a look at where it all began with

Make It Count

and

Make It Right

Make It Count

Kat Caruso wishes her brain had a return policy, or at least a complaint hotline. The defective organ is constantly distracted, terrible at statistics, and absolutely flooded with inappropriate thoughts about her boyfriend's gorgeous best friend, Alec . . . who just so happens to be her brand-new math tutor. Who knew nerds could be so hot?

Kat usually goes through tutors like she does boyfriends—both always seem to bail when they realize how hopeless she is. It's safer for her heart to keep everyone at arm's length. But Alec is always stepping just a little too close.

Alec Stone should not be fantasizing about Kat. She's adorable, unbelievably witty, and completely off-limits. He'd never stab his best friend in the back . . .

But when secrets are revealed, the lines of loyalty are blurred. To make it count, Alec must learn messy human emotions can't be solved like a trigonometry function. And Kat has to trust that Alec may be the first guy to want her for who she is, and not in spite of it.

KAT CHEWED ON her pen and studied her tutor's bent head. Ashley's shiny black hair was pulled back into a ponytail, held in place by a . . . scrunchie.

Seriously? Was that really a sparkly teal scrunchie? Kat bit down harder on her pen in concentration. Did they even sell those anymore? The last time she'd seen one, she'd been six and wrapped it around her side ponytail, pretending to be Kelly Kapowski while watching *Saved by the Bell* reruns.

Ashley droned on about something, and Kat yawned. She looked down at her notes but some of the words blurred, increasing her headache, so she gazed around the library. Through the windows, the late-January wind rattled the bare trees.

"Kat? Did you hear me?" Ashley's voice needled into her ear.

Kat snapped her head back. "Um . . . yeah?"

Ashley slumped her shoulders with a sigh. "Look, I'm going to be honest here. I like you, okay? But I don't think you're getting anything out of these sessions. I think my time would be better spent with someone else."

Kat opened her mouth but then snapped her jaw shut. It wasn't like she hadn't heard it before. Her inability to stay focused had annoyed plenty of tutors. Not to mention just about everyone else in her life. She jutted out her chin with as much confidence as she could muster. She'd find another tutor.

"I think that's a good idea, Ashley. I'd planned to say the same thing." The lie came easily. "I'm doing better in statistics anyway, so I don't need the help anymore."

Ashley raised an eyebrow while gathering her papers. "Okay, well, it was . . . nice to meet you." She winced, as if it was painful to say, then waved meekly and left.

Kat groaned softly. She was in the second semester of her sophomore year at Bowler University and already on academic probation. If she failed another course, she would be kicked out. This semester's bane of her existence—statistics.

She hated her brain. Absolutely hated the way it could never make sense of words and numbers on the page in front of her. How it wandered and couldn't focus on one thing for very long. How it was to blame for the dumb blonde jokes that had followed her like an unfunny comedian her whole life.

She wasn't even blonde. Not really. She held up a wavy curl and picked at the ends. It was more like a light brown. Caramel. Or whiskey. With blonde highlights. Were those split ends? She needed a haircut, stat. And a root touch-up because her highlights were growing out. And maybe an eyebrow wax. There was that place over on Lexington that took walk-ins . . .

Her cell phone vibrated on the table, announcing an incoming text message from her boyfriend. She swiped her thumb across the screen, automatically launching the text-to-speech app she'd downloaded after repeatedly reading her text messages incorrectly. She'd thought downloading it was genius at the time, until a clearly audible *Your ass looks hot today* text read in a sexy male Australian accent scandalized an unfortunate seventy-year-old at the drugstore.

Luckily, this message was tame.

Come over tonight.

She muttered to herself, "And that's an order, Private." Would it kill him to type *please*? It was only an extra six letters.

Max Payton didn't know she had a tutor. He didn't know much about her at all, really. But he was hot—really hot—and fun and as a junior, lived in a house off campus with his own room. And he liked to bake. Seriously, the man baked her chocolate-chip cookies. They were really good, too. When she asked him about the secret ingredient, he'd laughed and said *flour*. She was pretty sure he was making fun of her. But she'd learned at an early age to pretend mocking was just teasing.

She gathered her books and stuffed them into her plaid Burberry messenger bag, then headed toward the front doors, smoothie from the library snack shop in hand. Head bent, fiddling with the clasp of her bag, she stumbled into a wall of human on the pavement outside.

"Oh, I'm sorry—" Her voice dropped out when she realized the solid flesh belonged to Alec, Max's best friend.

She'd only met him once or twice before he'd moved in with Max this semester and every time, he cocked his eyebrow with a half frown like he knew something she didn't. Which he actually did, since he had brainy super-powers. Smarter than a speeding Einstein. Able to leap over C-minus students like her in a single bound.

She didn't trust people that smart. And she didn't trust a guy who didn't ogle her ass or leer at her boobs like every other member of the straight male species on the planet.

She once asked Max if Alec was gay, and Max had laughed so hard, she feared he'd pop a blood vessel in his forehead. Then he assured her his friend was in fact, very straight.

She'd believe it when she saw it.

Right now, that raised-eyebrow frown pinned her where she stood. His pale green eyes behind thick black frames roamed over her shoulder to the library and then back to her. With his pin-stripe button-down, dark jeans with Converse shoes and hair styled in a short, messy pompadour, he looked like a nerdy Elvis.

His frown morphed into a smile when he spotted the smoothie in her hand, and she *definitely* didn't notice his full lips. "You know, you don't have to venture into the forbidden zone just to get a smoothie."

Oooh. The jerk. She glanced around surreptitiously, then leaned in and spoke in a low voice. "Just play it cool. Don't let it slip someone like me snuck in the library." She gripped his forearm and whispered. "Password today is *rosebud.*"

His face blanked and he looked at her like he'd never seen her before. Kat debated whether or not that was an improvement over his other look.

But then those intelligent eyes narrowed and a smirk curled his lips. "I know. We nerds get an e-mail every morning."

See? He always needed the last word. She propped a hand on her hip and leaned in. "Well, sounds like you have a mole. Might want to look into that."

He opened his mouth but she cut him off. "Just looking out for you guys. Anyway, see ya around!"

Before he could shoot back a snarky comeback, Kat skirted around him and bounded down the stairs. She chalked that up as Kat 1, Alec 0.

She pulled out her phone and texted Max.

Come get me. At campus entrance in 10.

Kat stuffed her hands in the pockets of her fabulous—bought for a total steal—red peacoat, and took the long walk to the head of campus. The air was cold, that damp chill typical for Maryland. She glared sullenly at the bare trees on campus, wishing for spring, when they'd bloom again. She'd visited the campus in the spring of her junior year of high school with her parents, and everything about the university and nearby town of Bowler felt right. During her first year as a student, she'd built friendships and kept a decent reputation.

This second year was proving to be a huge pain.

Kat arrived at the large stones marking the entrance

of the campus, BOWLER carved into them and painted red. She began to worry about the condition of her frozen toes until Max pulled up to the sidewalk in his old truck.

"Babe, get in."

She didn't need the invitation as she wrenched open the rusted door and hopped inside, smiling at him.

The first time she saw Max, he was standing on a table in the middle of a raging house party in October, fist at his mouth as he belted the chorus to "Don't Stop Believin'." He was gorgeous in that confident, cocky way. And he looked like he belonged on the cover of a romance novel, wearing nothing but unlaced football pants and artistically placed eye black, the right amount of sweat running down the middle of his tanned pecs.

Their gazes had met and when he winked those big brown eyes at her, flashing a wide easy smile, she was a goner.

And one of the things she liked most about him was he didn't ask her too many questions about herself. So she didn't pry into his life.

She wasn't going to marry the guy. But she liked his kisses and his cookies.

"Your roommates around?" She buckled her seat belt.

"Uh, I think Cam went home for the weekend. Alec is around, I guess." He squeezed her thigh. "You know, he'll be busy studying like always. Should be quiet if you want to spend the night."

She sighed and wondered if Max was fed up with her evasion of sex. It wasn't that she didn't like sex. She loved it, actually. And while she was attracted to Max, something was holding her back.

"Maybe," she said.

Max sighed, and she absorbed the sting of his disappointment.

Kat gingerly placed her feet on crumpled fast food bags. Something oozed out of a damp corner and she hoped it was ketchup. The color suggested otherwise.

"I thought we agreed you were going to clean out your car." She eyed the suspicious substance and wished she had one of those hazardous-waste trash cans from a doctor's office.

Max snickered and nodded toward the bags. "I'm saving that for later."

Kat wrinkled her nose and he laughed harder. Organization was key to her life. She could control that—her bedroom tidy and her calendar neatly filled out with color-coded highlighter. Of course, it was a stark contrast to the riot of chaos that was her mind. But fake it 'til you make it, right?

Max parked along the sidewalk outside of his townhome off campus and as they crossed the street, Kat tried to grab his hand. He evaded it like always and wrapped a beefy arm around her neck. She huffed under her breath. For once, she wished he didn't act too cool to hold her hand.

Max's place was on the end of a row of four townhomes. The high ceilings made the already large living room feel even bigger. The kitchen was a decent size but outdated, with old appliances, a crumbling tile floor and a ceiling-fan light you had to tug just so if you wanted to see your hand in front of your face.

The staircase leading to the bedrooms upstairs was ornate, with a thick, solid railing Max often straddled and slid down with a whoop. There was one bathroom on the second floor, which for a guys' place was relatively clean.

When they walked inside the front door, Max headed right to the kitchen while Kat settled on the couch in the living room, running her hands over the ugly, fuchsia-flowered fabric. Max and his roommate Cam had found it by a Dumpster before they moved in. Kat was still unsure if sitting on it would give her a rash.

Minutes later, Max plopped down beside her with a can of beer and promptly turned on the TV to a hockey game.

Kat yawned. Hockey was boring to watch. The guys didn't wear tight clothes and lot of them were missing teeth. Playoff hockey was even worse because the players didn't shave and had scraggly neck beards. *Gross.*

When she'd had enough of trying to find the tiny puck on the screen, she said, "I'm going to make a sand-wich. You want one?"

"Yeah, I think we have some peanut butter and jelly."

As she walked into the kitchen, he called to her back, "Hey, I made some cookies for my brothers earlier today, bring us in a couple, yeah?"

Kat gave a thumbs-up over her shoulder. Max worked at his dad's auto mechanics shop almost every weekend along with his older brothers. And they always demanded Max's treats.

In the kitchen, she searched through the thin plywood

cabinets until she found the peanut butter, then pulled the jelly and the bread out of the puke green-colored refrigerator.

The front door opened and closed and low voices carried in from the living room. She shifted to the edge of the counter to grab a towel and ran smack into someone.

"Ouch!" She whirled around to face her opponent and met Alec's eyes. She frowned at him, rubbing her shoulder. "Seriously? Twice in one day?"

He rolled his eyes and held his hands up. "Yep, I'm following you around so I can get poked in the ribs by your bony elbows."

Her mouth dropped open. "Bony?! You think my elbows are bony?" She bent her arm and eyed the joint. "I think my elbows are quite attractive, thank you very much."

He looked at her as if she were one of those bugs you tolerate only because it eats worse bugs. Then his lips twitched into a grin and he leaned down, his lips near her elbow like it was a microphone. "I'm sorry, Kat's Elbow. You're the sexiest elbow on campus," he said in a deep, sexy voice. Wait, what? When did she start attributing Alec with anything sexy?

With him stooped for his elbow apology, their eyes met. His green irises studied her, making her feel naked. Not clothes naked but brain naked. Like he pried off the top off her head to look inside.

She didn't want anyone to peek inside the top of her head. Her brain was probably all weird colored and deformed. It looked better covered by her skull, scalp and in-need-of-a-dye-job hair.

She steeled herself against the rush of heat flooding her face, because it was really wrong to be a creeper about her boyfriend's best friend.

Didn't mean she couldn't look at his nice eyes. And big hands. And good profile with one of those Roman or Greek noses or whatever they were called. And thick dark hair she wanted to run her hands through, grip and pull. Just to see if it turned him on.

Oh sugar-snacks, now she was having dirty thoughts about her boyfriend's nerdy roommate.

Clearly, her brain was deformed.

She huffed in annoyance and backed away from him to resume her task, spreading four slices of bread on the counter and digging in the tub of peanut butter.

A hand crept into view and grabbed a banana off the counter while she slathered peanut butter on two slices of bread and reached for the jelly.

A throat cleared behind her. "If you put peanut butter on both sides of the bread, then the jelly doesn't make it soggy."

He apparently didn't even think she was capable of making a flipping peanut-butter-and-jelly sandwich.

She stuck a peanut-butter-covered finger in her mouth turned to face him. When his eyes tracked her finger and lingered on her lips, she felt as if she won this small battle of the sexes. Kat 2, Alec 0.

She smirked. "I'm so glad you're around to show me the error of my sandwich-making ways. What would I do without you, Alec?"

He took a bite of banana, chewed and swallowed. "I guess you'd have a soggy sandwich."

She rolled her eyes and turned back to her task.

He finished his banana and threw the peel in the trash.

"Do you want me to make you one, too?" she asked.

He paused with his hand on the door. "Sure. Thanks."

When he walked out of the kitchen, she pulled two more slices of bread and spread peanut butter on all the slices before squeezing on the jelly.

She carried the finished sandwiches and cookies out to the guys, then sat down beside Max. The hockey game was still on and even though she didn't give two flips about it, she pretended to care since Max did. That was pretty much Good Girlfriend 101.

She took a bite of her sandwich and squinted at the TV. "So, what quarter is this? What teams are playing?"

"Babe, this is hockey. There are no quarters. There are periods and—*What the fuck, ref! That was tripping!*—anyway, I think you ask me that question every game. Either remember or stop asking." His focus returned to the game. "That should have been a damn penalty," he muttered.

Well then. Apparently she had to retake Good Girlfriend 101.

She thought about telling him she didn't remember because she really only half listened to his answer. She cared about hockey about as much as she cared about what an absolute risk was in statistics. But it wasn't worth it, and she was hungry. Kat focused on her sandwich because the double-peanut-butter trick was pretty dang good . . .

Alec cleared this throat and she looked up. "Kat, there

are three twenty-minute periods in hockey. This is the first period. The Ducks are playing the Redhawks. Ducks are green jerseys; Redhawks are black. Ducks are winning." His tone was light and almost cautious. Like he thought she was going to take off his head. It was one of the few times he had spoken to her and his attention—those intelligent eyes fixed on her—caused a rush of heat to flare in her face.

"Thanks, Alec," she mumbled, eyes down on her sandwich to hide the color in her cheeks.

But she raised her head when her spine prickled, and they locked gazes for a moment. Kat was very aware of the air growing hot and heavy around her. Alec's lips twitched slightly, and her eyes were drawn to their fullness.

Max murmured at the TV, drawing her attention before a *bow chicka-bow-wow* soundtrack could play in her head.

She was so screwed.

Alec rose stiffly. He grabbed his book bag off the couch and said, "I have some studying to do. I'll be in my room."

"Later." Max waved him off, his attention unwavering from the game. Alec walked up the stairs, and Kat willed herself not to watch him. But her willpower was only so strong. At the top of the stairs, he turned around and immediately met her eyes.

Shoot! She quickly whirled her head around and stared blindly at the TV.

"Game's getting good, huh, babe?" Max grabbed the rest of her abandoned sandwich.

"Yep," she muttered. "Great game."

Make It Right

Max Payton would like nothing more than to forget his junior year of college . . . and yet, being a senior isn't looking much better. After graduation he'll still be under his overbearing father's thumb, helping run the family business as he's always been expected to do.

When Max volunteers to help teach a self-defense class after a rash of assaults and thefts on campus, one of the other instructors is the pixie-faced girl he hasn't been able to stop thinking about since last year. His dad taught him that size and strength always win a fight. But while Max is lying on the mat at Lea Travers' feet after a skilled blow to his carotid artery, he begins to revise that thought.

Lea Travers avoids guys like Max—cocky jocks who assume she's a fragile doll because of her short stature and disability from a childhood car accident. She likes to be in control, and Max challenges her at every turn. But during the moments he lets his guard down, she sees a soul as broken inside as she is outside. Trusting him is a whole other problem . . .

When the assaults hit close to home, both Max and Lea have to change their assumptions about strength and weakness before they can get the future they want—together.

MAX DRAINED HIS cup of beer and closed his eyes to let the sounds of the party sink into his skin and down into his bones.

This usually worked—the alcohol in his veins, the music, the friends. The girls.

He fed off others' energy, always had. His favorite thing to do to unwind was to head out to a bar or party and just let loose.

So when his roommate Cam found him cursing and pacing his room like an animal after a particularly *delightful* phone call with his father—Max curled his lip in a sneer just thinking about it—he'd encouraged Max to go out. That's what his friends did. They knew him better than he knew himself sometimes.

But for once, Max hadn't wanted to. He'd wanted to go to the gym and sweat out all the anger, but Cam was persistent. So Max relented.

He knew now he shouldn't have.

Because the beer tasted skunked and the music hurt his head and even the girls weren't interesting.

The redhead beside him right now was still talking. He'd asked her one question about her major, and she was still rambling on about it five minutes later.

He'd said maybe two sentences to this girl, both questions about herself, but she was clearly still into him, pressing her chest against his folded arms. The lace of her bra peaked out the top of her neckline, and he could feel the textured fabric through her thin shirt when it brushed against his knuckles.

He hadn't even been in the mood to lay on the charm. He knew how to stand, how to smile with his eyes. *Smize*, one of his brother's ex-girlfriends had called it with a giggle.

Whatever it was. He knew how to do it. And knew how to get the girl. Too bad he didn't want her.

Fuck this shit.

He set his empty beer cup on a window ledge. "Um, Kelly," he said, cutting in when she finally took a breath. He remembered her name, because he always remembered names. Kelly blinked and peered up at him through her lashes, lips parted. She was hot. Big rack. A year ago, she would have been his type. Hell, most girls were his type. But lately, they'd reminded him of how much he'd almost fucked up his life.

Except that one girl . . .

He shook his head, and leaned down to speak into her ear. He heard a stuttered inhale and resisting rolling his eyes. "I gotta head out. I forgot I need to get home. Early morning." He leaned back and shot her a smile. Or smize. Whatever.

Confusion crossed her face, but he was over this scene. "Sorry," he said with a shrug and turned away before she could respond.

Max searched the sea of bodies for Cam. The guy was over in the corner with a girl, flashing his dimples while she looked up at him with pure infatuation. Max rolled his eyes and hollered, "Ruiz!"

Cam turned his head and Max gave him the sign he was heading out. Cam waved in acknowledgment and turned back to his girl of the night.

Max made his way through the crowd, feeling a couple of touches on his arms or shoulders, some "Hey Max" 's, but he kept walking because he wasn't in the mood and enough people already thought he was an asshole.

He wished Alec, his best friend, was around, but he'd decided to stay home with his girlfriend, Kat, tonight. Kat, who used to be Max's girlfriend. Before he fucked it up.

Life was complicated.

Once he stepped outside, he pulled up the collar of his jacket against the early October air and walked briskly back to the townhouse he shared with Alec and Cam. The phone call with his dad still rankled, the words poking him with their sharp edges.

He'd mentioned changing his major, had barely even spoken the words when his dad proclaimed *Paytons stick together!* and Max was expected to complete his business degree and then work at his dad's mechanic shop, helping with the books and business side of things.

Max didn't want to, but the obligation to work with his dad and two brothers weighed heavily on his shoulders. Plus, his dad said he wouldn't hesitate to withdraw his tuition help, and Max couldn't afford to cover it, despite his two jobs.

The bastard.

The lights of the convenience store near his house caught his eye and he changed direction, suddenly hungry for those super-greasy pizzas they made in the back and kept in a warmer on the counter.

He was still a little drunk but hopefully the cheese, dough and sauce would mop up the rest of the awful beer sitting like acid in his stomach.

He crossed the parking lot and then stopped beside the front doors, fumbling inside his pockets. His phone fell out and he cursed as it clattered on the sidewalk. He shoved it back in his coat pocket and then dug his wallet out of his back jeans pocket. He blinked at it blearily and tried to count his bills.

He kept losing count of his ones and had to start over. Fucking beer.

The bell on the convenience store door tinkled and he heard a voice—that damn musical voice that hit him in the gut every time he heard it. And he couldn't figure out why.

He looked up from his wallet and there she was, Lea Travers, talking to some tall blond guy, his arm around her slender shoulders.

Max must have made a sound or movement because Lea turned her head, her long, dark straight hair swirling around her shoulders. In the glow of the streetlights, her eyes were even bigger, rounder and darker than normal, staring at him from under her thick fringe of bangs.

She wore low-heeled knee-high boots and tight jeans and a thigh-length pink jacket that cinched at the waist.

Her full lips were parted and her cheeks flushed, probably from the warmth of the convenience store she just left.

For a moment, he enjoyed the way she looked at him, a little bit of curious hope.

He'd met her last year, because she was friends with Kat. There was something about Lea, this power or strength that lurked below the surface of her small, fragile frame. He wanted to grab that strength, roll around in it like a cat in catnip.

Max looked to the guy who stood next to her, a proprietary arm around her shoulders—which Max glared at—and a pizza box in the other hand. The guy was tall and blond and had big blue eyes and looked like he just came from Wimbledon, where he had front-row seats because he was the heir to his dad's pharmaceutical business. He was the kind of kid whose dad drove some fancy BMW or Mercedes into the shop and then looked down on Max and his brothers, with their grease-stained clothes and fingernails.

He looked vaguely familiar but Max couldn't place him, and the guy's perfect hair and collared polo made him want to hurl.

So she had a boyfriend. And Max was done, absolutely positively fucking done with girls who were attached. He'd almost lost his best friend over the last time he'd let himself get involved with one.

So, like always, he fell back on what he knew. He curled his upper lip into a smirk, opened his mouth, and let out the asshole. "Hey there, doll."

Lea's eyes narrowed and her lips pressed into a thin

line. Well, it'd been nice while it lasted. His fault. Her lips parted one time to sigh. "Hi, Max."

He didn't want it to be this way between them. He wanted to saunter up next to her, wrap an arm around her neck and look down into those dark eyes while they filled with lust . . .

Shit. Fucking drunken daydreams. None of that was happening because somehow, around Lea, he turned into a six-year-old boy, teasing the girl he wanted the most.

And no matter how hard he tried, he couldn't curb the asshole. He jerked a thumb at the convenience door. "Might want to find a new boyfriend, there, Travers. Clearly Polo Boy can afford to take you to a nicer place." The words were coming, coming up like vomit, and with them came a heavy helping of self-loathing. He couldn't stop them. "Although, if a convenience-store pizza is all it takes to get a date with you, even I can afford that."

Polo Boy opened his mouth but Lea tapped his chest with the back of her hand, so he clamped his jaws shut.

Max's mouth just had a mind of his own now. "Oh, he replies to hand signals, too? Got 'em trained."

"Max, why are you always such an asshole?" The worst part about it was that Lea wasn't angry, her voice wasn't biting, it was dripping with disappointment and that was worse. He wanted her to be angry and stomp in a huff. He wanted a reaction.

He didn't want pity.

He spread his arms wide. "That's who I am, doll." It was a lie, but he'd perfected being an asshole to an art.

Just like the charmer role. It was easier than trying to figure out who he really was or wanted to be.

Her eyes narrowed more, and then Polo Boy spoke up. "Look—"

Lea cut him off. "It's fine, Nick. Let's go."

They walked away, Polo Boy's arm around her shoulders, Lea's limp from a childhood car accident more pronounced in the cold weather.

Max gritted his teeth. For once keeping his mouth shut from calling after them to ask what would buy him second base.

He looked at his wallet again in his hands and shoved it back into his pocket. He wasn't hungry for pizza anymore.

LEA STARED AT her boots as she walked and curled her hands into fists in the pockets of her jacket. Nick was silent beside her, lost in his own thoughts.

She hadn't known Max long, and what she knew of him wasn't so great. He'd dated Kat and hadn't been a very good boyfriend. And everything about Max, from his swagger to his snug T-shirts to his cocky smirk, screamed confident asshole.

Which meant he wasn't for her.

But tonight, for a brief moment, those big, expressive brown eyes had showed a glimmer of hope before he blinked. Then the alcohol haze clouded over them, and that little sliver of another Max disappeared with one curl of his lips.

She wondered if he realized how much those eyes gave him away when he wasn't careful. She wondered if anyone ever tried to look deeper.

She wondered if he wanted anyone to.

Nick squeezed her shoulder. "You all right?"

She chewed her cheek. "Yeah, just thinking."

"You know I went to high school with him, right?"

Lea looked up at her cousin and saw his blond stubble catching the rays of the streetlights. "What? Who?"

Nick gestured behind them. "Max Payton. He went to Tory High School."

She frowned. "But—"

"I'm three years younger. I mean, I doubt he has any idea who I am. I only know him because, well, everyone knew Max when he was a senior. Popular guy."

"Why didn't you say anything just now?"

Nick shrugged. "What's the point? So he can say, 'I don't remember you?' I was just a freshman. Doubt he ever saw me." He picked at his shirt. "And he was glaring holes in my polo shirt like it personally offended him."

"He was just drunk."

"I don't know, maybe he hates horses."

Lea laughed. "I don't think that's it."

"But can you imagine him on a horse? Max is a big dude. Poor horse."

Lea elbowed Nick in the ribs. "Stop."

"He'd probably try to bench-press the horse."

Lea elbowed him harder. "Nick, stop!"

Nick chuckled and squeezed her shoulder again before

dropping his arm. "So, that's kind of funny he thought we were dating."

Lea wrinkled her nose. "Ew."

Nick scrunched his lips to the side. "I mean, we're not actually related by blood, so . . ." he waggled his eyebrows.

"Seriously, ew. And you have a girlfriend."

"Threesome?"

"Nick."

He bumped her with his hip and laughed as they climbed the stairs to his place. When they opened the door, Nick's girlfriend, Trish, bounded up from the couch. "Finally! What took you guys so long? I'm starving."

She grabbed the box from Nick and immediately began to dish out slices onto paper plates. Lea took her plate and sat on the beanbag chair, tucking her legs under her. Trish sat across from her and when Nick sat down, he gave Trish a soft kiss on the forehead. They'd started dating sophomore year in high school, and the affection between them melted Lea's heart every time.

"So, Lea and I are together now," Nick started, "and my name is Polo, and I am a crappy boyfriend who takes her on convenience-store dates."

Trish froze with her pizza halfway to her mouth. "What are you talking about?"

"We ran into Max Payton and . . ." Nick turned to Lea. "Wait, how do you know him?"

"He used to date my friend Kat, who is now dating his friend Alec."

Nick blinked.

Lea picked off a slice of pepperoni and dropped it into her mouth. "It's kind of a long story."

"Alec Stone goes here too?" Nick asked.

"Oh yeah, I guess you know him, too. He and Max went to high school together."

"Small world," Trish said.

Nick shrugged. "A lot of kids from surrounding high schools apply here." He looked at Lea. "And can we talk about how he was flirting with you?"

Lea snapped her head back. "In what world was that flirting? He was an asshole."

"Wait, what happened?" Trish asked.

Nick held up a hand. "Okay, I admit it was a poor attempt. But he didn't like my arm around her shoulder, I'll tell you that," Nick muttered.

Lea rolled her eyes. "I don't think Max has a problem picking up girls, so if he wanted to be effective, he would have been."

Nick picked at the cheese on his pizza. "I don't know, maybe he didn't want to be."

"I'm really confused right now," Trish said.

Lea shifted on the beanbag chair. "Me too."

Nick looked up. "I'm not saying it's mature, but sometimes, when a guy wants a girl but knows he doesn't have a shot? Well, he's kind of a dick."

Lea narrowed her eyes. "Max has no interest in me."

Nick cocked his head.

"Seriously!" Lea threw up her hands. "There is no way."

"Why?"

"Because . . ." She pressed her lips together. Nick's previous girlfriend was Kat. Beautiful, effervescent, nothing serious—until she met Alec—Kat. Lea was . . . well, cynical and a little grumpy sometimes and wouldn't stand by while Max acted the asshole. She waved her hands. "I think I'm done with this conversation."

Nick's opened his mouth, but Trish knocked his knee with hers, so he rolled his eyes and took another bite of pizza.

But as they talked about classes and Nick imitated his professor's deep tenor, all Lea could think about was that hopeful glint she'd seen in Max's eyes for that brief moment.

No matter how much she tried to deny it to herself, she wanted to see it again.

It's graduation at Bowler University, but that doesn't mean we have to say goodbye. Megan Erickson is back with the first book in her sexy new series, The Mechanics of Love!

Dirty Thoughts

Cal was a bad boy from the
wrong side of the tracks.
Jenna was a classy good girl who
got anything she asked for.
She was all he ever wanted. He was
the only thing she needed.
They were everything to each other once,
but that was a long time ago . . .

Coming Summer 2015

About the Author

MEGAN ERICKSON grew up in a family that averages 5'5" on a good day and started writing to create characters who could reach the top kitchen shelf.

She's got a couple of tattoos, has a thing for gladiators and has been called a crazy cat lady. After working as a journalist for years, she decided she liked creating her own endings better and switched back to fiction.

She lives in Pennsylvania with her husband, two kids and two cats. And no, she still can't reach the stupid top shelf.

www.meganerickson.org

Give in to your impulses . . .
Read on for a sneak peek at seven brand-new
e-book original tales of romance
from Avon Impulse.
Available now wherever e-books are sold.

HOLDING HOLLY
A LOVE AND FOOTBALL NOVELLA
By Julie Brannagh

IT'S A WONDERFUL FIREMAN
A BACHELOR FIREMEN NOVELLA
By Jennifer Bernard

ONCE UPON A HIGHLAND CHRISTMAS
By Lecia Cornwall

RUNNING HOT
A BAD BOYS UNDERCOVER NOVELLA
By HelenKay Dimon

SINFUL REWARDS 1
A BILLIONAIRES AND BIKERS NOVELLA
By Cynthia Sax

RETURN TO CLAN SINCLAIR
A CLAN SINCLAIR NOVELLA
By Karen Ranney

RETURN OF THE BAD GIRL
By Codi Gary

An Excerpt from

HOLDING HOLLY
A Love and Football Novella
by Julie Brannagh

Holly Reynolds has a secret. Make that two. The first involves upholding her grandmother's hobby of answering Dear Santa letters from dozens of local schoolchildren. The second . . . well, he just came strolling in the door.

Derrick has never met a woman he wanted to bring home to meet his family, mostly because he keeps picking the wrong ones—until he runs into sweet, shy Holly Reynolds. Different from anyone he's ever known, Derrick realizes she might just be everything he needs.

"Do you need anything else right now?"

"I'm good," he said. "Then again, there's something I forgot."

"What do you need? Maybe I can help."

He moved closer to her, and she tipped her head back to look up at him. He reached out to cup one of her cheeks in his big hand. "I had a great time tonight. Thanks for having pizza with me."

"I had a nice time too. Th-thank you for inviting me," she stammered. There was so much more she'd like to say, but she was tongue-tied again. He was moving closer to her, and he reached out to put his drinking glass down on the counter.

"Maybe we could try this again when we're not in the middle of a snowstorm," he said. "I'd like a second date."

She started nodding like one of those bobbleheads, and forced herself to stop before he thought she was even more of a dork.

"Yes. I . . . Yes, I would too. I . . . that would be fun."

He took another half-step toward her. She did her best to pull in a breath.

"Normally, I would have kissed you good night at your front door, but getting us inside before we froze to death seemed like the best thing to do right then," he said.

"Oh, yes. Absolutely. I—"

He reached out, slid his arms around her waist, and pulled her close. "I don't want to disrespect your grandma's wishes," he softly said. "She said I needed to treat you like a lady."

Holly almost let out a groan. She loved Grandma, but they needed to have a little chat later. "Sorry," she whispered.

He grinned at her. "I promise I'll behave myself, unless you don't want me to." She couldn't help it; she laughed. "Plus," he continued, "she said you have to be up very early in the morning to go to work, so we'll have to say good night."

Maybe she didn't need sleep. One thing's for sure, she had no interest in stepping away from him right now. He surrounded her, and she wanted to stay in his arms. Her heart was beating double-time, the blood was effervescent in her veins, and she summoned the nerve to move a little closer to him as she let out a happy sigh.

He kissed her cheek, and laid his scratchier one against hers. A few seconds later, she slid her arms around his neck too. "Good night, sweet Holly. Thanks for saving me from the snowstorm."

She had to laugh a little. "I think you saved *me*."

"We'll figure out who saved who later," he said. She felt his deep voice vibrating through her. She wished he'd kiss her again. Maybe she should kiss *him*.

He must have read her mind. He took her face in both of his hands. "Don't tell your grandma," he whispered. His breath was warm on her cheek.

"Tell her what?"

"I'm going to kiss you."

Her head was bobbing around as she frantically nodded yes. She probably looked ridiculous, but he didn't seem to care. Her eyelids fluttered closed as his mouth touched hers, sweet and soft. It wasn't a long kiss, but she knew she'd never forget it. She felt the zing at his tender touch from the top of her head to her toes.

"A little more?" he asked.

"Oh, yes."

His arms wrapped around her again, and he slowly traced her lips with his tongue. It slid into her mouth. He tasted like the peppermints Noel Pizza kept in a jar on the front counter. They explored each other for a while as quietly as possible, but maybe not quietly enough.

"Holly, honey," her grandma called out from the family room. Holly was *absolutely* going to have a conversation with Grandma when Derrick was out of earshot, and she stifled a groan. All they were doing was a little kissing. He rested one big hand on her butt, which she enjoyed. "Would you please bring me some salad?"

Derrick let out a snort. "I'll get it for you, Miss Ruth," he said loudly enough for her grandma to hear.

"She's onto us," Holly said softly.

"Damn right." He grinned at her. "I'll see you tomorrow morning." His voice dropped. "We're *definitely* kissing on the second date."

"I'll look forward to that." She tried to pull in a breath. Her head was spinning. She couldn't have stopped smiling if her life depended on it. "Are you sure you don't want to stay in my room instead? You need a good night's sleep. Don't you have to go to practice?"

"I'm sure your room is very comfortable, but I'll be fine out here. Sweet dreams," he said.

She felt him kiss the top of her head as he held her. She took a deep breath of his scent: clean skin, a whiff of expensive cologne, and freshly pressed clothes. "You, too," she whispered. She reached up to kiss his cheek. "Good night."

An Excerpt from

IT'S A WONDERFUL FIREMAN
A Bachelor Firemen Novella
by Jennifer Bernard

Hard-edged fireman Dean Mulligan has never been a big fan of Christmas. Twinkly lights and sparkly tinsel can't brighten the memories of too many years spent in ramshackle foster homes. When he's trapped in the burning wreckage of a holiday store, a Christmas angel arrives to open his eyes. But is it too late? This Christmas, it'll take an angel, a determined woman in love, and the entire Bachelor Firemen crew to make him believe . . . it is indeed a wonderful life.

He'd fallen. Memory returned like water seeping into a basement. He'd been on the roof, and then he'd fallen through, and now he was . . . here. His PASS device was sounding in a high-decibel shriek, and its strobe light flashed, giving him quick, garish glimpses of his surroundings.

Mulligan looked around cautiously. The collapse must have put out much of the fire, because he saw only a few remnants of flames flickering listlessly on the far end of the space. Every surface was blackened and charred except for one corner, in which he spotted blurry flashes of gold and red and green.

He squinted and blinked his stinging eyes, trying to get them to focus. Finally the glimpse of gold formed itself into a display of dangling ball-shaped ornaments. He gawked at them. What were those things made from? How had they managed to survive the fire? He sought out the red and squinted at it through his face mask. A Santa suit, that's what it was, with great, blackened holes in the sleeves. It was propped on a rocking chair, which looked quite scorched. Mulligan wondered if a mannequin or something had been wearing the suit. If so, it was long gone. Next to the chair stood half of a plastic Christmas tree. One side had melted into black goo, while the other side looked pretty good.

Where am I? He formed the words with his mouth, though no sound came out. And it came back to him. Under the Mistletoe. He'd been about to die inside a Christmas store. But he hadn't. So far.

He tried to sit up, but something was pinning him down. Taking careful inventory, he realized that he lay on his left side, his tank pressing uncomfortably against his back, his left arm immobilized beneath him. What was on top of him? He craned his neck, feeling his face mask press against his chest. A tree. A freaking Christmas tree. Fully decorated and only slightly charred. It was enormous, at least ten feet high, its trunk a good foot in diameter. At its tip, an angel in a gold pleated skirt dangled precariously, as if she wanted to leap to the floor but couldn't summon the nerve. Steel brackets hung from the tree's trunk; it must have been mounted somewhere, maybe on a balcony or something. A few twisted ironwork bars confirmed that theory.

How the hell had a Christmas tree survived the inferno in here? It was wood! Granted, it was still a live tree, and its trunk and needles held plenty of sap. And fires were always unpredictable. The one thing you could be sure of was that they'd surprise you. Maybe the balcony had been protected somehow.

He moved his body, trying to shift the tree, but it was extremely heavy and he was pinned so flat he had no leverage. He spotted his radio a few feet away. It must have been knocked out of his pouch. Underneath the horrible, insistent whine of his PASS device, he heard the murmuring chatter of communication on the radio. If he could get a finger on it, he could hit his emergency trigger and switch to Channel 6, the May Day channel. His left arm was useless, but he could try with his right. But when he moved it, pain ripped through his shoulder.

Hell. Well, he could at least shut off the freaking PASS device. If a rapid intervention team made it in here, he'd yell for them. But no way could he stand listening to that sound for the next whatever-amount-of-time it took. Gritting his teeth against the agony, he reached for the device at the front of his turnout, then hit the button. The strobe light stopped and sudden silence descended, though his ears still rang. While he was at it, he checked the gauge that indicated how much air he had left in his tank. Ten minutes. He must have been in here for some time, sucking up air, since it was a thirty-minute tank.

A croak issued from his throat. "I'm in hell. No surprise."

Water. He needed water.

"I can't give you any water," a bright female voice said. For some reason, he had the impression that the angel on the tip of the Christmas tree had spoken. So he answered her back.

"Of course you can't. Because I'm in hell. They don't exactly hand out water bottles in hell."

"Who said you're in hell?"

Even though he watched the angel's lips closely, he didn't see them move. So it must not be her speaking. Besides, the voice seemed to be coming from behind him. "I figured it out all by myself."

Amazingly, he had no more trouble with his throat. Maybe he wasn't really speaking aloud. Maybe he was having this bizarre conversation with his own imagination. That theory was confirmed when a girl's shapely calves stepped into his field of vision. She wore red silk stockings the exact color of holly berries. She wore nothing else on her feet, which had a very familiar shape.

Lizzie.

His gaze traveled upward, along the swell of her calves. The stockings stopped just above her knees, where they were fastened by a red velvet bow. "Christmas stockings," he murmured.

"I told you."

"All right. I was wrong. Maybe it's heaven after all. Come here." He wanted to hold her close. His heart wanted to burst with joy that she was here with him, that he wasn't alone. That he wasn't going to die without seeing Lizzie again.

"I can't. There's a tree on top of you," she said in a teasing voice. "Either that, or you're very happy to see me."

"Oh, you noticed that? You can move it, can't you? Either you're an angel and have magical powers, or you're real and you can push it off me."

She laughed. A real Lizzie laugh, starting as a giggle and swooping up the register until it became a whoop. "Do you really think an angel would dress like this?"

"Hmm, good point. What are you wearing besides those stockings? I can't even see. At least step closer so I can see."

"Fine." A blur of holly red, and then she perched on the pile of beams and concrete that blocked the east end of his world. In addition to the red stockings, she wore a red velvet teddy and a green peaked hat, which sat at an angle on her flowing dark hair. Talk about a "hot elf" look.

"Whoa. How'd you do that?"

"You did it."

"I did it?" How could he do it? He was incapacitated. Couldn't even move a finger. Well, maybe he could move a finger. He gave it a shot, wiggling the fingers on both hands. At least he wasn't paralyzed.

But he did seem to be mentally unstable. "I'm hallucinating, aren't I?"

"Bingo."

An Excerpt from

ONCE UPON A HIGHLAND CHRISTMAS

by Lecia Cornwall

Lady Alanna McNabb is bound by duty
to her family, who insist she must marry a
gentleman of wealth and title. When she meets
the man of her dreams, she knows it's much
too late, but her heart is no longer hers.

Laird Iain MacGillivray is on his way to propose
to another woman when he discovers Alanna
half-frozen in the snow and barely alive. She isn't
his to love, yet she's everything he's ever wanted.

As Christmas comes closer, the snow
thickens, and the magic grows stronger.
Alanna and Iain must choose between
desire and duty, love and obligation.

Alanna McNabb woke with a terrible headache. In fact, every inch of her body ached. She could smell peat smoke, and dampness, and hear wind. She remembered the storm and opened her eyes. She was in a small dark room, a hut, she realized, a shieling, perhaps, or was it one of the crofter's cottages at Glenlorne? Was she home, among the people who knew her, loved her? She looked around, trying to decide where exactly she was, whose home she was in. The roof beams above her head were blackened with age and soot, and a thick stoneware jug dangled from a nail hammered into the beam as a hook. But that offered no clues at all—it was the same in every Highland cott. She turned her head a little, knowing there would be a hearth, and—

A few feet from her, a man crouched by the fire.

A very big, very naked man.

She stared at his back, which was broad and smooth. She took note of well-muscled arms as he poked the fire. She followed the bumps of his spine down to a pair of dimples just above his round white buttocks.

Her throat dried. She tried to sit up, but pain shot through her body, and the room wavered before her eyes. Her leg was on fire, pure agony. She let out a soft cry.

He half turned at the sound and glanced over his shoulder, and she had a quick impression of a high cheekbone lit by the firelight, and a gleaming eye that instantly widened with surprise. He dropped the poker and fell on his backside with a grunt.

"You're awake!" he cried. She stared at him sprawled on the hearthstones, and he gasped again and cupped his hands over his— She shut her eyes tight, as he grabbed the nearest thing at hand to cover himself—a corner of the plaid— but she yanked it back, holding tight. He instantly let go and reached for the closest garment dangling from the line above him, which turned out to be her red cloak. He wrapped it awkwardly around his waist, trying to rise to his feet at the same time. He stood above her in his makeshift kilt, holding it in place with a white knuckled grip, his face almost as red as the wool. She kept her eyes on his face and pulled her own blanket tight around her throat.

"I see you're awake," he said, staring at her, his voice an octave lower now. "How do you feel?"

How did she feel? She assessed her injuries, tried to remember the details of how she came to be here, wherever here might be. She recalled being lost in a storm, and falling. There'd been blood on her glove. She frowned. After that she didn't remember anything at all.

She shifted carefully, and the room dissolved. She saw stars, and black spots, and excruciating pain streaked through her body, radiating from her knee. She gasped, panted, stiffened against it.

"Don't move," he said, holding out a hand, fingers splayed, though he didn't touch her. He grinned, a sudden flash of white teeth, the firelight bright in his eyes. "I found you out in the snow. I feared . . . well, it doesn't matter now. Your knee is injured, cut, and probably sprained, but it isn't broken," he said in a rush. He grinned again, as if that was all very good news, and dropped to one knee beside her. "You've got some color back."

He reached out and touched her cheek with the back of his hand, a gentle enough caress, but she flinched away and gasped at the pain that caused. He dropped his hand at once, looked apologetic. "I mean no harm, lass—I was just checking that you're warm, but not too warm. Or too cold . . ." He was babbling, and he broke off, gave her a wan smile, and stood up again, holding onto her cloak, taking a step back away from her. Was he blushing, or was it the light of the fire on his skin? She tried not to stare at the breadth of his naked chest, or the naked legs that showed beneath the trailing edge of the cloak.

She gingerly reached down under the covers and found her knee was bound up in a bandage of some sort. He turned away, flushing again, and she realized the plaid had slipped down. She was as naked as he was. She gasped, drew the blanket tight to her chin, and stared at him. She looked up and saw that her clothes were hanging on a line above the fireplace—all of them, even her shift.

"Where—?" she swallowed. Her voice was hoarse, her throat as raw as her knee. "Who are you?" she tried again. She felt hot blood fill her cheeks, and panic formed a tight knot in her chest, and she tried again to remember what had happened, but her mind was blank. If he was—unclothed, and she was equally unclothed—

"What—" she began again, then swallowed the question

she couldn't frame. She hardly knew what to ask first, Where, Who, or What? Her mind was moving slowly, her thoughts as thick and rusty as her tongue.

"You're safe, lass," he said, and she wondered if she was. She stared at him. She'd seen men working in the summer sun, their shirts off, their bodies tanned, their muscles straining, but she'd never thought anything of it. This—he—was different. And she was as naked as he was.

An Excerpt from

RUNNING HOT
A Bad Boys Undercover Novella
by HelenKay Dimon

Ward Bennett and Tasha Gregory aren't on the
same team. But while hunting a dictator on the
run, these two must decide whether they can trust
one another—and their ability to stay professional.
Working together might just make everyone safer,
but getting cozy . . . might just get them killed.

"Take your clothes off."

He looked at her as if she'd lost her mind. "Excuse me?"

"You're attracted to me." Good Lord, now Tasha was waving her hands in the air. Once she realized it, she stopped. Curled her hands into balls at her sides. "I find you . . . fine."

Ward covered his mouth and produced a fake cough. She assumed it hid a smile. That was almost enough to make her rescind the offer.

"Really? That's all you can muster?" This time he did smile. "You think I'm fine?"

He was hot and tall and had a face that played in her head long after she closed her eyes each night. And that body. Long and lean, with the stalk of a predator. Ward was a man who protected and fought. She got the impression he wrestled demons that had to do with reconciling chivalry and decency with the work they performed.

The combination of all that made her wild with need. "Your clothes are still on."

"Are you saying you want to—"

Since he was saying the sentence so slowly—emphasizing, and halting after, each word—she finished it fast. "Shag."

Both eyebrows rose now. "Please tell me that's British for 'have sex.'"

"Yes."

He blew out a long, staggered breath. "Thank God, because right now my body is in a race to see what will explode first, my brain or my dick."

Uh? "Is that a compliment?"

"Believe it or not, yes." Two steps, and he was in front of her, his fingers playing with the small white button at the top of her slim tee. "So, are you talking about now or sometime in the future to celebrate ending Tigana?"

Both. "I need to work off this extra energy and get back in control." She was half-ready to rip off her clothes and throw him on the mattress.

Maybe he knew because he just stood there and stared at her, his gaze not leaving her face.

She stared back.

Just as he started to lower his head, a ripple moved through her. She shoved a hand against his shoulder. "Don't think that I always break protocol like this."

"I don't care if you do." He ripped his shirt out of his pants and whipped it over his head, revealing miles of tanned muscles and skin.

"You're taking off your clothes." Not the smartest thing she'd ever said, but it was out there and she couldn't snatch it back.

"You're the boss, remember?"

A shot of regret nearly knocked her over. Not at making the pass but at wanting him this much in the first place. Here and now, when her mind should be on the assignment, not on his chest.

She'd buried this part of herself for so long under a pile of work and professionalism that bringing it out now made her twitchy. "This isn't—"

His hands went to her arms, and he brushed those palms up and down, soothing her. "Do you want me?"

She couldn't lie. He had to feel it in the tremor shaking through her. "Yes."

"Then stop justifying not working this very second and enjoy. It won't make you less of a professional."

That was exactly what she needed to hear. "Okay."

His hands stopped at her elbows, and he dragged her in closer, until the heat of his body radiated against her. "You're a stunning woman, and we've been circling each other for days. Honestly, your ability to handle weapons only makes you hotter in my eyes."

The words spun through her. They felt so good. So right. "Not the way I would say it, but okay."

"You want me. I sure as hell want you. We need to lie low until it gets dark and we can hide our movements better." The corner of his mouth kicked up in a smile filled with promise. "And, for the record, there is nothing sexier than a woman who goes after what she wants."

He meant it. She knew it with every cell inside her.

Screw being safe.

An Excerpt from

SINFUL REWARDS 1
A Billionaires and Bikers Novella
by Cynthia Sax

Belinda "Bee" Carter is a good girl; at least, that's
what she tells herself. And a good girl deserves
a nice guy—just like the gorgeous and moody
billionaire Nicolas Rainer. Or so she thinks,
until she takes a look through her telescope
and sees a naked, tattooed man on the balcony
across the courtyard. He has been watching
her, and that makes him all the more enticing.
But when a mysterious and anonymous text
message dares her to do something bad, she
must decide if she is really the good girl she has
always claimed to be, or if she's willing to risk
everything for her secret fantasy of being watched.

An Avon Red Novella

I'd told Cyndi I'd never use it, that it was an instrument purchased by perverts to spy on their neighbors. She'd laughed and called me a prude, not knowing that I was one of those perverts, that I secretly yearned to watch and be watched, to care and be cared for.

If I'm cautious, and I'm always cautious, she'll never realize I used her telescope this morning. I swing the tube toward the bench and adjust the knob, bringing the mysterious object into focus.

It's a phone. Nicolas's phone. I bounce on the balls of my feet. This is a sign, another declaration from fate that we belong together. I'll return Nicolas's much-needed device to him. As a thank you, he'll invite me to dinner. We'll talk. He'll realize how perfect I am for him, fall in love with me, marry me.

Cyndi will find a fiancé also—everyone loves her—and we'll have a double wedding, as sisters of the heart often do. It'll be the first wedding my family has had in generations.

Everyone will watch us as we walk down the aisle. I'll wear a strapless white Vera Wang mermaid gown with organza and lace details, crystal and pearl embroidery accents, the bodice fitted, and the skirt hemmed for my shorter height. My hair will be swept up. My shoes—

Voices murmur outside the condo's door, the sound piercing my delightful daydream. I swing the telescope upward, not wanting to be caught using it. The snippets of conversation drift away.

I don't relax. If the telescope isn't positioned in the same way as it was last night, Cyndi will realize I've been using it. She'll tease me about being a fellow pervert, sharing the story, embellished for dramatic effect, with her stern, serious dad—or, worse, with Angel, that snobby friend of hers.

I'll die. It'll be worse than being the butt of jokes in high school because that ridicule was about my clothes and this will center on the part of my soul I've always kept hidden. It'll also be the truth, and I won't be able to deny it. I am a pervert.

I have to return the telescope to its original position. This is the only acceptable solution. I tap the metal tube.

Last night, my man-crazy roommate was giggling over the new guy in three-eleven north. The previous occupant was a gray-haired, bowtie-wearing tax auditor, his luxurious accommodations supplied by Nicolas. The most exciting thing he ever did was drink his tea on the balcony.

According to Cyndi, the new occupant is a delicious piece of man candy—tattooed, buff, and head-to-toe lickable. He was completing armcurls outside, and she enthusiastically counted his reps, oohing and aahing over his bulging biceps, calling to me to take a look.

I resisted that temptation, focusing on making macaroni and cheese for the two of us, the recipe snagged from the diner my mom works in. After we scarfed down dinner, Cyndi licking her plate clean, she left for the club and hasn't returned.

Three-eleven north is the mirror condo to ours. I

straighten the telescope. That position looks about right, but then, the imitation UGGs I bought in my second year of college looked about right also. The first time I wore the boots in the rain, the sheepskin fell apart, leaving me barefoot in Economics 201.

Unwilling to risk Cyndi's friendship on "about right," I gaze through the eyepiece. The view consists of rippling golden planes, almost like . . .

Tanned skin pulled over defined abs.

I blink. It can't be. I take another look. A perfect pearl of perspiration clings to a puckered scar. The drop elongates more and more, stretching, snapping. It trickles downward, navigating the swells and valleys of a man's honed torso.

No. I straighten. This is wrong. I shouldn't watch our sexy neighbor as he stands on his balcony. If anyone catches me . . .

Parts 1 – 6 available now!

An Excerpt from

RETURN TO CLAN SINCLAIR
A Clan Sinclair Novella
by Karen Ranney

When Ceana Sinclair Mead married the youngest
son of an Irish duke, she never dreamed that
seven years later her beloved Peter would die.
Her three brothers-in-law think she should
be grateful to remain a proper widow. After
three years of this, she's ready to scream. She
escapes to Scotland, only to discover she's so
much more than just the Widow Mead.

In Scotland, Ceana crosses paths with Bruce
Preston, an American tasked with a dangerous
mission by her brother, Macrath. Bruce is too
attractive for her peace of mind, but she still
finds him fascinating. Their one night together
is more wonderful than Ceana could have
imagined, and she has never felt more alive.

The darkness was nearly absolute, leaving her no choice but to stretch her hands out on either side of her, fingertips brushing against the stone walls. The incline was steep, further necessitating she take her time. Yet at the back of her mind was the last image she had of Carlton, his bright impish grin turning to horror as he glanced down.

The passage abruptly ended in a mushroom-shaped cavern. This was the grotto she'd heard so much about, with its flue in the middle and its broad, wide window looking out over the beach and the sea. She raced to the window, hopped up on the sill nature had created over thousands of years and leaned out.

A naked man reached up, grabbed Carlton as he fell. After he lowered the boy to the sand, he turned and smiled at her.

Carlton was racing across the beach, glancing back once or twice to see if he was indeed free. The rope made of sheets was hanging limply from his window.

The naked man was standing there with hands on his hips, staring at her in full frontal glory.

She hadn't seen many naked men, the last being her husband. The image in front of her now was so startling she couldn't help but stare. A smile was dawning on the stranger's full lips, one matched by his intent brown eyes. No, not quite brown, were they? They were like the finest Scottish whiskey touched with sunlight.

Her gaze danced down his strong and corded neck to broad shoulders etched with muscle. His chest was broad and muscled as well, tapering down to a slim waist and hips.

Even semiflaccid, his manhood was quite impressive.

The longer she watched, the more impressive it became.

What on earth was a naked man doing on Macrath's beach?

To her utter chagrin, the stranger turned and presented his backside to her, glancing over his shoulder to see if she approved of the sight.

She withdrew from the window, cheeks flaming. What on earth had she been doing? Who was she to gawk at a naked man as if she'd never before seen one?

Now that she knew Carlton was going to survive his escape, she should retreat immediately to the library.

"You'd better tell Alistair his brother's gotten loose again. Are you the new governess?"

She turned to find him standing in the doorway, still naked.

She pressed her fingers against the base of her throat and counseled herself to appear unaffected.

"I warn you, the imp escapes at any chance. You'll have your hands full there."

The look of fright on Carlton's face hadn't been fear of the distance to the beach, but the fact that he'd been caught.

She couldn't quite place the man's accent, but it wasn't Scottish. American, perhaps. What did she care where he came from? The problem was what he was doing here.

"I'm not a governess," she said. "I'm Macrath's sister, Ceana."

He bent and retrieved his shirt from a pile of clothes beside the door, taking his time with it. Shouldn't he have begun with his trousers instead?

"Who are you?" she asked, looking away as he began to don the rest of his clothing.

She'd had two children. She was well versed in matters of nature. She knew quite well what a man's body looked like. The fact that his struck her as singularly attractive was no doubt due to the fact she'd been a widow for three years.

"Well, Ceana Sinclair, is it all that important you know who I am?"

"It isn't Sinclair," she said. "It's Mead."

He tilted his head and studied her.

"Is Mr. Mead visiting along with you?"

She stared down at her dress of unremitting black. "I'm a widow," she said.

A shadow flitted over his face "Are you? Did Macrath know you were coming?"

"No," she said. "Does it matter? He's my brother. He's family. And why would you be wanting to know?"

He shrugged, finished buttoning his pants and began to don his shoes.

"Who are you?" she asked again.

"I'm a detective," he said. "My company was hired by your brother."

"Why?"

"Now that's something I'm most assuredly not going to tell you," he said. "It was nice meeting you, Mrs. Mead. I hope to see more of you before I leave."

And she hoped to see much, much less of him.

An Excerpt from

RETURN OF THE BAD GIRL

by Codi Gary

When Caroline Willis learns that her perfect
apartment has been double-booked—to a
dangerously hot bad boy—her bad-girl reputation
comes out in full force. But as close quarters
begin to ignite the sizzling chemistry between
them, she's left wondering: Bad boy plus bad
girl equals nothing but trouble . . . right?

"I feel like you keep looking for something more to me, but what you know about me is it. There's no 'deep down,' no mistaking my true character. I am bad news." He waited, listening for the tap of her retreating feet or the slam of the door, but only silence met his ears, then the soft sound of shoes on the cement floor—getting closer to him instead of farther away.

Fingers trailed feather-light touches over his lower back. "This scar on your back—is that from the accident?"

Her caress made his skin tingle as he shook his head. "I was knocked down by one of my mother's boyfriends and landed on a glass table."

"What about here?" Her hand had moved onto his right shoulder.

"It was a tattoo I had removed. In prison, you're safer if you belong, so—"

"I understand," she said, cutting him off. Had she heard the pain in his voice, or did she really understand?

He turned around before she could point out any more scars. "What are you doing?"

She looked him in the eye and touched the side of his neck, where his tattoo began, spreading all the way down past his shoulder and over his chest. "You say you're damaged. That you're bad news and won't ever change."

"Yeah?"

To his surprise, she dropped her hand to his and brought it up to her collarbone, where his finger felt a rough, puckered line.

"This is a knife wound—just a scratch, really—that I got from a man who used to come see me dance at the strip club. He was constantly asking me out, and I always let him down easy. But one night, after I'd had a shitty day, I told him I would never go out with an old, ugly fuck like him. He was waiting by my car when I got off work."

His rage blazed at this phantom from her past. "What happened?"

"I pulled a move I'd learned from one of the bouncers. Even though he still cut me, I was able to pick up a handful of gravel and throw it in his face. I made it to the front door of the club, and he took off. They arrested him on assault charges, and it turned out he had an outstanding warrant. I never saw him again."

Caroline pulled him closer, lifting her arm for him to see a jagged scar along her forearm. "This is from a broken beer bottle I got sliced with when a woman came into my bar in San Antonio, looking for her husband. She didn't take it well when she found out he had a girlfriend on the side, and when I stepped in to stop her from attacking him, she sliced me."

He couldn't stop his hand from sliding up over her soft skin until it rested on the back of her neck, his fingers pressing into her flesh until she tilted her chin up to meet his gaze.

"What's your point with all the show-and-tell, Caroline?"